# DETROIT NOIR

### EDITED BY
### E.J. OLSEN & JOHN C. HOCKING

# DETROIT

Palmer Woods

HIGHLAND
PARK

Grandmont–
Rosedale

94

Rouge Foundry

Delray

75

75
94
Hamtramck
Chrysler Freeway
Alter Road
94
New Center
Woodward Avenue
East Grand Boulevard
Brush Park
Rivertown
Belle Isle
Grand Circus Park
Downtown
Corktown
DETROIT RIVER
CANADA

*Detroit turned out to be heaven, but it also turned out to be hell.*
—Marvin Gaye

# TABLE OF CONTENTS

# TABLE OF CONTENTS

*Detroit turned out to be heaven, but it also turned out to be hell.*

—Marvin Gaye

# PART III: SILENCE OF THE CITY

# PART IV: EDGE OF THE PAST

# INTRODUCTION
## REFLECTIONS FROM THE DARK SIDE

D etroit.
The name comes from "*les étroits*" (the narrows), for the river straits that flow between Lake St. Clair and Lake Erie. The city was founded as French wilderness outpost Fort Pontchartrain du Détroit in 1701 by Antoine de la Mothe Cadillac. Memorialized in true Detroit fashion, his coat of arms was used as the logo of the Cadillac automobile. The past as viewed through the lens of the auto industry.

Despite the twentieth-century dominance by manufacturing, Detroit has been many things in its 300-year history. A young settlement in the face of an often hostile western wilderness, it was a frontier town where settlers fought for valuable property along the waterway, the only reliable connection with the cities to the east.

It was a city in dispute. In 1760, during the French-Indian War, the British took control of the region. In 1796, a treaty brought Detroit into the United States. During the War of 1812, Detroit was again captured by the British, and in 1813 it was retaken by the Americans, this time permanently.

Detroit was a Gilded Age boom town. By the late nineteenth century, the city had become a prosperous transportation hub, bolstered by the rise of shipping, shipbuilding, and manufacturing. During this period, Detroit was known as the Paris of the West for its beautiful architecture. In 1896, Henry Ford built his first automobile in a workshop on Mack Avenue, and the city became the birthplace of a transportation revolution which would change the face of Detroit, and America, forever.

It was a bootlegger's town, where the Purple Gang and their competitors might drive a car filled with Canadian alcohol across the frozen surface of the Detroit River. A prohibition city, where the forbidden liquor flowed so freely that there were those who believed some of the city's more enterprising gangsters had laid, beneath the dark waters of the river, a pipe that stretched all the way across from Canada to furnish Detroiters with bootleg whiskey on tap.

It was the Motor City, Sugartown, the City of Basements, where a working man or woman from anywhere could find a steady job and the promise of the middle-class American Dream. But the dream always had a dark side.

Factory shifts were long and often dangerous. In 1935, the United Auto Workers was founded, and the union went on to fight a bitter, often bloody battle with General Motors and the notoriously brutal strikebreakers from the Ford Service Department.

During World War II, Detroit was the Arsenal of Democracy, and the auto plants retooled to manufacture munitions, planes, and tanks. Wartime also gave Detroiters a preview of the social strife to come when racial tensions, primarily among black and white migrant workers from the South, exploded into a full-scale riot in 1943.

By the '60s, Detroit had become Motown, the city with a pulsing beat where melodies that enchanted the world were born and endured. But this decade also saw the beginning of a long economic decline, and the city was often cited as a symbol of urban blight and "white flight" to the relatively homogenous suburbs across Eight Mile Road. In 1967, racial tensions again boiled over, and 12th Street erupted into riots that spread throughout the city. The rioting lasted five days and killed forty-three people. More than two thousand buildings were destroyed, and the city has never recovered from the exodus of fleeing residents and businesses.

In the economically depressed landscape of the 1970s, it finally became Murder City, where the dreams of industry and the working man collapsed into urban decay, crime, drugs, and desperation, where many would say it languishes to this day. The capital of the rust belt.

Detroit is an old and wounded city, broken into wildly diverse splinters, but it is not dead, for it is possessed of a unique vitality rooted in its complex history and in its hardy people.

Detroit is noir, shadowed and striving, grim and powerful. It is impossible to truly know the city and not respect it. This collection of stories is a rich reflection of Detroit's dark side, offering a variety of perspectives on both the city and noir style.

Here you will find noir in many forms, embodied by many characters. From a driven detective with a mystery to solve to a working man just trying to make it through another day, from a bemused outsider seeking a thrill to one so deeply inside the city as to see no outside at all. Urban professionals, night watchmen, tarot card readers, waitresses, caretakers, and criminals, all bound together by the city and by a dark dilemma that looms just ahead.

A moment awaits each of them, a moment of truth or violence or epiphany or change. A noir moment.

This is *Detroit Noir.*

*E.J. Olsen & John C. Hocking*
*Detroit, Michigan*
*August 2007*

# PART I

*ANIMAL FARM*

# KILL THE CAT

BY Loren D. Estleman

*Rivertown*

I
t was right at dark, one of those evenings when you saw it
as a black diagonal against the light, like the title sequence
of the old soap opera *The Edge of Night*. The river smelled
like iron, and the People Mover—Coleman Young's electric train
set—chugged along several stories above the street, empty as
usual, shuttling around and around in its endless circle as in one
of those post-apocalyptic science-fiction stories about a depopulated world, still going about its automated business decades after doomsday, jungle vines crawling up the sides of vacant glass
buildings. Detroit had a start on the last, in weedy empty lots
where pheasants roosted among the rats and cartridge casings. I
was thirty seconds from downtown and might have been driving
through Aztec ruins.

The address I'd scribbled in my notebook belonged to a barely renovated pile in the shrinking warehouse district, one of the
last places where the city still shows its muscle: miles of railroad
track and a handful of gaunt brick buildings where steering gears
and coils of steel once paused for breath on their way to becoming automobiles. In a year or two it'll be gone. City Hall and
the Chamber of Commerce are busy gentrifying it into riverfront
condominiums. This address was poised square in the middle,
the edge of the edge of night.

I was working on a teenage runaway. Mark Childs had slid
through a crack in the *über*–upper class of Grosse Pointe, getting
the boot from the University of Michigan three weeks into his
first semester and then falling in with low company, in this case

three boys studying at Wayne State University. I'd gotten the last from a kid who hung doors at Chrysler in order to attend classes in library science at WSU. Childs had taken his place when he'd opted out of sharing rent so he could sleep in his parents' house and save money for cigarettes and tuition.

Where the new roomie found cash to keep up his end, I didn't know and never did, although the family suspected an indulgent aunt. Childs was seventeen, a young high school graduate coming into a trust fund when he turned eighteen in two months. The family didn't like that, thought if they got him back under the parental roof they could teach him some responsibility in sixty days so he wouldn't blow it all on Internet poker or the Democrats. I hadn't said anything to that. When work comes your way you don't get into a debate situation with the client.

A simple job: Confirm the kid's location and notify the parents so they could call the cops and tell them to take a mixed-up boy off the streets and deliver him to their door.

I parked on gravel off Riopelle and walked down to the river to finish a cigarette, stepping carefully over chunks of brick and Jell-O pudding tops. The lights of Windsor, Ontario made waffle-patterned reflections on the surface where the Detroit River squeezes between countries. The spot where I stood hadn't changed since Prohibition, when rum boats docked there and men who weren't dressed for the work off-loaded the cargo into seven-passenger touring cars with a man standing sentry holding a tommy gun. It was late August and already the air felt like October. We were in for one of those winters that shut up the global-warming people for a while.

The place I wanted stood fifty yards away, with all the character sandblasted off the brick and yellow solar panels replacing the multiple-paned windows. The concrete loading dock was intact, but above it someone had substituted a faux–wrought iron carriage lamp for the original bare bulb. It was an amateur facelift, done on the cheap by a landlord who'd seen too many local renaissances fizzle out to put any faith in the current one.

The big bay doors were chained and padlocked, but decks had been built around the corner with steps zigzagging up four stories and doors cut into each level for the tenants, with small windows added to let in light and accommodate the occasional window-unit air conditioner. The only lights burned on the ground floor. The kid at Chrysler had said none of the other apartments was ready for occupancy.

When no one answered I tried the knob. It turned freely.

There might have been nothing in that; college housing is always getting burgled because the students are careless about locking up. The boxy window unit that stuck out of the nearest window was pumping full out. I didn't like that. The damp air off the river was too cool to bother running up the utility bill. I went back to my car and transferred the Chief's Special from its special compartment to my pocket.

Still no answer. I opened the door as quietly as I could, just wide enough to step inside around the edge with my hand on the revolver. It was like walking into a refrigerator truck.

The first one lay on a blown-out sofa near the wheezing air conditioner. He was in his underwear, lying on his side facing the back of the sofa, as if he'd been caught sleeping. I found the next one on his back in an open doorway connecting to a hallway and had to step over him to inspect the rest of the apartment. I had the gun out now.

Number three was twisted like a rag on the floor halfway down the short hallway. I eased open the door to a small bath-room, dirty but unoccupied, found an untidy bedroom with no one in it, checked out a narrow closet with sports equipment piled on the floor, and finished the inventory in another bedroom at the back. This one, more cautious than the others, sprawled on the bed with his legs hanging over the footboard, arms splayed. When I stepped in for a closer look, my toe bumped into something that rolled: an aluminum baseball bat. He'd dropped it when he fell backward. He was naked, the others nearly so. No one wears pajamas anymore.

I put away my weapon. There was nobody left to shoot.

I noticed the smell then, faint but bitter, mixed with the slaughterhouse stink. They'd all been blasted at point-blank range by a heavy-caliber shotgun.

Checking for pulses would have been redundant. I went back to the first corpse. The back of his head was a mass of pulp; stray pellets had torn fresh holes in the upholstery, but he'd taken most of the charge. The others had been struck in the chest or abdomen. Mr. Sofa was the only white victim. Mark Childs was white.

I wished it was that easy, but I had a report to make. Setting my jaws tight, I grasped his bare shoulder to pull his face into view. The skin was cold and the body turned all as one piece, stiff as a plaster cast. Death alters features, but he looked enough like his picture to give him a name. The birthmark on his upper lip settled the question.

The front room was as big as the rest of the apartment. The sofa was part of a rummage-sale set facing a home theater from a box, with a kitchen at the other end. Disposable food cartons littered a folding card table with four mismatched folding chairs around it, but plastic forks and smeared paper napkins suggested more nomadic dining habits. My breath made gray jets. I thought about turning down the air conditioner but didn't. Whoever had touched the controls last wasn't present.

The place didn't seem to be wired for a telephone. I found a cell on the sticky kitchen counter and called police headquarters. I bypassed 911 and asked for Lieutenant Mary Ann Thaler.

"Why felony homicide?" she asked. "Why not plain homicide?"

"It looked like a drug thing," I said.

"It still looks like it."

"So I called you to avoid a handoff."

"I appreciate it. I've been on duty thirteen hours now."

She sat across from me at the folding table, dangling a tea bag on a string in a big cardboard cup with a Powerpuff Girl printed on it. Now that she no longer wore glasses the tiredness showed, but she was still the best-looking thing I'd seen all day, and mine had started as early as hers. Her skin was fair, she had her light brown hair tied in a ponytail with a yellow silk scarf, and a fitted jacket and pleated slacks didn't distract the admiring male gaze from the rest. Her SIG Sauer would be on the left side of her belt, the gold shield on the right. Her brown eyes were as big as wheel covers.

The place buzzed with assorted professionals. A happy Asian medical examiner hummed show tunes and probed at wounds with the nightmare tackle from his tin box. Young people of both sexes measured spatter patterns and bumped into a big black radio-car cop who kept grunting and moving out of their way and into someone else's. Every light was on and a couple of arcs had been brought in for a better look.

Finally the air conditioner stopped. A fingerprint tech had lifted latents off the controls with a gizmo that took pictures like a camera phone.

"That should wrap this," Thaler said. "The heat wave broke night before last; the tenants had no reason to crank up the cold. Whoever did wanted to keep them from getting ripe long enough to split and set up an alibi. I figure these boys have been dead since early this morning or they wouldn't have been undressed for bed."

She sipped tea and twisted in her chair to gesture with the cup. "Your boy Charles died in his sleep. The next two came running when they heard the noise and Shotgun popped them, one, two, like birds. Number Four stuck it out in his room in batter's position, but rock breaks scissors. That how you see it?"

"Clear as gin. Can I smoke?"

She nodded, watched me light up while she rotated the cup

between her palms. She kept her nails short and polished clear. "What else you see?"

"Not a thing. I called you right after I ID'd my runaway." I drew in a lungful and staggered it out through my nostrils.

"You didn't snoop around for dope? Funny money? Stolen rubies?"

"I'm not as curious as I used to be."

"Who else you call?"

"The client. It's all in your notebook."

"Before or after you called me?"

"After."

She was still deliberating my case when a sergeant or something in a sharp suit and cowboy boots came over carrying two Ziploc bags. The one he dropped on the table contained four spent shotgun shells. "Twelve-gauge double-O buck, L.T.," he said. "Nothing surer, richer or poorer."

"Rick McCoy, Amos Walker. Walker called it in."

He took my hand in a hickory grip. He wore his hair to his collar and a soul patch in the hollow of his chin. I figured he was working undercover with a Wild West show.

"What else?" Thaler said.

McCoy flipped the other bag onto the table. We didn't have to open to smell what was inside. "In the fridge."

"Nothing harder?" Thaler asked.

"The gunner left with it if so. But if my honker is working this isn't nickel-bag stuff. There's right around six or seven grand in there." He had an accent, Arkansas or farther.

"How'd he miss it?"

"Maybe he found another stash and stopped looking."

"Okay. Tag both bags and get them to the Poindexters downtown."

"Who's McCoy?" I asked when he left with the evidence.

"Narcotics. He caught the squeal and hitched along. He thought the same thing you and I did when it came down."

"I did then."

"You saw the pot. Either a buy went wrong or word got out the stuff was here. You've seen it before."

"Not over pot. Not even the premium kind. Someone who knows his way around a shotgun might stick them up, but he wouldn't cut loose for anything less than heroin, or high-grade coke on the outside. He was methodical, if not professional. And any idiot who's ever seen *Cops* knows enough to look in the refrigerator."

"McCoy's people will run a check on the stiffs as we make them. One of 'em will cash back."

"That sounds like racial profiling."

"Not if it turns out it's Childs."

"His family never said anything about drugs."

"That's reliable." She raised and plunged the tea bag a couple more times; the contents of her cup were nearly black. "You're out at first base, Walker. If you think Homicide rides its fence you don't know anything about those cowboys in Narco."

I dragged in everything but the filter and put it out in a carton of moo shu pork. "I told you I'm not as curious as I used to be."

"You were more convincing the first time."

Mark Childs was the product of a broken home; the home in his case being a nine hundred square foot house in old Delray. At age three he'd traded it for a Cape Cod on Lake St. Clair, with grass and clay courts and a skiff tied up at the dock out back with *Childs' Plaything* scripted on its transom. Orson Childs, Swedish on one side, English on the other, with equal shares in Volvo and British Petroleum, had adopted Mark after his mother's divorce and her marriage to Orson. If I understood right, Orson's own mother had commemorated the occasion by endowing the boy with a trust fund that after nearly fifteen years of compound interest looked like the annual budget for the state of Rhode Island.

The houseman, a fine-featured Micronesian in a white coat, left me standing in the entrance hall while he found out if anyone was home at 11 o'clock on a weeknight. It was a room meant for standing, despite the presence of a row of straight shieldback chairs and an antique oak hall tree with a bench. I got the nod finally and followed him into a carpeted living room with a sunken conversation pit and Mrs. Childs drinking from an umbrella stand in a white leather armchair. She was a horsey-looking woman of fifty, not horsefaced but the type you pictured riding to hounds in a red habit and black helmet, and to hell with the animal rightists, in a gray silk blouse, black stirrup pants, tasseled loafers on her bare feet; fencerail-lean with high cheekbones and straight auburn hair swept behind her ears. She'd been crying. She offered me a drink. I said no thanks and she threw out the houseman with her bony chin.

I remained standing. "I'm sorry."

"Why should you be? You didn't kill him. Did you?" She had a flat Midwestern accent. In those surroundings, with her features, it should have been New England, but then she'd been married to a construction worker before Orson came along.

"Have the police been here?"

"They just left. They were polite; sincere, even. They asked if Mark was into drugs. I said no. They didn't believe me, but they were polite about it, so I didn't throw anything at them. I suppose we owe you money."

"We're square. You gave me a three-day retainer but I only used two days. Actually, it's your husband I wanted to talk to. Is he around?"

She said he was in his workshop and gave me directions. Then she swirled the ice in her glass and drank from it and I stopped existing.

It was a metalworking shop in a small building behind the house, a shed that was supposed to be an old carriage house that had been converted into a shed but had always been a shed. It was one of the newer estates in Grosse Pointe, less than sixty years old; no vintage auto money there of the Dodge and Ford and Durant type. I knocked, but it was noisy inside, so I let myself into a room filled with blue smoke and the sharp stench of scorched metal and sparks from Childs's cutting torch. He was a hobbyist who made sculpture from rescued driveshafts, leaf springs, and gold dental retainers scrounged from salvage yards and dumpsters behind schools. At the moment he was cutting up a length of steel pipe clamped in a vise bigger than my head.

I waited, hands in pockets, not wanting to startle him while he was handling dangerous equipment. When he saw me he jumped a little anyway, then tipped up his visor and screwed shut the valve on the acetylene tank. I said I was sorry about Mark.

"Yes." He spoke in clipped tones: stiff-upper-lip Brit by way of Vancouver, where the American branch of his family emigrated after the colonies declared independence from England. "I consider our transactions at an end, barring outstanding expenses. If you'll submit a statement, we can put an end to this sad business." He produced a checkbook from a hip pocket. He had it on him with a leather apron.

"We're fine," I said. "I just wanted to clear up some details before I type my report."

"Clarissa's the detail person. Why don't you come back when she's in a condition to answer your questions?"

"Stepfathers tend to be more objective considering their wives' children. Was there anything about Mark's behavior that suggested he might have been into the drug scene?"

He tugged off his gauntlets. He was a good-looking man creeping up on sixty, with a receding hairline and a long upper lip fighting the old battle between pickled youth and premature old age. "I liked Mark," he said. "I couldn't really love him, because he came to me fully assembled, but I think we might have been friends if I hadn't married his mother. It never occurred to me he had anything to do with drugs, but then I didn't pay as much attention to that sort of thing as I suppose I should have. It would explain some things, wouldn't it?"

"Things such as what?"

"Well, his poor academic performance and his running off. He wasn't a rebellious boy. He was a sickly child, always on some kind of medication. Maybe that's where it started."

"His real father might know something."

"Hank? I doubt it. They haven't seen each other in years."

"That's what he said when I called to ask if Mark had moved in with him. Then he hung up."

"That's Hank Worden. I suppose I should be grateful he's such a miserable son of a bitch. He's made me look like the ideal husband by contrast."

I thanked him and thought of some more words of sympathy, but he had his gloves back on and the visor down and was firing up the torch for another go at his project. People grieve all sorts of ways.

The houseman was standing in the path between the house and the workshop when I let myself out. His hands hung at his sides and his white coat glowed blue under a mercury light mounted on top of a tall pole.

"We talk," he said.

He asked me to call him Truk. That was the name of the archipelago where he'd grown up; he said his real one was even harder to pronounce than it was to spell. His room in the walk-out basement contained popular fiction on the shelves and stacks of *People*. I guessed he read them to improve his English. He sat cross-legged on a neatly made twin bed, showing bare ankles and the smooth brown line of his throat when he tipped his head back to draw on the cigarette he'd bummed. I smoked and waited in a wicker armchair and wondered how old he was, thirty or sixty. His bowl-cut hair was glossy black, but Micronesians are a long time going gray.

"Police?" he asked.

"Private," I said.

His face crumpled into a wrinkled mask. Sixty, definitely. "I don' know what this is, *private*."

"It means I can't shoot if you run away from me. Apart from that the work's the same."

He smiled, showing gold teeth and smoothing out his face. Thirty, maybe. "I thought Mark is dead before this."

"Bad habits?"

He puffed and said nothing. He didn't inhale, just filled his mouth and let it out like cigar smoke. His grin set like plaster of Paris. Forty, probably. I got out a twenty, folded it lengthwise, and held it up between two fingers. He drew his lip down over his teeth and shook his head.

I started to put it away.

"Kidneys," he said.

I stopped. "What about them?"

"Like he didn't have none. None that worked."

"He didn't die because his kidneys failed. His kidneys failed because he died."

"I mean before. Three year, four. He got a new one."

"His mother and stepfather didn't mention that."

"He didn't get it from them."

"Who donated it?"

He dropped the filter into a jar lid on the nightstand and asked for another cigarette. I tucked the twenty into the pack and flipped it onto the bed. I'd guessed the answer, but I might have to come back for more later.

He pocketed the pack with the bill inside. He didn't take out a cigarette. "His father, the real one."

"The mother's type didn't match?"

He shrugged.

I said, "I heard Mark and his father weren't that close."

He smiled again and patted his pocket.

I misunderstood. "That's all you get. I'm dipping into capital."

"Money's what I meant. They pay."

"Hank Worden sold one of his kidneys? For how much?"

He lifted and dropped his shoulders again. I asked him how he knew about the deal.

"I didn', then. Later, Worden comes back, drunk, loud. Mr. Childs he say, 'I call police.' Then he leave."

"What was he mad about?"

"I think maybe he wants more and Mr. Childs says no. I guess. My English is not so good as now."

"Was Mrs. Childs here at the time?'

"She is out. It is after the operation, she goes to see Mark in the hospital."

I got up and put out my cigarette in the jar lid. "Anything else?"

"Nothing else. I hear you talk to Mrs. Childs, I think maybe you want to know." I was at the door when he spoke again. "You no police?"

"When's the last time a cop gave you money?"

He lifted his bangs to show me a thin white scar on his scalp. "Sixteen stitch, ten year ago. All I ever got. So why you want to know about Mark?"

"I'm more curious than I thought I was."

The radio news had more details on the victims in the apartment. Du'an Reeves, twenty, was a sophomore at Wayne State. Gordon Samuels and LeRon Porter, both twenty-one, were juniors. Porter had done short time in County for nonpayment of child support to a seventeen-year-old former girlfriend in Redford Township. None of the others had a record, including Mark Childs. The police were still investigating drug connections. I switched off.

Hank Worden, Mark Childs's father and Clarissa Childs's ex,

lived in a bungalow that needed a new roof on West Vernor, the old Delray section, now mostly Mexican. The disrepair wasn't uncommon in houses where construction workers lived; the work is all outgo and no income. His lights were on at midnight, so I knocked on his door. I had my gun with me on a hunch, but I didn't need it to get in. I accomplished that by sticking my foot in the door and pushing a twenty through the gap.

He sat in a quagmire sofa drinking Diet Pepsi from a can, a man in his middle fifties but fit, tan from rugged outdoor work, in jeans and run-down tennis shoes and a plaid flannel shirt with the sleeves rolled up past his elbows. He had all his hair, splintered with silver, and from the look of him it was easy to see why his kidney passed muster. But you don't have to socialize with a vital organ.

"So you got the boy killed." That's what he opened with.

I remained standing. All the seats in the place looked like sinkholes and I didn't want to have to wallow my way out of one to clock him. "According to the cops he was dead almost before I started looking for him. Do you want to fight? I sure don't. It's been a day."

He shook the last drops onto his tongue and tossed the can toward a raveled straw laundry basket heaped over with empties. "I don't want to fight. I been in fights and I never got a thing out of them, not even the sense to stop picking 'em. Last time I saw Mark he was in Pampers. I know I ought to feel something, but I don't. Bastard, ain't I?"

"Who told you, the cops?"

"They make the family rounds when something like this happens. Greasers next door get a visit every time one of their uncles gets squiffed. They got more uncles than a rabbit. Ought to loan 'em out to colored boys that got no daddies."

"You thought enough of Mark to give him a kidney."

"First thing I thought when they told me. 'Well, there's a piece of me wasted.' You know about that, huh?"

"I told you, I'm a detective. So what about it?"

"That was strictly a business deal. Ten thousand bucks and all expenses paid. See, Mark and me was a perfect match. Is that a hoot? Clary took him when she left and she had less in common with him than me."

"Ten grand doesn't go as far as it used to. That was true even three or four years ago. So you went back for more, and Childs threw you out."

His face darkened under the tan. "That what he said?"

"It's what I heard."

"I ought to go back up there and bash in his skull with one of them nutty statues he makes out of scrap."

I didn't like the way he said it. He was too calm. "If the cops heard you say that, they'd be down here tossing the place for a shotgun."

"Go ahead, it's in that closet. I used to bring it along when I had a job in the country, in case I saw a deer. Now I just keep it around to punch holes in the sky on New Year's Eve."

It was a Remington twelve-gauge in good condition. The barrel smelled oily and there was a little dust in it when I turned it toward the light. It hadn't been fired recently. I put it back. "Of course, it could be one of a set."

He made a kazoo with his lips. "I can barely afford to buy pop in six-packs. Get me one, will you? Take one for yourself. I ain't had a real drink in twelve years; that's why my kidney was so rosy pink." He took one of the two I got from the refrigerator in the kitchenette and watched me snap the top on mine. "If Childs told you I got greedy, then he's a liar on top of a deadbeat. I only went to that barn of his to get what was promised me. That check he wrote me ought to be tied to a paddle with a string."

"It bounced?"

"Man, I had to duck when I tried to cash it." He popped open his can. "I guess his insurance took care of the hospital bill, but I don't go in to get carved on just for the rush."

"You didn't take it to court?"

"No contract. He said it was dicey legalwise. What you think of that, man lives like that, hanging paper like some goldbrick?" He poured half the can down his throat.

"Maybe he lives better than he is off." I sipped. No matter what they put in place of sugar it always tastes like barbed wire left to steep. "I don't guess you told any of this to the police."

"I would've, if they asked. Why should I cover up for a squirt like Orson Childs?" He spoke the name with an effete accent.

"No reason, except they might look at it as motive for murder. You made a deal to save Mark's life, Childs reneged, so you decided to repossess."

He paused in mid-guzzle, swallowed. "Jesus, that's cold."

"It should be. I just took it out of your refrigerator."

"I mean what you said. So why'd I wait four years?"

"Murder plots have been known to stew a lot longer than that."

He drank off the second half and flipped the can toward the basket. It wobbled but didn't fall off, as some of the others had. "Do I *look* like somebody who'd wait that long?"

I drove away from there, yawning bitterly and hoping Barry Stackpole's lights would be out so I could go home and go to bed. But Barry lived without sleep, a journalistic vampire who that season had sublet lodgings downtown, five minutes from each of the city's three legal casinos. He had a theory that the owners were building a Mafia outside the Mafia, with no ties to what the gaming commission interpreted as organized crime, but with all the benefits attendant. He might have had something, at that; the owners were exclusively male, and the mob is not an equal opportunity employer. Traditional gangsters had taken one of his legs, some fingers, and put a steel plate in his skull, so he was less than reasonable on the subject of thugs incorporated. In that vein of mind he'd hacked into every hundred-thousand-dollar bank account between Puget Sound and Puerto Rico. Thirty minutes after I dropped in on him and his computer arsenal, I found out Orson Childs had been selling off his family's stock for five years, trying to bolster investment losses and personal indulgences, from *Childs' Plaything* to a racehorse named Light-year that couldn't hold its own beside a California redwood. I promised Barry a case of Scotch and left him to his obsession of the season.

The rest was as glamorous as it gets. I caught a few hours' sleep in my hut on the west side of Hamtramck, got up at the butt-crack of dawn with black sludge in a thermos, and camped out across the street from the Childs house in Grosse Pointe. That morning happened to be trash collection. I was out of the car the second Truk wheeled the household refuse bin to the curb and started back up the drive, puffing smoke from one of the cigarettes I'd given him.

I worked fast, because the trash truck was snorting its way up Lake Shore Drive, the collectors evaluating the inventory for personal aggrandizement before feeding it to the crusher. I found what I wanted among the empty single-malt bottles and plain garbage, put it in my trunk, and went home to hose off and change. Rich people are never available before 9:00 anyway; not even rich people who aren't really rich, mathematically speaking. In America, even the broke are divided into classes.

Truk let me in with no expression on his face to indicate he knew me from anyone else who came to the door. He didn't even glance at the red and blue gym bag I was carrying. After a little absence he came back and led me through a room I hadn't been in and outside to a flagged courtyard where Orson and Clarissa Childs sat in fluffy white robes drinking coffee; Mrs. Childs's out-of-focus gaze said there was as much Kentucky as Colombian in her cup.

The houseman faded and I set down my bag, which clanked when it touched the flagstones. Childs, looking up from the *Free*

*Press*, glanced back at it, then at me. Portrait shots of the shooting victims bordered a grainy picture of the murder scene on the front page.

"Anything new?" he asked. "There was nothing on the radio that wasn't there last night."

"There wouldn't be. The press doesn't know yet about the kidney."

The woman started, spilling coffee on the table. Childs folded the paper and laid it on the vacant chair. "It didn't have anything to do with what happened. I assume you've been talking with Worden."

"What happens to Mark's trust fund now that he isn't around to collect it?"

"It goes to his heirs and assigns. Before you go any further, you might want to consider the penalty for slander."

"What lawyer would press the case after your retainer check came back from his bank?"

The couple locked gazes. He blinked first. She set down her cup with a double click.

Childs said, "You should be having this conversation with Worden. He's an angry man and simple. His thought processes are easy to predict when he thinks he's been cheated. Not that there is anything to whatever he told you. Buying organs is shaky from a legal standpoint."

"So's murder. His shotgun tests clean. How about yours?"

"I don't own a shotgun."

"Not anymore. You decided to get rid of it after you used it on Mark and then his roommates to make it look like he wasn't the only target."

He lengthened his upper lip. "Evidence?"

"Me, for starters. I'm a witness." I leaned down, unzipped the bag, and took out one of the pieces I'd retrieved that morning. The barrel had been cut into eight-inch lengths, then split down the middle. When I laid it on the table, Mrs. Childs squeaked, got up, and half ran inside, holding a hand over her mouth. I let her. "If I'd known this was what you were slicing up last night, it would've saved me a dive in your dumpster. No wonder you jumped when I walked in on you."

Childs turned his head slowly from side to side, as if he were trying to get out of my shadow. "Assuming that's where you found it, what's it prove? You can't trace scrap."

"You know a lot less about shotguns than you do about metalwork. Cutting up the barrel's a waste of time; it's smooth, leaves no striations on the pellets. In order to connect the weapon to the murder, all the cops have to do is match the firing pin to the marks on the shells found on the scene." I was holding the bag now. I took out the heavy Browning receiver and laid it on the table. The incriminating evidence was intact.

He stared at it while I let the bag drop with the rest of the pieces inside.

"Planting that high-grade pot was smart," I said. "It should have been coke or heroin, but maybe a man in your circumstances doesn't know how to go about finding them. Smart, and stupid: It diverted the investigation, but it put it in the hands of a narc named McCoy, who'll have all the upper-end dealers in the area in his data bank. The one you bought it from will turn you if it means ducking four charges of homicide."

"It's true," he said. "I don't know much about dope *or* shotguns."

"Don't say anything, Orson. All you did was buy marijuana."

I turned around. Clarissa Childs was standing in front of the door to the house with the twin of the chopped-up Browning raised to her shoulder. The barrel looked as big as a culvert.

"He wasn't lying to you, Mr. Walker," she said. "Orson has never fired a shotgun in his life. My first husband taught me how to hunt. I've been putting game on the table for years."

I thought about the revolver in my belt. She read my mind. The shotgun twitched. I held my hands out from my body,

"Clarissa—" Childs began.

"I said don't say anything!" She kept her eyes on me. "Nothing that ever came from Hank was any good. His son was defective; even his kidney didn't fix what was really wrong with Mark. After everything Orson and I did for him, he turned his back on his education and ran away. Why should he fall into money when we've got three mortgages on this house?"

"Clarissa?" This time his throat throbbed with warning.

"Drop it!"

We turned our heads together. Childs sat motionless, staring at Lieutenant Mary Ann Thaler, Rick McCoy, and three uniforms standing with sidearms pointed at the woman with the shotgun. I'd called them early enough to avoid a standoff, but they must have taken the long way around the house.

"Drop it!" Thaler shouted again.

Clarissa Childs hesitated, then lowered the shotgun. The officers were advancing when she swiveled the butt down to the ground, jammed the muzzle up under her chin, and tripped the trigger with the toe of her slipper.

"We got a partial off that air conditioner knob that puts the mother on the scene," Thaler said while my statement was being typed up. "For what it's worth."

"It closes the case. That must be worth something to someone."

She was drinking tea again, from one of those mugs they sell downstairs with the police seal on it. Headquarters is running a boutique to catch up on repairs. Today she had on a grayish-pink suit; ashes of rose, I think they call it. She looked less tired. "All we've got on Orson Childs is attempting to destroy evidence. I don't think we can make accomplice after the fact stick. Some mother, huh? I used to think there was something to maternal instinct. I thought I was missing something."

"Not wanting kids and killing the one you have don't walk under the same sun."

"Plus three other mothers' sons just for garnish. Sometimes I hate this town. Other times I just dislike it a little."

"It started in Grosse Pointe."

"It's all Detroit." She worked the tea bag. "I'd sure like to know how you confirmed the Childses had money troubles. If I thought you knew your way around a computer I might ask the boys in white-collar crime to keep an eye on you."

"You don't have to log in to run a bluff."

"*On,*" she said. "You log on to the Internet, not in. But you knew that. You're overdoing it."

"The less people think you know, the better for you."

"If that's true you'll live forever."

I said nothing.

She said, "I know about you and Barry Stackpole. You two are the evil twins of amateur law enforcement." She took out the tea bag and dumped it into her wastebasket. "Any questions?"

"None I can think of."

"Well, you know what they say about curiosity." She sipped.

# PRIDE

BY P.J. PARRISH

*Brush Park*


Tonight I have the windows open to catch what little breeze there is, and as I lay in my damp sheets, my face turned toward the gauzy glow of the streetlight outside, I can hear them. The lions are roaring.

It starts low, a moaning prelude. Then it builds, drifting to me in my bed with the shifts of the heavy August air, until it becomes a distant but full-throated roar.

*Aaaa-OUUU. Aaaa-OUUUUUU.*

I listen, my body tense, until it finally dies into a series of staccato grunts.

*Huh, huh, huh.*

I am two miles away from the lions, safe in my basement studio apartment just a block off Woodward Avenue. I know the lions are secured behind a moat. They are fed twice a day, cosseted by their caretakers at the Detroit Zoo. They want for nothing.

So why do they roar at night?

It starts again.

*Aaaa-OUUU. Aaaa-OUUUUUU.*

I look toward the corner where the yellow-white beam from the streetlight falls across the bureau and brings the steel of my gun to life.

I press my palms over my ears and close my eyes.


Baker was waiting at my desk when I got to work the next morning. He had made my coffee for me.

"You look like hell," he said, holding out my chipped white mug. The rim still had yesterday's lipstick on it, but I didn't care.

"I couldn't sleep," I said.

"You need to do something about that," he said.

I nodded as I sipped the coffee. He had even remembered the Splenda. After four years riding together, it made me feel good that he remembered how I took my coffee. My ex had never seemed to get that one down.

"Drink up, we have a call," Baker said.

I looked at him over the rim of the mug. "How bad?"

He held my eye for a moment but didn't say anything before he turned away to pick up his jacket off the chair. That explained the waiting coffee. It was going to be a really bad one.

We drove through a sticky morning rain, moving away from the Central District station house on Woodward. For once, I hadn't put up a fight when Baker told me he was going to drive. I just sat back in the seat, watching the slow sweep of the windshield wipers.

Baker took a right into Brush Park. A century ago, the neighborhood had been home to the city's elite. But now it was block after block of decaying Victorians, weedy empty lots, and the collapsing brick caverns of abandoned boarding houses. We called it The Zone, the nickname coming from the government E-Zone program that was funneling millions of dollars into Detroit's decaying core. The E stood for Empowerment, the politicians said, and there were signs of life here and there—a new Blimpie over on Mack, an old factory being converted to lofts, a few rehabbed mansions reclaimed from ruin. And at night, when the Tigers had a home game, the southern horizon burned bright with the lights from Comerica Park. But for most of the people here, the empowerment hadn't trickled down enough to ease the pain of their daily lives. To most people in The Zone, E still meant empty.

Literally empty, I thought as I stared out the window.

Over the past couple decades, in the name of renewal, whole blocks of blighted and burned-out houses had been demolished, leaving vast stretches of weeds and grass. Untrimmed trees formed tunnels over the pocked streets. Wild pheasants had taken to roosting in the rafters of the rotting houses. The Zone had the aching loneliness of an abandoned prairie town.

As we turned onto John R, I found myself looking for the small reminders of the lush life that had once thrived here. A set of stairs leading up to nowhere, the ornate carvings still visible in the crumbling concrete. A listing red brick chimney covered with the creeping pink blooms of wild sweet pea vines. A rusted stop sign standing sentry on a corner where no one came anymore.

But then, the surprise of a lone house, bars on the windows and plastic flowers in the yard. And another, its sagging porch strung with Christmas lights. People hanging on, barricading themselves in their homes against the drug dealers and prostitutes, waiting for the city fathers to figure it all out.

I stole a look at Baker's Sharpei profile, with the ever-present mint-flavored toothpick hanging from his lip. None of this ever seemed to bother him. He was driving slowly, like he always did, a sharp contrast to my own gas-brake-gas-brake style. Baker kept an even flow on most everything. Even on calls like this, even when he knew what we were going to see.

"How old?" I asked.

"Four months," he said.

The rain had stopped by the time we pulled up to the house. There was a small crowd gathered by the steps, women mostly, their arms crossed over their chests or clutching kids to their thighs. The low tire-whir of the nearby Fisher Freeway filled my ears.

Baker turned toward me. "You ready?"

Usually someone—often the mother but on rare occasions the male in the house—takes the child to the emergency room. Driven by a fleeting clarity of what they have done, they hope that the limp body in their arms can be miraculously transformed back into a baby.

That was not what had happened in the house on John R.

When the responding officers arrived, the child was still in its bed. By the time I entered the blue bedroom, the eyes of three stuffed animals—a bear, a rabbit, and a zebra—looked down upon an empty crib. With its broken slats, it resembled a wooden cage.

Baker nudged me, indicating I should step aside to let the photographer do his job. The camera flash brightened the blood on the yellow tangled blanket. The air smelled of sour diapers.

I heard a woman crying. Between her sobs, she whispered the name *Tommy*. I followed the sound back to the living room, pulling my notebook from my jacket.

The woman sat on a green sofa. When her eyes came up, she focused first on Baker, then on me, making that female-to-female connection. I knew from experience she had some vague hope that I was the one person in this group of stone-faced strangers who might understand why her baby died at the hands of her man. I resented it and I wanted to slap her. Instead, I sat down next to her.

"What was your son's name?" I asked.

"Justin."

"And your boyfriend's name?"

"Tommy Freeman." It was his name she had called out from the bedroom, not her baby's.

"Do you know where he is right now?" I asked.

"Probably at his brother's."

I took down all the information in my small notebook. I wrote slowly, postponing the final part of my interview, the part that in all my years as a cop had never gotten any easier. I learned a long time ago that these woman often changed their stories when they realized that their boyfriend or husband was going to go to prison. Sometimes, they recanted everything. Sometimes, they took the full blame themselves.

I set a small tape recorder on the scarred coffee table near the woman's knees.

"Can you tell me what happened?"

"The baby stressed Tommy out. He works nights, and the constant crying . . ."

I nodded, my eyes closing over a burn of tears. I knew I wouldn't cry. I had this way of absorbing tears back inside my head. Baker once told me that if I didn't let them out once in a while, they'd back up into my brain and begin to ferment. He had meant it as a joke, but I didn't laugh.

"Please don't hurt him when you pick him up," the woman whispered.

I said nothing and stood up. The creamy scent of formula was in my nose and I took a look around. A blue plastic baby bottle sat on the end table.

"You'll need to go with the officers down to station, ma'am," I said.

She looked to me in confusion. "But I didn't do anything."

"I know," I said.

Baker was stopped at a traffic light. The heat rose in wavering vapors from the hot asphalt, dissipating into the pale yellow sky. There was a sulphurous smell in the air that pricked my nostrils even through the closed car windows.

"Can we stop at Angela's?" I asked Baker.

He nodded and turned right, heading to an apartment building over on Winder. I had met Angela about three years ago. She was working in a strip club up on Eight Mile, trying to do the best she could for her twelve-year-old daughter. Angela had just married Curtis Streeter, a mostly unemployed construction worker with flat black eyes and the names of his two ex-wives tattooed on his bicep. As a wedding gift, he had added Angela's name to his arm.

It was two nights after the wedding that Baker and I made our first visit to their place. We found Angela crumpled in the corner of the tiny yellow kitchen, bloody hand prints smearing the oven door. The daughter was in her bed with a split lip and her hair chopped off above her ears by dull scissors. Punishment by her stepfather for sassing back.

Angela had been strong at first, fueled by her pain and the sight of her daughter's ragged hair. But in the days after, she began to withdraw, the pain turning to regret and self-blame. I knew that without Angela's testimony, Streeter would walk free.

For the first time in my career, I went the extra mile for a victim. I spent nights digging into Streeter's past, but I didn't find anything that could send him away. Though I did find something I hoped might steel Angela's resolve.

A few years before he hooked up with Angela, Streeter had been living with a woman who had an infant son. Six weeks into the relationship, the mother carried her dead son into an emergency room. The baby died of a head injury, like his brain had ricocheted around inside his skull, the doctors said. The mother said the baby had fallen down some stairs. No one believed her. But when Streeter's alibi was backed up by three of his punk friends, the only thing the cops could do was charge the mother with neglect.

I pulled out the coroner's photos of the dead child and I showed them to Angela, telling her Streeter had shaken that baby to death. A week later, Angela stood in court and begged the judge to put Streeter away. Because Streeter had a record and his battery charge on Angela violated his probation, an impatient judge gave him seven years.

In the four years I had been working the special crimes unit, I could count on one hand the number of abuse cases that came close to a successful resolution. Angela's was one of them, and I had been keeping loose tabs on her ever since. Maybe I took a sort of pride in the fact that I had helped her turn some corner.

That's why I had asked Baker to swing by. That, and I needed something to wipe the image of Justin's bloody crib from my head.

* * *

The outside of Angela's building was as bad as I remembered. But behind the triple deadbolts she had fixed up her place. Fresh mauve paint, rose-patterned curtains I knew she had made herself. The place smelled of simmering beef and green beans.

Baker posted himself at the window to watch the cruiser below. Last week on this same street a squad car had been stripped while the officer was inside taking a report.

Angela emerged from the kitchen carrying a can of Vernors ginger ale. She looked good, even with a few extra pounds. Her hair was bright yellow with a recent coloring. Men tipped well for blond hair, she had once told me.

When she handed me the can of pop, an odd scent drifted off her body. Someone who had given birth would have recognized it more quickly, but it wasn't until I picked up on Angela's expression—child-bright with a secret—that it hit me. The smell was breast milk.

"I had a baby," she said.

I scanned the room for evidence that a man now lived here. I saw nothing except a baby seat pushed into the corner near the television.

"When?"

"Three months ago. Want to see him?"

She didn't give me time to answer and I followed her back to the bedrooms. The first room was painted pink, adorned with posters of pop singers and kittens. The daughter's room. She'd be fifteen or so now.

At the door of Angela's room, I slowed, but she waved me over to the bassinet near her bed.

A halo of curls around a chubby face. Long brown lashes that fluttered with dreams. His tiny body filled only a third of the mattress.

"Who's the father?" I asked.

Angela picked up the baby and placed a soft kiss on his

cheek. "He's out of the picture," she said. "He was married, and I'm okay with that. He paid for everything, though. Still sends me money when he can."

I found the news oddly comforting. "So you're doing okay?"

Angela nodded, yet wouldn't meet my eyes. There was something she wasn't telling me, but I wasn't sure I should push. Baker had said I couldn't be both protector and friend to the victims I met. The line between the two was too thin.

"Sheffield," Baker called out.

Something in the way he said my name compelled me quickly back to the living room. I stopped short, staring into a pair of flat black eyes.

Curtis Streeter stood there, smiling at me.

I didn't smile back.

"Curtis has been paroled."

Angela's voice was small behind me. I didn't turn to look at her, just kept my eyes on Streeter.

Angela sidled past me, still carrying the baby and going to Streeter's side. He gave her an odd hug, his hand gently pushing the baby to Angela's hip so he could flatten himself against her body. When he broke the embrace, his eyes came back to my face. He wasn't smiling anymore. It was clear he remembered me.

"He doesn't have anyplace to go," Angela said. "I'm letting him move back in."

My eyes flicked to Baker, still standing at the window. He wasn't watching Streeter. He was watching me. He gave me a subtle shake of his head. I turned away.

*Tonight I have the windows closed, even though it is still eighty degrees. I lay here in my narrow bed, staring at the shadows. Finally, I can't stand it anymore and go to the window, throwing it open. The heavy night air pours over my body.*

*I stand at the small casement window, looking up at the ground*

*that encloses me, and then up further to the small slice of night sky I*
*can glimpse. No stars, no moon.*

*I crawl back to my bed, my head thick with sleeplessness. Just*
*as I dare to close my eyes, it starts, a single low roar. Then another*
*in answer, and finally a third, forming a raw chorus of overlapping,*
*repetitive bellows.*

*Closer, a night bird calls, its tiny sharp pleading punctuating the*
*roaring.*

*The night has awakened, and its creatures—large and small—are*
*proclaiming themselves to the world.*

"What's with you today?"

I stayed silent. A part of me was glad that Baker picked up
on my mood because I hadn't been able to think of a way to tell
him what I needed to.

"Sheffield, what the hell is wrong?"

I let out a long breath. "I'm thinking of bagging it."

"Bagging what?"

"This. I can't do it anymore. I can't take it anymore."

Baker was quiet, chewing on his toothpick, his hands steady
on the wheel. The soft chatter from the radio filled the car.

"This got anything to do with Angela?" he asked.

"No. Maybe. Shit, I don't know."

"Sheffield, for chrissake . . ."

I held up a hand. "I can't do this anymore, all right? I can't
keep telling myself that what I do makes any difference in this
shithole place."

Baker was quiet.

I was afraid I would cry. "I'm tired," I said. "I'm tired and I
just feel so alone."

Baker still said nothing, just put the car in gear and we moved
slowly forward. I leaned my head back and closed my eyes.

I don't know how long I stayed like that, in a half-sleep
state, lulled by the murmur of the radio and the movement of

the car. When I realized we had stopped, I opened my eyes.

We were in a deserted parking lot. The peeling white façade of Tiger Stadium loomed in the windshield. Baker was gone. Then I saw him coming toward the car carrying two Styrofoam cups. He slid in and handed me a cup and a pack of Splenda.

For several minutes we sat in silence, sipping our coffees.

"My dad used to bring me here for games," Baker said, nodding toward the stadium. "We were in the bleachers for the seventh game of the '68 series when Northrup hit a two-run rope into center to win. It was great."

"I wasn't even born then, Baker," I said.

He gave me a half-smile, set his coffee in a holder, and put the car in gear. We headed down Michigan Avenue, past empty office buildings with paper masking their storefront windows. It had started to rain again, and in distance I could see the gleaming glass silos of the Ren Cen.

Baker slowed and pointed to the abandoned hulk of the Book-Cadillac building. "My mom took my sister and me to have tea there once," he said, nodding. "I guess she was trying to give me some class. I guess it didn't take."

I stared at the old hotel's boarded-up windows. There was a sign in one saying, FRIENDS OF THE BOOK-CADILLAC, with a website for donations.

At Grand Circus Park, Baker swung the cruiser around the empty square and slowed as we moved into the shadows of the People Mover overhead. "My dad used to bring us down here to the show," Baker said. "The Madison is gone now but the old United Artists is still there. That's where I saw Ben Hur."

I stared out the windshield at the abandoned theater's art deco–like marquee, now covered with gray plywood. I knew that Baker had grown up in Detroit and that after his wife died fifteen years ago, he had sold their house in Royal Oak and moved back. But he never talked about the city or its steady deterioration.

Baker pulled to a stop at the curb. We were in front of the

Fox Theatre now. In the gloom of the rain and late afternoon, the ten-story neon marquee with its winged lions pulsed with light. Tickets were now on sale for *Sesame Street Live.*

"They almost tore this place down, you know," he said. "But that millionaire pizza guy bought it. Fixed it up, reopened it, and then relocated his business offices upstairs."

I looked out over the empty street. "Why would anyone with any brains invest in this place?"

"Maybe he couldn't take seeing one more good thing die," Baker said.

I stared at the winged lions. I heard the snap of Baker undoing his seat belt and looked over.

He reached under his seat and came up with a crumbled brown paper bag, molded in a distinctive shape I instantly recognized.

He pulled the gun from the bag and handed it to me. It was an older S&W Model 10 revolver. The bluing was chipped along the barrel. The gun was clean but it had seen its share of street time.

"Remember me telling you about Hoffner?" Baker asked.

"Your first partner," I said. My mind flashed on the photograph of the jowly man on the memorial wall at the Beaubian station. Shot to death during a drug bust.

"That was . . ." Baker paused, searching for the word he wanted. Cops had a way of doing that, selectively choosing words that could be interpreted one way by other cops and another more benign way by the rest of the world.

"Hoffner and me, we called that gun our third partner," Baker said.

I turned the weapon over. The serial number had been acid-burned away. But this gun was so old I doubted it had a registered owner anywhere. I knew why. Hoffner's gun was a throw-down, a handy way of fixing the worst mistake a cop could make— shooting an unarmed suspect.

"Did this partner ever have to do any work?" I asked.

"Not on my watch."

"Why are you giving it to me?"

"Because every officer should have one."

"And you think I might need it one day?"

"No," Baker said. "I think you need it now."

*I need to know why. I need to know why they do it.*

*So I find this book about lions and I read it, because I have this idea that if I can find out why they roar I can figure out a way to stop it.*

*I read about the lions of the Serengeti, how they have different sounds to mark their territories, to attract female lions, to find each other when they are separated, to call their cubs when they are lost.*

*But that awful group roaring that comes every night. What is that?*

*I read on.*

*. . . When a strange male lion comes into a pride he kills all the cubs too small to escape him. He kills because it ends the mother lion's investment in her cubs and brings her back into fertility sooner.*

*But . . .*

*Sometimes the female lions band together and roar as a group to drive the killer male away. They roar as one to make sure their cubs survive.*

*That night, when the roaring builds to its crescendo, I lay there and listen. I listen, trying hard to interpret the sounds, trying hard to hear my own heart.*

I was sitting in my personal car, Hoffner's old chipped gun on the seat next to me. I hadn't brought my service weapon or either of the other two guns I had locked up at home. I didn't want to take any chances that I would somehow screw it up and use the wrong one.

I had never worried about things like that before.

Confusing guns or being seen somewhere I shouldn't or worrying about performing my duties in the way I had been trained. I was a professional.

But I had never killed someone before.

Not even in the line of duty. Until now, I had been grateful for that. But somewhere in the last few days, and more so in these last few hours spent sitting outside Angela's apartment building, I had the unforgivable yearning to know what it felt like to kill.

I checked my watch. Nine p.m.

Angela had left earlier for her job, turning to blow a kiss to her teenage daughter who stood in the doorway holding the baby.

I was relieved that Angela had not left the baby alone with Streeter, but I was worried for the daughter.

I knew I couldn't go up there. I needed to be invisible right now, to Streeter and to my fellow cops. I only hoped that I could make my move before Streeter made his.

If he made one.

My thoughts were shifting again, drawn to that basic human hope that men were not wild animals. And for a moment, I questioned what I was doing. But only for a moment, because this job had taught me different.

I checked my watch again. Nine-twenty.

A light went out in the apartment. I knew it was in Angela's bedroom and I let out a breath, thinking that Streeter was going to bed. I would have to wait. Wait and hope he didn't do anything.

I had just reached for the keys when the apartment door opened and Streeter hustled out. His leather jacket caught the orange beam of the streetlight before he disappeared into the darkness.

I started my car and followed slowly, hugging the curb but keeping my distance. He seemed intent on his destination, his pace quickening as he crossed the street and made a turn south.

I thought he may be heading to the bar over on Woodward,

but then he just jagged east, head down, hands sunk deep into his jacket pockets. As he entered a block of abandoned houses, he slowed, looking to the structures as if he wasn't sure which one he wanted. I knew then what he was doing.

Out of prison three days and already sniffing out a new supplier.

He found it at the corner.

It was a listing shingle-sided house missing half its porch. The windows were boarded up but a faint light was visible behind a web of curtain in the small upper-story window.

Streeter stopped on the sidewalk, half-hidden behind a mound of trash. He stood in a glistening puddle of broken glass, his head swiveling in a nervous scan of the street. I had stopped halfway down the block and was slumped low in my seat, confident my rust-pocked Toyota didn't stand out in the ruins around us.

He went inside.

I waited.

He was out again in less than three minutes, hand again in his pocket, unable to resist fondling the rock of crack as he walked. I slipped down in the seat but he didn't even look my way as he hurried past. He was already tasting his high. It would be the only thing on his mind.

I rose, and in my rearview mirror I watched his retreat. I started the car and eased away from the curb.

He was going home.

And I would get there before him.

In the few seconds before he arrived, I took small, calming breaths and I hoped for things I had no right to hope for.

I hoped the T-shirt I had brought to put over the gun would muffle the sound. I hoped the people who lived here were too used to gunfire to even hear it anymore. I hoped no one had seen me move from my car to the shadows at the side of the apartment building. I hoped Angela would not grieve for this man too long.

I heard his footsteps before I saw him.

It kicked my heart up another notch and I drew what I knew would be my last full breath for the next few minutes.

I raised the gun. Kept it close to my side so it was partially obscured.

The sheen of his leather jacket caught the glow of the street-light first. Then I saw a slice of skin and the glint of an eye that for a second looked more animal than human.

Two steps further and his entire body came into focus. He was walking straight toward me, but the emptiness of the night made me invisible to a man seeing only the weak yellow light of his front door.

He stopped at the stoop, nose and ears turned up to the air, as if he could smell my presence.

I stepped from the darkness.

I waited one second for my face to register in his brain because I wanted him to know who I was and why he had to die.

When I saw the fearful recognition in his eyes I fired. Once.

Trusting my ability to hit him in the heart. Knowing one shot would attract far less attention than six.

He fell straight down, his knees hitting the pavement with a bone-jamming thud. His hand went to his chest, and for a second he was frozen in that position, eyes locked open, blood pouring from between his fingers.

He fell face first with a fleshy smack to the concrete.

I made myself a cup of tea and took it to my bed. The television was on, the sound low but the light putting out something close to a comforting glow.

My hand trembled as I brought the cup up to my lips and took a drink.

There was nothing about Streeter on the 11 o'clock news

but I knew there wouldn't be. A crack addict getting shot on a random Detroit street didn't merit a mention. Still, I watched.

The talking heads lobbed it over to sports. I hit the mute and leaned back on my pillows as the silence filled my small basement room.

I would go see Angela in a day or two. Give her enough time and space. Give myself enough time and space.

My head was pounding with fatigue. I set the cup aside and closed my eyes.

The ring of the phone jarred me awake. The TV was still on. I caught the green dial of the clock as I went for the receiver. Twelve-fifteen.

"Yeah, hello?"

"Detective Sheffield?"

The voice was deep but definitely female, with an authoritative calm that sent a small chill through me.

"Yes," I said.

"Detective, this is Lieutenant Janklow over at the Western District."

I felt my heart give an extra beat.

"We had a report tonight of a shooting in your district, a Curtis Streeter."

I closed my eyes.

"Detective Sheffield?"

"A shooting, yes . . ."

"We know what you did."

I couldn't move.

"Don't worry, detective, you're not alone."

I brought a shaking hand up to my sweating face.

"There are six of us now," the woman said. "The others asked me to call you and welcome you to our group."

There was a long silence on the other end of the line. Then the woman's voice came back, softer now.

"Good night, detective."

A click, then silence.

I opened my eyes. My hand was still shaking as I set the receiver back in its cradle.

*Something wakes me. A sound in my dreams or something outside? I can't tell. I jerk awake, my eyes searching the darkness.*

*But it isn't really dark. There is a gray light in the corners of my room, creeping in from the edges of the window. I throw the sheet aside and go to the window.*

*Not dawn. Not yet. Still night but almost there.*

*And then I hear it. The roaring. But it sounds different now, still edged with anger, still deep with pain. But now with a strong pulse of relentless strength. The lions will never be quieted.*

*I go back to my bed. The sound is in my ears. I sleep.*

# PANIC

BY JOYCE CAROL OATES

*Chrysler Freeway*

He knows this fact: It was a school bus.

That unmistakable color of virulent high-concentrate urine.

A lumbering school bus emitting exhaust. Faulty muffler, should be ticketed. He's gotten trapped behind the bus in the right lane of the Chrysler Freeway headed north at about the exit for I-94, trapped at forty-five goddamned miles an hour. In disgust he shut the vent on his dashboard. What a smell! Would've turned on the A/C except he glimpsed then in the smudged rear window of the school bus, a section of which had been cranked partway open, two half-heifer-sized boys (Hispanic? Black?) wrestling together and grinning. One of them had a gun that the other was trying to snatch from him.

"My God! He's got a—"

Charles spoke distractedly, in shock. He'd been preparing to shift into the left lane and pass the damned bus but traffic in that lane of the freeway (now nearing the Hamtramck exit) was unrelenting, he'd come up dangerously close behind the bus. Beside him Camille glanced up sharply to see two boys struggling against the rear window, the long-barreled object that was a gun or appeared to be a gun, without uttering a word or even a sound of alarm, distress, warning. Camille fumbled to unbuckle her safety belt, turned to climb over the back of the seat where she fell awkwardly, scrambled then to her knees to unbuckle the baby from the baby's safety seat, and crouched on the floor behind Charles. So swiftly!

In a hoarse voice crying: "Brake the car! Get *away!*"

Charles was left in the front seat, alone. Exposed.

Stunned at how quickly, how unerringly and without a moment's hesitation, his wife had reacted to the situation. She'd escaped into the backseat like a panicked cat. And lithe as a cat. While he continued to drive, too stunned even to release pressure on the gas pedal, staring at the boys in the school bus window less than fifteen feet ahead.

Now the boys were watching him too. They'd seen Camille climb over the back of her seat, very possibly they'd caught a flash of her white thigh, a silky undergarment, and they were howling with hilarity. Grinning and pointing at Charles behind the wheel frozen-faced in fear and indecision, delighted as if they were being tickled in their most private parts. Another hulking boy joined them thrusting his heifer face close against the window. The boy waving the gun, any age from twelve to seventeen, fatty torso in a black T-shirt, oily black tight-curly hair, and a skin like something smudged with a dirty eraser, was crouching now to point the gun barrel through the cranked-open window, at an angle that allowed him to aim straight at Charles's heart.

Laugh, laugh! There were a half-dozen boys now crowded against the bus window, observing with glee the cringing Caucasian male, of no age in their eyes except old, hunched below the wheel of his metallic-gray Acura in the futile hope of minimizing the target he made, pleading, as if the boys could hear or, hearing, be moved to have pity on him, "No, don't! No, no, God, no—"

Charles braked the car, desperately. Swerved into the highway shoulder. This was a dangerous maneuver executed without premeditation, no signal to the driver close behind the Acura in a massive SUV, but he had no choice! Horns were sounding on all sides, furious as wounded rhinos. The Acura lurched and bumped along the littered shoulder, skidded, began to fishtail. Both Camille and Susanna were screaming. Charles saw a twisted heap of chrome rushing toward them, tire remnants and broken glass, but his brakes held, he struck the chrome at about ten miles an hour, and came to an abrupt stop.

Directly behind Charles, the baby was shrieking. Camille was trying to comfort her, "Honey, it's all right! We are all right, honey! We're safe now! Nothing is going to happen! Nothing is going to happen to you, honey. Mommy is right here."

The school bus had veered on ahead, emitting its jeering exhaust.

*Too fast. It happened too fast.*

*Didn't have time to think. Those punk bastards . . .*

Had he seen the license plate at the rear of the school bus? He had not. Hadn't even registered the name of the school district or the bus company in black letters coated in grime at the rear of the bus.

Hamtramck? Highland Park? As soon as he'd seen the gun in the boy's hand he'd been walloped by adrenaline like a shot to the heart: rushing blood to his head, tears into his eyes, racing his heart like a hammering fist.

He was shaken, ashamed. Humiliated.

It was the animal panic of not wanting to be shot, not wanting to die, that had taken over him utterly. The demonically grinning boys, the long-barreled object, obviously a gun, had to be a gun, the boy crouching so that he could aim through the cranked-open section of the window straight at Charles. The rapture in the thuggish kid's face as he prepared to pull the trigger.

Camille was leaning over him, concerned. "Charles, are you all right?" He was cursing the boys on the bus. He was sweating now, and his heart continued to beat erratically, as if mockingly. He told Camille yes, of course he was all right. He was fine. He was alive, wasn't he? No shots had been fired, and he hadn't crashed the car. She and Susanna were unhurt.

He would climb out of the overheated car as, scarcely more

than a foot away, traffic rushed by on the highway, and he would struggle with the goddamned strip of chrome that had jammed beneath the Acura's front bumper, and then with mangled hands gripping the steering wheel tight as death he would continue to drive his family the rest of the way home without incident.

Camille remained in the backseat, cradling and comforting the baby.

Comforting the baby—she should be comforting *him*. She'd abandoned him to death.

He laughed. He was willing to recast the incident as a droll yet emblematic experience. One of the small and inexplicable dramas of their marriage. Saying, teasing, "You certainly got out of the passenger's seat in record time, Camille. Abandoned your poor husband."

Camille looked at him, eyes brimming with hurt.

"Charles, I had to protect Susanna. I only—"

"Of course. I know. It was remarkable, what you did."

"I saw the gun. That's all I saw. I panicked, and acted without thinking."

"You acted brilliantly, Camille. I wish we had a video."

Camille laughed. She was still excited, pumped up.

Susanna, eighteen months old, their first and to-be-only child, had been changed, fed, pacified, lain gently in her crib. A miracle, the baby who usually resisted napping at this hour was sleeping.

She'd cried herself into exhaustion. But she would forget the incident in the car, already she'd forgotten. The bliss of eighteen months.

Camille was saying, in awe of herself, "Charles, I don't think I've ever acted so swiftly. So—unerringly! I played high school basketball, field hockey. I was never so fast as the other girls."

Ruefully Camille rubbed her knees. She was slightly banged

up—she would be bruised, she guessed. Lucky for her she hadn't broken her neck.

Yet Camille was marveling at what she accomplished in those scant several seconds. While Charles had continued to drive the car like a zombie, helpless. She had unbuckled her seat belt and crawled over the back of the seat and unbuckled the baby and crouched with the baby behind Charles. Shielded by Charles.

Charles understood that Camille would recall and reenact her astonishing performance many times, in secret.

He said, "You hid behind me, which was the wise thing to do. Under the circumstances. The kids had a target, it would have been me in any case. It was purely nature, what you did. 'Protecting the young.'"

"Charles, really! I didn't hide behind you. I hid behind the car seat."

*But I was in the car seat.* "Look, you were acting instinctively. Instinct is impersonal. You acted to save a baby, and yourself. You had to save yourself in order to save the baby. It must be like suddenly realizing you can swim." Charles spoke slowly, as if the idea were only now coming to him, a way of seeing the incident from a higher moral perspective. "A boat capsizes, you're in the water, and in terror of drowning you swim. You discover that you can swim."

"Except you don't, Charles. You don't just 'swim.' If you don't already know how to swim, you drown."

"I mean it's nature, impersonal. It isn't volitional."

"Yet you seem to resent me."

"Resent you? Camille, I love you."

The truthful answer was yes. He did resent her, unfairly. Yet he knew he must not push this further, he would say things he might regret and could not retract. *You don't love me, you love Susanna. You love the baby not the father. You love the father but not much. Not enough. The father is expendable. The father is last season's milkweed seed blown in the wind. Debris.*

Camille laughed at him, though she was wanting to be kissed by him, comforted. After her acrobatics in the car, after she'd demonstrated how little she needed him, how comical and accessory he was to her, still she wanted to be kissed and comforted as if she was a wistful girl of about fourteen. Her smooth skin, her face that was round and imperturbable as a moon, maddening at times in its placidity. Charles had been attracted initially by the calmness of the woman's beauty and now he was annoyed. Camille was thirty-six years old, which is not so young, and yet even in unsparing daylight she looked at least a decade younger, her face was so unlined, her eyes so clear. Charles, forty-two, had one of those fair-skinned "patrician" faces that become imprinted with a subtle sort of age: reminding Charles, when he had to consider it, of calcified sand beneath which rivulets of fresh water are running, wearing away the sand from within.

He was a corporation lawyer. He was a very good corporation lawyer. He would protect his clients. He would protect his wife, his daughter. How?

"Camille, don't misunderstand me. Your instinct was to protect Susanna. There was nothing you could have done for me if one of those kids had fired the gun."

"If you had been shot, we would have crashed anyway. We might all be dead now."

Camille spoke wistfully. Charles wanted to slap her.

"Well. We're not, are we?"

Instead, they were in their bedroom in Bloomfield Hills. A large white colonial on a hill in Baskings Grove Estates, near Quarton Road. Leafy hilly suburb north of the derelict and depopulated city of Detroit where, years ago as a boy, Charles had lived in a residential neighborhood above Six Mile Road near Livernois until his parents, afraid of "coloreds" encroaching upon them, had panicked, sold their property, and fled. They were now living in Lake North, Florida. Charles thought of them as he tugged off his noose-necktie and flung it down. *Some of*

*them, they'd kill you as soon as look at you. They're crack addicts,
animals.*

In the car returning home, Camille had tried to call 911 but
the cell phone hadn't worked, and now that they were home,
and safe, Charles debated whether to report the incident to Detroit police, now that the emergency had passed. No one had
been hurt, after all.

Camille objected, "But they—those boys—might hurt someone else. If they play that trick again. Another driver might really
panic seeing the gun aimed at him, and crash his car."

Charles winced at this. Really panic. As if he, Charles, had
panicked only moderately. But of course he had, why deny it?
Camille had been a witness. The swarthy-skinned boys laughing
like hyenas in the rear bus windows had been witnesses.

While Camille prepared their dinner, Charles made the call.
He spoke carefully, politely. His voice did not quaver: . . . *calling
to report an incident that happened at about 4:15 this afternoon on
the Chrysler Freeway headed north at about the Hamtramck exit. A
very dangerous incident involving a gun, that almost caused an accident. High school boys. Or maybe junior high . . .* Charles spoke
flatly describing in terse words what had happened. What had
almost happened. Having to concede he hadn't seen a license
plate. Had not noticed the name of the school district. No dis-
tinguishing features on the bus except it was an old bus, probably not a suburban school bus, certainly not a private school
bus, very likely an inner-city bus, rust-flecked, filthy, emitting
exhaust. No, he had not gotten a very good look at the boys:
dark-skinned, he thought. But hadn't seen clearly.

In the kitchen, Camille seemed to be opening and shutting
drawers compulsively as if looking for something that eluded her.
She was in a fever, suddenly! She came to a doorway to stare at
Charles who had ceased speaking on the phone, which was their
land phone; he stood limply, arms at his sides, staring at the car-
pet at his feet. Camille said, "Charles?"

"Yes? What?"

"Didn't whoever you spoke with have more to ask? Didn't he ask for our number?"

"No."

"That seems strange. You weren't on the phone very long."

Charles felt his face darken with blood. Was this woman eavesdropping on him? She'd left him to die, abandoned him to jeering black boys with a gun, now she was eavesdropping on his call to the police, staring at him so strangely?

"Long enough."

Camille stared. A strand of hair had fallen onto her forehead; distractedly she brushed it away. "'Long enough'—what?"

"On the fucking phone. *You* call, if it's so important to you."

In fact, Charles had not called the police. Even as he'd punched out the numbers on his phone, he'd broken the connection with his thumb before the call went through. He hadn't spoken with any police officer, nor even with any operator. None of what happened that afternoon seemed very important to him now. The boys (Hispanic? Black?) were punks of no consequence to him, living here on Fairway Drive, Bloomfield Hills; his revenge was living here, and not there, with them; his revenge was being himself, capable of dismissing them from his thoughts. The gun had (probably) not been a real gun and whatever had happened on the Chrysler Freeway . . . after all, nothing had happened.

"But I didn't get a good look at them, Charles. As you did."

There was nothing on the local Detroit news stations, of interest to them, at 6 p.m. But at 11 p.m. there came *BULLETIN BREAKING NEWS* of a shooting on I-94, near the intersection with Grand River Avenue: a trucker had been shot in the upper chest with what police believed to be a .45-caliber bullet, and was in critical condition at Detroit General. The shooting had occurred at approximately 9:20 p.m. and police had determined the shot had been fired by a sniper on an overpass, firing down into traffic.

Camille cried, "It was him! That boy!"

Charles switched stations. Film footage of I-94 near Grand River Avenue was just concluding. "Why should it be I-94? An overpass? The boys on the bus were headed in the other direction. They'd have been off the bus, wherever they were going, hours before. And miles away. It's just a coincidence."

Camille shuddered. "Coincidence? My God."

"You still love me. Don't you?"

"Don't be ridiculous."

"*Don't* you?"

"Shouldn't I?" A pause. "I'm so tired . . ."

Knowing he wouldn't be able to sleep, but he must sleep, he had an early meeting the next morning: 8 a.m., breakfast. At his company's headquarters. Must sleep. They'd gone to bed, exhausted and creaky-jointed as an elderly couple, and Charles lay now stiff as a wooden effigy, on his back. He'd dismissed the incident (urine-colored school bus, smudge-skinned young punks, the ambiguous long-barreled weapon) from his mind, it was over. Beside him Camille lay warm-skinned, ardent. Wanting to push into his arms, to make love, with him, or wanting at least to give the impression of wanting to make love, which, in a long-term marriage, counts for the same gesture, in theory. *See? I love you, you are rebuffing me.* Charles was polite but unreceptive. What pathos in lovemaking, in stark "physical" sex, when life itself is at stake! Civilization at stake! Charles's head was flooding with images like the screen of a demonic video game. (He had never played such a game. But he'd observed, in video arcades.) The ugly lumbering school bus he'd been trapped behind. The stink of the exhaust. How had it happened, had Camille been speaking to him? He'd become distracted, hadn't seen the bus in time to switch to another lane, and if he'd done that, none of this would have happened. Seeing now the rear window of the bus: craning his neck upward, to see. What were those boys doing? The rear window was divided into sections and only the smaller panes could be cranked open. The pane at the left, directly in front of, and above, Charles, had been opened and it was through this window that the long-barreled revolver had been pointed. *No! Don't shoot! Not me!* Now Charles saw vividly, unmistakably, the faces of the boys: They were probably not more than twelve or thirteen years old, with dark, demonic eyes, jeering grins, oily-dark hair. As he stared up at them, pleading with them, the gun discharged, a froth-dream washed over his contorted face like an explosion of light. Was he already dead? His face was frozen. And there was Camille screaming and pushing—at him—trying to get away from him, as he restrained her. *Brake the car! Get away!* He'd never heard his wife speak in so hoarse, so impatient a voice. For the baby was somewhere behind them, and nothing mattered except the baby.

Charles was alone now in the speeding car. A limping-speeding car, as if one of the tires was going flat. Where was he? One of the freeways? Emerging out of Detroit, in a stream of traffic. And there was the school bus, ahead. He'd been abandoned by his family to die in their place. You are born, you reproduce, you die. The simplest equation. No choice except to drive blindly forward even as the gleeful boys, one of them pudgy-fat-faced, a faint mustache on his upper lip, knelt on the bus seat to aim a bullet into his head.

He heard the windshield shatter. He cringed, trying to shield his face and chest with his arms.

It is said that when you are shot you don't feel pain, you feel the powerful impact of the bullet or bullets like a horse's hooves striking you. You may begin to bleed in astonishment for you did not know you'd been hit. Certainly you know with a part of your brain, but not the conscious part of your brain, for that part of your brain is working to deny its knowledge. The work of mankind is to deny such knowledge. The labor of civilization, tribal life. Truth is dissolved in human wishes. The wish is an acid powerful enough to dissolve all knowledge. He, Charles, would die; must die at the hands of a grinning imbecile in a black T-shirt. Yet he seemed to know, and this was the point of the dream, that he could not allow himself such knowledge for he could not bear his life under such circumstances. In middle age he had become the father of a baby girl. He had neither wanted nor not-wanted a baby, but when the baby was born he'd realized that his life had been a preparation for this. He loved this baby girl whose name in the dream he could not remember far more than he loved his own ridiculous life and he would not have caused such a beautiful child to be brought into a world so polluted, so ugly a world. As the bullets shattered the windshield of the car, a sliver of glass flew at the baby's face, piercing an eye for she'd been left helpless, strapped in the child safety seat.

Charles screamed, thrashing in panic.

"Charles? Wake up."

He'd soaked though the boxer shorts that he wore in place of pajamas. The thin white T-shirt stuck to his ribs and his armpits stank, appallingly.

"You've been dreaming. Poor darling."

Camille understood: Her husband had ceased to love her. He would not forget her behavior in the car, her "abandonment" of him. He was jealous of her acrobatic prowess, was he?—as he was jealous of her way with Susanna who would rather be bathed by and cuddle with Mommy than Daddy.

It wasn't the first time in nine years of marriage that Charles had ceased to love Camille, she knew. For he was a ridiculous man. Immature, wayward in emotion, uncertain of himself, anxious-competitive in his profession, frightened. He was vain. He was childish. Though highly intelligent, sharp-witted. At times, handsome. And tender. He had a habit of frowning, grimacing, pulling at his lips, that Camille found exasperating, yet, even so, he was an attractive man. He was shrewd, though he lacked an instinctive sense of others. And yet Camille herself was shrewd, she'd loved one or two other men before Charles and understood that she must comfort him now, for he needed her badly. She must kiss his mouth, gently. Not aggressively but gently. She must hold him, his sweaty, frankly smelly body, a tremulous male body, she must laugh softly and kiss him as if unaware that he was trembling. At first Charles was resistant, for a man must be resistant at such times. For his pride had been wounded. His male pride, lacerated. And publicly. He'd been having a nightmare just now, yet how like Charles not to want to have been wakened from it, by Camille.

Panic can only be borne by a man if there is no witness.

Charles's skin had turned clammy. Camille could feel his heart beating erratically. He was still shivering, his feet and hands were icy. He'd had a true panic attack, Camille thought. She was holding him, beginning to be frightened herself. But she must not let on, of course. "Darling, I'm here. I've got you. You'll be fine."

Eventually, well before dawn when the baby in the adjoining room first began to fret and flail in her crib, this was so.

# LITTLE HORSES

BY NISI SHAWL
*Belle Isle*

T he white candle on top of her dresser had burned dirty that morning. When she stood up from her prayers she saw its glass sooting up black. Big Momma would say that meant danger of some kind. But what? To who? Not Carter. It was after Carter's funeral that Big Momma had made her promise to burn it.

Uneasily, Leora turned her gaze away from the boy beside her on the car's backseat. Sometimes it was hard not to stare at him. And sometimes, for the same reasons, it hurt.

It was her job, though, keeping an eye on him. Leora did her duty. Especially today; might be him who the candle had been warning her about. If Big Momma had a phone, she could have called her and found out.

If it was her own self in danger, that didn't matter. Not that she'd commit the sin of suicide, but it wasn't natural she should be living on after her child.

In case her suspicions were right, Leora had stayed close as she could by the door to the boy's room when his teacher came that morning. She'd cut his sandwich in extra tiny pieces, even lifting the bread to check the chicken salad surreptitiously with her finger for bones. Left the lunch dishes for the maid to clear while she fussed at nothing in the basement, keeping an eye on him building his boat models till his mother came and insisted they go outside.

"Take the car," the mother had suggested, standing on the stairs in one of her floaty chiffon numbers designed to hide her weight. Against Mr. McGinniss's wishes, his wife had hired a new chauffeur. Now she needed to prove he wasn't a waste of money.

Outside the car's windows, Belle Isle's spare spring beauty waltzed lazily around them as they followed the road's curves. The chauffeur seemed to understand his business. Not real friendly, but then he wasn't getting paid to talk to the nanny. The 1959 Cadillac was the McGinnisses' third best car, last year's model. He had it running smooth and fine; she could barely hear the engine.

He had known the best way to take to the park, too, staying on course as the street name changed from Lake Shore to Jefferson, and passing up the thin charms of Waterworks Park without hesitating one second. And he had circled the stained white wedding cake of the Scott Fountain as many times as the boy asked him. Now he steered them past some people fishing, practicing for the Derby coming in June.

Without looking, Kevin's hand sought and found Leora's. He was all of six years old. Six and a half, he would have said. His fingers stretched to curl over the edge of her pinkish palm, the tips extending between her knuckles. Not such a high contrast in color as it could have been. His daddy was what they called "Black Irish," which was only about his hair being dark and curly and his eyes brown and his skin liable to take a tan easier than some white folks.

A gentle turn, and the road ran between the waters of Lake Tacoma and the Detroit River. Kevin's hand nestled deeper into her own. She let her eyes sweep slowly away from the window, over the car's plush interior and the back of the driver's head, the pierced-glass barrier dividing him from the rear seat, to the boy's snub-nosed profile. A pause; then she slid her glance past him through the far window to the Canadian shore. So much the same. But different. A different country. Slaves had escaped to Ontario a hundred years ago. Some of them settled there and never came back.

The driver spoke unexpectedly. "Here's the boat museum site coming up, Mester McGinniss." A pile of bricks, low and flat, ugly even in the late afternoon sun, occupied the road's left side. Holes gaped for windows. The driver honked his horn at a man sitting hunched over on a sawhorse with his back to them and turned sharply onto Picnic Way, stopping right on the road. Two red trucks and a beat-up black-and-purple sedan squatted on the muddy lot around the half-finished museum. "You want to get out, Mester McGinniss, take a look around?" What was there to look at that they couldn't see from where they were sitting? With Kevin's clean loafers in mind, Leora told the driver to keep driving. Time enough for them to visit when it was open; Kevin wasn't like most boys his age, excited by earthmovers and heavy machinery.

They headed for the island's center. The Peace Carillon loomed up, narrow and white like that black-burning candle. Usually Belle Isle's spacious vistas calmed Leora's spirit, but not today.

At Central they turned east again, toward the island's wilder end. "Will we see any deer?" Kevin asked.

"No tellin," Leora answered.

"I think we should get out when we get to the woods. They're never going to walk up close to a car." He took his hand back to hold himself up off the seat cushions with two stiff arms, a sure sign of determination. "We could hide ourselves behind some trees."

Leora was about to tell him about the one time she'd seen them here, a whole herd, eight or ten wild deer, crossing Oakway bold as you please. But the driver interrupted her thoughts. "A fine idea, Mester McGinniss," he said, as if he was the one to decide those sorts of things. "We'll do just that."

No one else on the road before them or behind them, and the driver took advantage of that to step on the gas again. What was the man's name? Farmer, she recalled, and was ready to speak up sharp to him, white or not, when he slowed down. Way down.

He grinned back over his shoulder at the boy, a nervous grin not coming anywhere near his pale eyes. "Like that?" he asked. Kevin nodded, grave as his uncle the judge. "You ever try driving?" Leora clamped her lips firmly shut to make sure she didn't call the man a fool to his face.

"Maybe when we get safe into the woods I'll take you up on my lap, let you to steer a bit afore we ambush them deer, Mester McGinniss." Farmer turned to the front. "If your mammy won't mind."

"I ain't his mammy."

"Beg pardon, but I thought that's what—"

"Mammies is Southern. I'm Kevin's *nanny*."

Farmer muttered something, his voice low, lost under the quiet engine's. She should have kept her own counsel. She should have, but there was only so much a body could take, and after nearly thirty years of passing up on pound cake and plucking her eyebrows and creaming her hardworking hands and pressing her hair and dyeing and altering her employers' worn-out gowns so you wouldn't hardly recognize them, Leora was not about to sit silent while some ignorant peckerwood called her after a fat, ragheaded old Aunt Jemima. And her so light-skinned. Even at forty-two, she was better-looking than that. Not long ago, she had been beautiful.

Mr. McGinniss had called her irresistible.

Shadows covered the car hood, the road ahead, the view out of either window. Thin shadows, thickening as she noticed them, leafless branches crowding together to warm their sap in the spring sun. They were in the woods, and suddenly that ignorant driver had swung onto an unpaved side road. The car slowed to a crawl, ruts and puddles rocking it along. Farmer stopped again, for no reason Leora could see.

"Is this where we hide to look for the deer? And I can learn to drive?" the boy asked.

"Yessir, Mester McGinniss. This here's the place. Just let me take you on my lap." The driver got out and went around the back to Kevin's side. As Farmer opened the door, the fear smell came off him in great stinking waves like a waterfall. Leora reached for Kevin. She got him by his waist and held him as Farmer grabbed his arm, lifting him half off the car seat.

The boy screamed. They were pulling him apart, hurting him. Leora loosened her grip, but only for a moment. Then she had him again, by his wool-clad thighs this time, and they were both out on the ground, Farmer yelling and yanking Kevin's arm, jerking him around so that Leora rolled in the mud. Sharp pains, blows to her sides that made her sick. Someone was kicking her and she screamed, held on tighter as if the boy could keep away the pain.

"Stop." It was a man's voice, sounding quiet above all the noise, like smoke above a flame. Leora held Kevin solidly in her arms, sat up on the muddy ground and looked.

There were three of them. The driver Farmer, or whatever his real name was, and two more. The others wore masks, but she recognized one by his sweater, a thick gray cardigan bunched up over his broad hips. He had been sitting on the sawhorse at the construction site. He had a gun. It was aimed at her. And beside him stood a thin man in a long coat with his hands in the pockets.

"What do you want?" Leora asked. The thin man snorted.

"Shut up, mammy." Farmer rolled his shoulder, wincing like she'd hurt him. Good.

"Bring the car closer," the thin man said. The driver went off out of sight down the dirt road, past the Caddy. That left two. Could she run away and lose them in the woods?

"Stay down," said the thin man. "And no more noise out of either of you." The one with the gun lifted it, like it was something she might have missed.

She didn't ask again what they wanted. They were kidnappers, had to be: the danger that dirty burning signified. That's what these men were up to, like in the papers; why else would they be doing this?

Kevin started crying and shivering, and Leora turned her attention back to him. "Shush now," she told him. "Ain't nobody gonna hurt you, baby. They just gonna ask your daddy to give them some money is all." She hummed the lullaby Big Momma had taught her, soft, no words, so only he would hear, and stroked his hair back from his face. No words. She had never been able to bring herself to sing them.

It worked well enough; his sobbing wound itself down to where she could listen in on their captors.

"—shoulda waited to give the signal on a day she wasn't riding along."

"Farmer said he'd be able to separate them. Said he'd have no problems." A short pause. "Find a way to tie and gag her too. Give me the gun. Somebody could come along any minute." Smart, that one in the long coat. In fact, she heard an engine now, getting louder, nearer. The police? They had a station on the island's other side.

"On your feet, mammy." She looked up from Kevin's dark-lashed eyes. The sweatered man held out one hand to help her up; a dingy-looking red bandana drooped from the other. She got her legs under her and stood up on her own, the boy a soft weight in her arms. She could see through the leafless trees now, and it was only the black-and-purple sedan from the construction site coming toward them. The man took her by the elbow. The sedan stopped, and he started to steer her to its back door.

"No." She planted her feet as firm as she could. Prepared to fight. The thin man had said it himself: Stay here and someone would come along eventually. No telling where they'd take her once they got her in the car. Not anyplace she'd want to go.

"I'll shoot you," the thin man said. He stepped nearer and the gun's muzzle dug into her neck. She couldn't tell if it was hot or cold or both. "I will. Give me half a chance," he said, and she decided she'd better believe him. Maybe he wouldn't; maybe a gun would make too much noise. She wasn't going to find out.

Leora laid Kevin down on the car seat the way she would for a nap. He looked up at her accusingly, as if the kidnapping was her fault, and opened his mouth to say something, but she shook her head and put her finger to her lips. She tried to get in next to him, but the gun pressed harder. "Hold up," the thin man told her. She stood as still as she could.

The driver got out with a short piece of clothesline hanging from his arm and went into the back on the other side.

"Farmer, my father's going to be *very* angry at you." Kevin's voice sounded firm and fragile at the same time, like pie crust. "You'd better bring us home right away."

"All in good time, Mester McGinniss. Give me your hands here, and put 'em together at the wrists. Don't make us have to shoot nobody, now—yes, that's the way. I'll have that gag now." The sweatered man moved to the other door. They stuck the dirty red bandana over the boy's mouth.

When they were done with Kevin, it was her turn. The thin man stepped back but kept the gun aimed at her face. "Take your jacket off. Now put it on again, backwards. Leave your arms out." He had Farmer jerk it down level with her elbows and tie the sleeves behind her. He searched the pockets, confiscating her keys, wadding up her gloves and handkerchief and throwing them in the dirt. Then he picked them up again and crammed the gloves in her mouth with her handkerchief on top, smashing her lips flat when he tied it in back. Farmer put her silk neck scarf over her eyes, knotted it too tight, and that was the last she saw for a while.

They shoved her in next to the boy, laying his head in her lap, she was pretty sure. That was what it felt like. The thin man crowded in beside her; she knew it was him by the gun muzzle he dug in her neck. He pulled her toward himself and pushed her face against his coat's shoulder. He smelled like Old Spice and dry-cleaning fluid.

Somebody started the car and backed it up the dirt road to where the pavement began again. They turned left and kept driving.

She could feel when they came from under the trees. The sun was so low it struck through the sedan's windows, warming the back of her head. Almost ready to set.

"They'll be taking off soon." That was the sweatered man talking.

"All right, we'll circle around the island a few times." The thin man. They didn't use each others' names besides Farmer's. As they talked more she figured out the discussion was about the boat museum's construction crew going home for the weekend. Farmer said something about ransom money. She had been right. Such a comfort.

Kevin began crying again. With his gag in she felt more than heard him: hot tears soaking her skirt, shoulders trembling. She tried humming the lullaby but this time her voice wouldn't cooperate. It cracked, wanted to rise up and up, roll out of her loud and high. The gunmetal pressing into her neck muscles put an end to that before it got properly started.

Where were they going? She lost track of the turns: angles, curves, left, right, hummocks and dips that might lead anywhere. Nowhere. The boy's weeping went on and on. She did her best to shut it from her mind and think how to escape.

The scarf was too tight. Her coat was untied and off; the wind blowing from the river cut through the thin material of her uniform. Her shoes, heavy with mud, slipped on the unseen ladder's rungs and she held herself on as best she could, arms half-numb from being pinned to her sides. Then she reached the floor. The wind died, and the smell of earth and concrete rose around her.

A shove on her shoulder sent Leora sprawling to the side,

but she stayed upright. What was happening? She had to know. She tore at the scarf, her short, blunt fingernails useless. Muffled sobs and shrieks came closer and closer, lower and lower, accompanied by the scrape of leather on wooden rungs.

"Dump him in the corner over there." That was the thin man, the one who had forced her down the ladder by telling her he had a gun aimed at her head. He gave most of the orders. He was the one she had to convince.

She needed to get calm, get ahold of herself. She had a plan. It had come to her in the car. She willed her hands away from the knotted silk blinding her weeping eyes. Worked instead on the gag, wet with her own drool. Quickly, while they were too busy with Kevin to notice. The handkerchief was cheap, a gift from Big Momma, flimsy cotton. It tore easily and hung in damp shreds around her neck.

"I got a confession," Leora announced. "About my boy." Swear words and fast steps filled the darkness. Air brushed her cheek; she flinched.

"Wait." The thin man again. No blow landed. "Let's hear her out. Yell for help and you die," he promised.

"You gone and took the wrong one. This here's my son."

More swearing. The thin man cut through it. "You're saying Farmer made a mistake?"

"I nivver did! That there's the McGinniss heir—on my life it is!"

"That's what you think." She spun them her whole sorry tale. Mr. McGinniss had got her in the family way, she said, and Big Momma sent her off to her sister Rutha's house in Ontario to have the baby boy and leave him there.

Then Mrs. McGinniss got pregnant too. But her child never drew breath in Leora's version of events, so Mr. McGinniss called Carter back to raise him as his son. Which he was. Had been.

It was true enough, and better than what actually happened.

"Well," said the thin man after she finished, "that's a very compelling narrative."

"What?" Farmer protested. "You believe that bullshit? I wouldn't raise some half-nigger as my kid no matter—"

"There are precedents . . . Of course, without proof—"

"We'll still collect us a ransom, won't we?" The least familiar voice, so it must be the sweatered man.

"Maybe," the thin man answered.

And that was when Leora realized what a bad mistake she had made.

The kidnappers didn't let them go. If the ransom never came, they weren't about to. Ever. Her lies had nearly made Kevin and Leora worthless. Only the kidnappers' disbelief kept them alive.

It was so cold. They had tied her arms with her coat again but that was no protection.

She and Kevin were together in the same corner. Her new understanding of the criminal mind helped her reject the notion that this had anything to do with how she or the boy felt. For whatever reason, it was simply more convenient this way for the kidnappers. Probably they had just the one gun.

The floor was cement, rough and uneven. Leora lay on her side, Kevin curled up in front of her like a question mark. His wool britches smelled like pee. His silent sobs were weak and hopeless, old-seeming.

At least no one had tried putting her gag back on. "You wanna hear a story, Kevin?" She waited while his sobs slowed. No other response came. That figured; no call for the kidnappers to take his gag off. She started anyway, her voice low and soothing. "Once there was a little boy. Now I'm talkin about *real* little, not a big boy like you. He lived far away, in another country, far away from his momma and his daddy . . . Why?" Leora made believe the boy had asked her a question, then answered it. "On account of he was a prince in disguise, and being off in another land was the best disguise his momma and daddy could come up with."

She stopped. Was this idea any better than her last one?

She had something else to try, something maybe a little easier; it depended on which kidnappers had been left to watch them. And how many. What seemed like hours ago she'd heard feet climbing up the ladder. Now she struggled to remember: One pair? Two?

"I need to use the lavatory," Leora said, loud enough that anyone nearby could hear her.

"That's a shame, since we got no such *facilities* on the *premises*." Farmer. Him she could handle. "Guess you'll have to wet yourself."

"It ain't that . . ." Leora let her sentence trail off, pretending embarrassment she wasn't far from feeling.

Farmer laughed, but the thin man interrupted. "Take her through to the other room." Him she was afraid of.

"What? She shits, I'm supposed to wipe her black ass?"

"Don't act any stupider than you are. Untie her, let her take care of it herself." A pause. "Do it."

A hand on her shoulder helped her clumsily up from the floor. "I'll be right back," she told the boy.

Her plan wouldn't work so well with two of them there. But maybe she could overpower Farmer when she was untied and alone with him in this other room, take away any weapon he had, or do something to get him on her side. She shuffled carefully through the darkness, grit crackling beneath her feet.

By the change in the echoes around her, Leora figured they had entered a smaller space. Farmer shoved her front against a cold, damp wall and freed her arms. He was out of reach by the time she turned around. She took a step forward, another, hands extended, without connecting.

"What's the hold up? Do your business!" It sounded like he was talking to a dog.

"It's . . . I think I'm gettin my monthlies . . ." Leora improvised. "I won't know just by touching myself. I'm gone hafta see—"

"Jesus *Christ*! I don't— You expect me to take off your blindfold too? That's a lot of nerve you got, nigger gal—"

"No!" He was closer now, she could tell by his voice, the noise of his breath. "No, only, how about you . . . reach in for me . . . and find out yourself." Lord knew what she looked like, lipstick smeared off, mascara and eyeliner and rouge running all down her face, mud caking her uniform.

She smiled anyway, and when he said, "Yeah," sounding half-strangled in spit, she opened her mouth in anticipation, as if this was something she had waited for her whole life, his callused hand hiking up her skirt and skinning down her nylon underwear, parting the tangled hair and inserting one finger where no one had been in years. She sighed and rode up and down on it a couple of times for good measure, and he said, "Jesus Christ," again, but in an entirely different tone of voice.

He had his pants unbuttoned in seconds, and replaced his finger without even laying her on the floor.

She felt a jackknife in his pocket as he scrabbled against the concrete. The blade wouldn't be longer than two or three inches, she judged, but good to have all the same. He slumped to one side, done. Before she could retrieve the knife he recovered and pushed himself away from her.

"You two having a nice time in there?" The thin man's voice sounded maybe forty feet off.

"Yeah. I'll be out in a jiffy." He tied her arms again without saying another word, not a bit won over, and Leora had no choice but to let him.

Time to put her new plan into action.

"Well," the thin man said as they reentered the first room, "I see you *did* have a nice time." Her face and neck went hot. "Unfortunately, you're not my type." He laughed at his own joke.

"Listen," Leora said. "I lied before. About the boy. I—"

"Sure you did. What happened—you had a chance to realize the consequences if it was true?"

"Well, some of it—"

"Sit down and shut up."

Farmer pushed her to her knees.

"I'll tell you the—"

"Shut up!" Farmer knocked her the rest of the way to the ground. "There must be something to— I'll stuff your drawers in your mouth, I don't care!" He rolled her back and forth, wrestling her skirt up again.

"The real one's still alive! I know where they hid him!"

"Will you—"

"Wait a minute! Why are you so determined to keep her from saying what she wants? Something you'd rather I didn't learn about?"

"But you told her to shut up!"

"I changed my mind. A gentleman's prerogative." The thin man bent over her. "All right. Upsy daisy." He helped her sit with her back to the wall. "Now talk."

"It . . . He's my son, but if you let us go I can tell you where they took the other to be raised."

"Let you go. That's rich. Yeah, that's exactly what we plan on doing, let you go and head off on some wild goose chase looking for a boy who died or don't even exist." Farmer slapped her hard. This time the thin man raised no objection.

Half her face was numb. She made her mouth work. "I told you the truth! We swapped them two at birth, and only they daddy ever knew. He was thinkin ahead to when somethin like this would happen. You want the ransom or you want Mr. McGinniss to be laughin at you? You already sent him the note, right? He ain't answered you yet, has he?" A guess. She hoped it was a good one. "And he ain't gonna. You know why? Cause he don't care!"

Silence. Then the unclear sounds of them moving around—

doing what? If only she could see. Their voices came from more of a distance, muffled and senseless. All she could tell was that they were angry, till they returned and the thin man said, "Here's the deal. You tell us where the heir is. We release you, but we keep your kid till we find the real one's hideout."

Leora breathed huge gasps in and out. Oh God, she wanted like hell to agree, to get out of that hole in the ground where they had her; she had done her duty and then some, and what was Kevin to her anyway? Just a job, and maybe even the reason her own boy Carter had died, lost in the woods when he wandered off from Great-Aunt Rutha's cabin because his momma hadn't been there to take care of him, gone and disappeared while Leora watched over this white child who she owed nothing, *nothing*! She was crying, crying hard, she couldn't do anything about that or what she heard herself saying, which was, "No! NO! You cain't take him! I won't letcha! No, I won't!"

Farmer hit her again, but it was the thin man's unbelieving laughter that brought her back to her right mind.

The kidnappers were standing her on her feet. "So we believe you now about this one being your kid," the thin man said. "Otherwise you would have taken us up on our offer. So let's have the rest of it."

Their test, and she'd passed it without knowing. "You gonna—"

"Tell us where the McGinniss heir is or we'll shoot your son and throw him in the river."

"Canada," Leora said. "Ontario."

"Windsor?"

"In the country. I can give you directions—"

"You'll do better than that. Here you are, Farmer." The thin man's voice moved away. "Keep it trained on her. I'll be back fast as I can. Try not to have too much fun." The sound of his feet rising up the rungs. Then another noise: wood on wood, something dragging, scraping, then falling loudly on the ceiling, the floor above her head.

She was alone in the basement with a rapist and a help-less, tied-up white boy. Who she should have left to his fate. At least she should have tried to. When Farmer yanked him out of the car seat like that, she could have let him. And she would have, too, if only she'd been thinking instead of feeling. Using her brain, not her heart. If Kevin hadn't looked so much like his brother. Carter.

She wasn't going to cry. Leora had done enough of that al-ready. Big Momma had taught her to be strong, to survive. Do whatever it took, even if it went against the Bible.

One more plan.

She struggled to remember the words to that lullaby. She had always known she'd need to use it someday, in the special way Big Momma had learned her. How did it go now? *Hush-a-bye, don't you cry, / Go to sleepy, little baby; / When you wake, you shall have—*

"Okay, turn around so I can take this thing off," Farmer interrupted her thoughts, tugging at her blindfold. Which was when she realized her arms were untied again. Why? She hadn't sung a note, and anyway, it wasn't supposed to work like that.

Maybe she wouldn't have to, after all.

The knots in her good scarf proved too tough for Farmer as well, and he sliced them apart with his knife. She heard him open it, felt the silk give way.

Her eyes hurt. They were in a cellar, big metal buckets over in one corner with a fat flashlight standing on one. In another corner lay a short, lumpy shadow, white patches showing where Kevin's skin contrasted with his clothes and the bandanas over his mouth and eyes.

No sign of the ladder they'd made her walk down.

She whirled quickly to find Farmer behind her but out of reach, and grinning like a natural-born idiot. He had the knife and the gun both, but the gun wasn't aimed. "You want another fuck?" he asked. "I think there's time before we head out."

With a one-minute man like him there'd always be time, Leora figured. She didn't say that, though, mindful of the weapons. She gave him her back and went to Kevin.

Farmer followed her, pushing her out of the way. He cut the line holding the boy's legs, then his hands. Leora took them up in her own, kneeling beside him. They were cold, and mottled-looking in the dim light. She rubbed them to start the blood moving. Farmer got rid of the boy's blindfold; she saw when she looked up at his face. *Bees and butterflies, flutterin round his eyes . . .* Those same long lashes—

"Why you doin this?" she asked Farmer. "You lettin us out of here?" She might be wrong about the man, and he'd taken a fancy to her, after all.

"So I am, after a fashion." He brought the knife up against Kevin's neck. "We'll be taking a drive over the border, and you're less likely to stick in folks' memories without the ropes and things. Think you can convince your kid to keep his mouth shut when we cross the bridge?" Dark eyes darted to hers and away in every direction, taking in the room. Leora couldn't talk. She nodded yes. The knife moved up to the bandana's edge and ripped its way through the stained fabric. Not the bruised white skin.

Kevin couldn't talk either. He'd been gagged much longer than Leora. He needed water. When she had him sitting up she asked Farmer for something to drink and got a flask of what smelled like cheap whiskey, the sort of thing the Purple Gang once smuggled in. She gave it to the poor child; better that than nothing. Then she made him walk a little. He stumbled like a baby. She held him by his arms, surreptitiously looking for the ladder or some other way out.

There were three rooms counting the main one, the one where Farmer had taken her earlier, and what amounted to a closet. Doorways opened between them without doors. None contained stairs or a ladder, and Leora suddenly recalled the sounds she'd heard as the thin man left, the scraping and bumping. Like a picture she saw it in her head: He had pulled the ladder up with him and put something over the hole he had climbed out of.

No wonder the kidnappers weren't worried about letting loose their hands.

After helping Kevin go the bathroom, she sat down with him in the corner furthest from the stink. "Now what?" he whispered, the first words he'd spoken since the gag came out.

A hopeful sign. "We wait, I guess."

"For what? What are they—"

"None of that now! Speak so I can hear you, or else!" Farmer stood from the bucket where he sat and took a threatening step toward them, gun up.

"He just wants me to finish the story I was tellin," Leora lied.

"Go on then. So I can hear."

She hadn't gotten far past the beginning before, she was pretty sure. "So this prince was sent to a foreign land—"

"What was his name?"

"Foster."

"That's a dumb name." Sounding more like himself every second.

"Anyway, he was a prince, so you don't have to feel sorry for him. And he lived on a farm with a kindly old couple who always let him have whatever he wanted." Even if what he wanted killed him. "They had rules, but when he broke them, those old people would never raise not a hand against him."

"No spankings?"

"Not a swat. He was a prince; hittin him was against the law. Now one day, the little boy got up early, before anybody else was awake. And he went down to the kitchen and fixed a bowl of cereal, and then he went outside and walked off into the forest all by himself, although he had been told not to." And told and told and told.

"Why wasn't he supposed to go in the forest?"

"Because he wasn't supposed to go anywheres. Remember, he was a prince in disguise. He couldn't be runnin around where folks would see and recognize him. Then, of course, he went and got lost." In the great Canadian wilderness, trees and rocks and marshes—miles and miles of loneliness. "Lost. And he was hungry and tired and miserable, and he wished he'd never, never left that kitchen table. But what he didn't know was his momma—"

"The queen?"

"Yeah, that's right, his momma the queen, she had lit a magic candle to proteck him." Like Big Momma said to do. If only she had done it instead of worrying it was conjuring, the devil's work. Well, that wasn't going to stop her now. "The sun went down. Night was fallin. All of a sudden he seen a light."

"The candle?"

"The candle! You such a smart boy!" Same as Carter. "That's right, the prince seen the flame of his momma's magic candle, and it led him straight home to the farm where he lived. The end."

Kevin stayed quiet, thinking the way he usually did when she finished a story. She always knew he was thinking by the questions he would ask later, long after she'd forgotten the things she said.

The candle she lit after the funeral had been for Carter. Not to protect him. Too late for that. It was to commemorate his spirit, Big Momma had said. And to be what she called a *conduit*, a way they could speak with one another.

Of course, Leora had never attempted such a blasphemous thing.

Banging and a blast of cold air from the ceiling told her the thin man was back. The ladder slid down to rest its foot on the floor's middle and the thin man descended it, aiming his thin smile and a second gun through the rungs at them.

It took her till the sweatered man came down, too, to work out what was different. No masks.

It took her till they'd exchanged some talk she didn't follow and herded her and Kevin between them up out of the cellar and into the black-and-purple sedan to understand why this made her sick to her stomach.

No mask to prevent her from seeing the thin man's blond mustache and the way his nose tipped up at the end and the squint lines radiating from the edges of his eyes. No mask to stop her noticing the sweatered man's freckled forehead and the crease in his chin he didn't look to bother shaving.

So what was to prevent her from describing them to the police when they set her and Kevin free?

But of course the kidnappers had never been going to do that, since there was nobody except Aunt Rutha and Uncle Donald at the cabin, no secret heir. No prince in disguise.

Only Leora knew that though. She had thought.

She had thought she could wait till they got there, but no telling what these white men had in mind.

As soon as Farmer stopped driving, she'd have to sing.

The black-and-purple sedan's motor made more noise than the Cadillac. It was older too. The island looked empty for a Friday night. Then they reached the mainland, and she saw all the traffic lights flashing yellow. No reds. That late. Or early; early Saturday morning.

And when would the kidnappers stop the car? Where? Would she even have time to open her mouth before they shot her?

Kevin snuggled up against her on her right, both arms wrapped around hers at the elbow. In the regular flare of streetlamps Leora saw him staring up at her, worry and trust tugging him back and forth in nervous twitches. If she saved his life, he was truly hers. That's what she'd heard the Hindus would say.

The thin man had stuck a gun under her left ribs. On Kevin's far side the sweatered man crowded against the fogged-up window, flicking some switch on the gun he held. Tense or bored? Both, she decided. Wait for a change in that, then.

The lights came less often. Fewer of them; they must be near the rail yards now. Maybe here— Leora discovered she'd been holding her breath and let it go. The sweatered man stopped fiddling with his gun, but only to light himself a cigarette.

"Put that thing out," the thin man told him. "Filthy habit." He reached past her and snatched it away to stub it in the ashtray. A sudden sharp left. Lights ahead, low and steady. "Get the toll ready, Farmer," the thin man ordered. He jabbed the gun harder into Leora's side, a silent reminder to keep quiet.

They sailed through the toll booth and onto the Ambassador Bridge almost without a pause. Golden lights hanging on either side swooped their shadows across her eyes. They passed under its two signs, the red letters first facing forward, then backward.

Slaves had crossed all along here. In winter the water froze and they walked to freedom. In the darkness, on the ice, they ran over the river to the land they'd been so long dreaming of . . . Leora loved that freedom, the kind that came only in your sleep.

And then they were in Canada. The gun switch clicked so fast it sounded like a bent fan blade hitting its frame. A low roof lit from beneath by blue-white fluorescents chopped the horizon in half. Customs check.

Farmer pulled up to a booth. The man inside raised his eyes from his magazine, frowned, and waved them toward the parking lot.

The clicking stopped. "Shit," swore the thin man.

"Should I go where he's pointing at, or maybe I oughta make a run for it—"

"See those cop cars waiting up ahead? Think you can outrace them?"

The kidnappers continued to quarrel as Farmer veered off the road into a parking place. He left the engine idling, but they weren't going anywhere for a while. Not before they got a thorough inspection.

She smiled down at the boy beside her. This would be her

best bet. Big Momma had taught her, and it was not a sin—
especially in self-defense. And if it worked she would light a second candle. She opened her mouth to sing the lullaby until they
shut their eyes, every mother's son.

> *Hush-a-bye, don't you cry,*
> *Go to sleepy little baby;*
> *When you wake, you shall have,*
> *All the pretty little horses.*
>
> *Blacks and bays, dapple grays,*
> *All the pretty little horses.*
>
> *Way down yonder, in the meadow,*
> *Lies a poor little lamby;*
> *Bees and butterflies, flutterin round his eyes,*
> *Poor little thing is crying "Mammy."*
>
> *Go to sleep, don't you cry,*
> *Rest your head upon the clover;*
> *In your dreams, you shall ride,*
> *While your mammy's watching over.*
>
> *Blacks and bays, dapple grays,*
> *All the pretty little horses;*
> *All the pretty little horses.*

# PART II

*FACTORY OF ONE*

# RED QUARTERS

BY CRAIG HOLDEN

*Hamtramck*

F uck yeah," said Ziggy. "We're in." A piece of cheek beneath his left eye jumped, then jumped again. It was a place I'd never been, right on Joseph Campau, around the corner from St. Ladislaus. But then it all felt new to me. I'd only been back in Hamtramck, city of my life, for six months. I had gone off to other places, tried other things. When I got back, my friend Danny Lewicki got me on at the Main. I would've never got on without him. Most of the places then were laying off.

By we, I hoped Ziggy meant him and Danny. I couldn't shoot so well. I tried to be invisible against the wall. It was 8 a.m., and we were just off shift.

"We break," said the long-necked regular.

It was a close narrow place, just enough room in the front for the bar and stools along one wall, and only the light from a single window throwing over the thing. In the back it opened to a room just big enough to hold the pool table, but they'd had to shorten the cues so you didn't hit the walls when you shot.

"*We* break," said Ziggy. He was an old-timer, due to retire in another year or two. He didn't take much shit off anyone.

"We break," said the long-necked regular. He was shiny, with thin hair that looked like he wiped it back with his palms. He wore a leather vest, and a chain secured his wallet to his trousers.

Beyond the table, a paneled hallway led off to nothing. It was just a wall at the end of it, and an old console TV sitting there all covered with the dust of a thousand shows. Through a little window cut in one of the walls, you could see into a kind of kitchen area. There was a big stove in there and some sinks. A cook, or somebody in a white T-shirt, sat at a steel counter, counting cash out onto a sheet of aluminum foil.

"Then fuck it," said Ziggy. His hand was twitching; the middle fingers kept snapping in toward the palm. He put his cue down and headed back for the bar, so he could sit down. He looked like he needed to. He wasn't the steadiest.

"Awright," said the regular. "You can break."

"Break, Dan," said Ziggy. Danny was only a few years older than me. Ziggy was our supervisor at the Dodge Main. Poletown, they called it. This was 1979. The winter was ending, but the rumors had just started that the Main was coming down. No one believed it. It'd been there since 1912. I heard it rolled off more than thirteen million cars in them sixty-seven years. The Dodge brothers themselves built it, after they left off working for Henry. It was like a city in there, its own fire department and hospital and roads and kitchens. You could've been born in there and grown up and stayed inside the whole time, never coming out, and lived just fine.

"Watch this," Ziggy said to me. The tick beneath his eye kept time, the same time as the automatic riveter or the arm that whipped the planes of sheet metal into place. Danny broke. Three dropped, two solids and a stripe.

"Solids," said Danny.

"Drop 'em," said Ziggy. And Dan did: two more.

The long-necked regular sank a few. Ziggy sank two. The regular's partner, a true hefty boy, and with a scraggy little mustache, missed altogether.

"Shithead," said the long-necked regular.

"They call you Hamtramck Fats?" Ziggy said. Danny snickered, then cleaned it off and sank the eight.

"That's a round," said Ziggy. "Three rums."

"Three?" said the regular. "Only two of ya's playin.'"

"Partner there," said Ziggy. "Eddy. He drinks too."

"Two plays, two drinks," said the long-necked regular. He bought two. I went out to the bar and bought my own, and sat there to drink it.

Down at the other end were two girls. I saw them when we came in. One, whose grin was half-empty of teeth, nodded at me now. And she kept eyeing me. At least, I thought she did. The light from the window made it hard to see. I looked away from them but my head kept turning back, like they were pulling a string.

"Again," I heard the regular say.

"Rack 'em," said Ziggy. When I heard him break, I got up and stood in the open doorway between the bar part up front and the pool room in back. I leaned against the jamb, so I could see the whole place at once.

Ziggy's break sank a couple. Solids again.

It went on. Ziggy and Danny cleaned up again, won by four balls. I kept turning my head away from the far end of the bar.

"Another round," said Ziggy.

"You still got your last drinks," said the regular.

"Back 'em up," said Ziggy.

"Markers," said the bartender. He'd been watching through a little window between the end of the bar and the pool room. He held up a quarter someone had painted red. "Trade these in for drinks."

"Rack 'em," said the long-necked regular as he paid for the markers. Hamtramck Fats racked.

It went on. A stack of red quarters grew up from the bar, leaned, split into two stacks. I couldn't figure why they'd have so many red quarters.

"Use 'em," said Ziggy to me. "Might as well." I traded one in. Switched from rum to beer.

It went on. Ziggy and Dan let them win a game, handed them a couple of our quarters. "Keeps 'em biting," Ziggy whispered to me. He'd come out to the bar to rest, and I sat beside him. He had on his UAW hat, and his shirt had a UAW patch on the sleeve. Many didn't dress like that anymore, but Ziggy always did, every shift.

I looked at him, then the girls at the other end, back and forth. I could see him looking down at them too.

Then he said something about Elaine. She was a hot one we knew from the plant. A front office secretary. I knew her from high school.

"Call her," Ziggy said. "You could sure use some of that."

"She'll be in bed by now," I said. She hadn't been interested in me at Hamtramck High, and she wasn't interested now.

"All the better," Ziggy said.

I fingered the stack of red quarters.

"You know what them're for?"

"No."

"Bars all have 'em. Nothing's happening, they drop a few in the pool table or juke box or whatever to get things rolling. Then when the vendor cleans out the boxes, he knows what was the bar's to start. Don't count it against their percent."

"Really?"

He nodded, then got up and went back to the table, and I heard another rack and break.

"Shit!" said Hamtramck Fats, and Danny was laughing.

They played again, again, and it didn't get any better for the regulars.

"Here," Ziggy said when it was over and the chalk dust had settled. He handed a couple more quarters to the long-necked regular.

"Big of ya," the regular said. He retreated with Fats to their end of the bar, where the girls sat waiting for them.

"Fuck it," Ziggy said.

Danny and I drank and Ziggy told us a story about a trucker he knew who bought it on a curve on I-75. "Twenty ton come down on him," Ziggy said. "Took 'em four hours to saw him out." His cheek jumped. "Five ton an hour."

The two girls got up now and scooted down the bar. I was sitting between Ziggy and Danny. The girls sat one on each side of us, the half-toothless one by Ziggy.

"Drink?" Ziggy said. He flipped them each a red quarter. The one with half her teeth did all the talking. The other one wouldn't say nothing. She had greasy hair and little zits all over her face you could only see close up. Dan was next to this one, the Mute, and he was flicking bits of napkin at her, watching how they stuck on her hair.

"You wanna drive us to Chicago?" said the half-toothless one.

"For?" Ziggy said. He slipped off his barstool and had to climb back on. A muscle in his neck started contracting and relaxing, pulling his chin around toward his shoulder and then releasing it.

"Cause it ain't here," she said.

"Maybe so," he said. "Got a car?"

"You do," she said.

"Eddy's drivin," Ziggy said. He pointed at me.

"Wanna drive us to Chicago?" she said to me.

I looked away. She pulled my eyes back and grinned in a half-toothless sort of way. I traded in another quarter and went back and started shooting around on the table. Couldn't hit a thing. It was all spinning. I had no control over my arms. I killed my Blatz and traded in another quarter.

Then I heard the half-toothless one scream and slap Ziggy. I went around to watch. She and the Mute got up and went back down to their end of the bar. Ziggy and Dan were giggling. The greasy gal talked to the long-necked regular and Hamtramck Fats and all of them started looking at us. I stuck the cue in the crotch of my arm, like it was a gun I was cradling. I was ready. I was looking at them too. Couldn't stop.

Ziggy and Danny each traded in another red quarter.

"Think you guys had enough?" the bartender asked.

"Still got five quarters left," said Ziggy. "You gonna take 'em away? Bought and paid for?" His fingers were snapping into his palm again, hard enough so I could hear it.

The bartender walked down to the other end of the bar.

I stepped out and leaned against the wall.

"Pool cues stay back by the table," the bartender said. I stood where I was. The cue raised itself, pressed its butt against my shoulder, and fired—one, two, three, four, five, it picked them off.

"Get outta here, why don'cha," said Fats.

Ziggy looked at them, then at me. His whole face was moving, different parts of it twitching at different times. I saw him raise his glass. He told the story once of how he cleared off a whole bar, up in Flint, with his empty glass, just like he was bowling.

I had set my glass on the bar. I picked it up and said, "Hey! Hey! I'm a fucking puppet." I poured the beer over my head. They all looked at me. Then Ziggy broke up laughing.

Danny tipped his head back and balanced one of the red quarters on his nose and said, "Hey, I got a quarter growing on me."

We cracked up. We were all laughing. Even the dipshits at the other end were laughing for not knowing what else to do. Then Ziggy gagged and pressed his palms to his face. He gagged again and stood up and his back arched; he began convulsing and spun around and smashed into the bar. Glasses and napkins and red quarters flew everywhere. He spun off the bar and fell into the stools and bounced around and finally hit the floor. He was lying face down, a line of blood running out from his mouth. I felt my arms rise up into the air and my hands rest on top of my head.

Danny said, "He's killed."

After the moment of dead quiet that followed, the half-toothless one got up and walked down to our end of the bar. She kicked at Ziggy a few times. She said, "He ain't dead."

Ziggy moaned and moved a little.

"Tol you," she said.

"I'm a fuckin puppet," said Danny.

Ziggy moaned again. He lifted his head and in the blood I could see some of his teeth. He rolled over on his back and I saw the blood on his face and I could see where he was an old man, older than I had ever pictured him.

"What is it?" I said. I was whimpering.

"Fit," the half-toothless one said. She kicked Ziggy harder, in his ribs.

I remembered hearing something once about Ziggy, some brain thing he had.

"Get up," she said. He got up. She handed him some napkins and he stuffed one inside his mouth and dried his gums. Then he sat down at the bar and propped his forehead in his hands.

"Ziggy," said Danny.

"Ziggy," I said.

But he would not answer us.

The half-toothless one had her hands on Ziggy's back and she was leaning over his shoulder, talking to him. "Shush," she told us.

"Ziggy," I said.

"Ziggy," said Danny.

But still he would not answer us, so we went outside to breathe. It was very bright, cloudless, a ringer of a morning. Joseph Campau, the main street of Hamtramck, stretched out in both directions, just like it always had. I had been living in some mountains before I came back but there was no good work there.

"I'm a puppet," Danny was saying. It made him laugh.

We hadn't believed the rumors about the Main when we heard them, but they were true. We would find out for sure in another couple months, and by June it would be all over. Chrysler was barely staying alive. They'd sell the whole thing to GM, which would up and tear it all down. And that would be that.

After a few minutes, Danny and me got up and were going to go back in to get Ziggy, but the front door was locked.

"Hey," I said. I rattled the door and knocked on it but it wouldn't open. I peered through the smudgy glass and could just make out the interior. There was Ziggy, sitting up at the bar with all the others, the long-necked regular and Hamtramck Fats and the Mute and the half-toothed girl. The bartender leaned on his elbows, grinning and listening, a tall stack of red quarters on the bar in front of him. Everyone was listening to Ziggy. He was telling them a story, probably about his days in the army or about one of the whores he knew or something. He was one of the best storytellers. He'd been around.

"Come on," Danny said. "Time to go."

I said, "But—"

"I know a bar," he said.

"But—"

He took my arm and led me out into Joseph Campau, and across and down the sidewalk. He knew a place, he said, where it would be only the two of us and a barmaid named Brenda, and she would laugh and tell us stories about the days before the layoffs, way back when things were so busy in the city you could hardly take it all in, and the young men would come in from their shifts and fight and swear and bite the necks from the beer bottles and she would slap them on their heads to straighten them out. And we would smile and nod, weary with the beers and the hours and her tired voice.

# MIGRATION

BY Craig Bernier

*Rouge Foundry*

Barry Biehn made his commute to the Rouge. He skirted along industrial sprawl, mostly forgotten properties of the Ford Motor Company. The route from his nearby Dearborn home consisted of surface streets: Oakwood to Fort, Fort to Miller, then Miller to an unnamed road leading to Old Gate Five. Each street was pitted from truck traffic and neglect, but Barry preferred them to taking his old Lincoln on the freeways. Every day edged closer to the vehicle's last.

He drove past a fallen gate and its adjacent unmanned guard shack. Rusting metal signs hinted a cryptic warning about trespassing. Barry headed toward the toxic river. He passed through the ghost town of his father's Rouge River Plant, archaic and obsolete. Barry turned onto a cement byroad that ran alongside the gray river and drove under the rusting legs of an old off-loading crane, past rows of stilted fuel tanks, then onto blacktop that veered him toward the switching yards.

The Mk V's snow tires whirred a different pitch on the blacktop, an uplifting but brief chord. The blacktop switched abruptly into a cinder path that split two groups of train tracks. A plume of dust kicked up as Barry hit the cinders, like he'd thrown a switch. He passed one dormant freight car after another, a smoke screen stretching out behind him then dissipating into the wind. He thought of James Bond.

Barry arrived at the opposite side of the switching yards, the Lincoln bottoming out as he banged over a series of low rollers onto another road. He made the linchpin turn of his entire shortcut, slowing to inch the car up into the mouth of a mammoth abandoned warehouse. Like a covered bridge for titans, it was missing its two short walls. A 707 could taxi through it. This was the only passage in the miles of fencing that separated the living, breathing Rouge from its old necropolis. Barry idled through the warehouse, then dropped out the other side. He punched the car back onto the main road, then slowed again to tool into the foundry lot, slow, like clockwork. It began to snow.

The foundry works had one longitudinal parking lot, large, like a soccer field, about a quarter-mile's walk from the main entrance. First shift had the up-close spots and most of his co-workers on second shift gobbled up the rest. Barry was not one for arriving early to the foundry, and as a consequence was often relegated to a long walk from the outskirts.

He parked the Lincoln, grabbed his brownbag, and killed the engine. The car began its routine, dieseling and knocking for more life. Barry gave it one thing: It was a survivor. Bought new in '73, it, along with the Dearborn house, was Barry's inheritance when his father died a few years back. The car continued sputtering even after Barry closed the door. He started toward the main and the car stopped with a backfire pop, loud, like a pistol had gone off. Barry made a mental note to put the carb back the way he found it before all the weekend tinkering—a quarter turn here, a half turn there. As of late, the car had taken on qualities akin to a curse.

Barry was enthralled with the exponentially increasing snowfall. The forecast had called for the year's first blizzard, twelve to sixteen inches starting in the afternoon and continuing through the night. The powder was already showing accumulation, and the wind had increased in force—doubling and gusting—since Barry had left his house. He pulled up his collar and squared his pea cap down over the ears. Again, he headed into another shift he wished was his last.

Material, Planning, and Logistics (M, P & L) for the Rouge

Foundry Works held an elongated storeroom aloft as headquarters. It was tidy and well organized, but impossible to keep clean from a layer of soot generated by the works running below. More than soot, really, it was like an invasive burnt dust, a fine, powdery, oil-based grime that stuck to things. It worked its way into mechanisms and crevices, up nostrils, down lungs. Workers gave in to it as reality, an absolute. Not something to be combated, as it covered all things.

M, P & L's workspace had one large wall of square-paned, segmented windows that looked out on one of the molding bays down in the works. Looking out over the scene, the contrasts produced by darkness and fire could trance a viewer. It was not unusual from such a vantage point to ponder the existence of heaven and hell—or at least the planes of hell, higher and lower. Loud by comparison to most workplaces, this room was like the foundry's scriptorium, its personnel like busy monks, interpreting and writing, interpreting and writing.

At changeover, first shift gave their pass-down to second. It was brief today: some procurement, but mostly shipping, incepts, and the dailies. First left second a few inspections, but all in all it would be an easy evening. The men, five from each shift, then sat on desks and squat filing cabinets to shoot the shit about the weather and the Lions.

The man closest to Barry's age was twice his twenty-nine. M, P & L was a retirement position. Barry's father knew people; he'd had a long run at the Rouge plant, forty-one years—thirty of those at the foundry. In an act his dad associated with grace, he pulled some strings. Since Mr. Biehn wasn't able to keep his son from Ford and the foundry, he could at least get him out of the pits. When his dad retired, Barry was transferred to the loft. It caused no end of resentment.

Barry's interest in his coworkers' chatter had waned. He looked down on the smelting bay as he'd done every day since coming to the loft. The infernal chiaroscuros, the sparks and fires, the molten pour of reality, his entire sweep of vision begged Barry to consider again the question he'd been asking for over nine years now, *What the fuck am I doing here?*

Barry couldn't focus lately. He was tired all the time. His daughter was six months old and not sleeping through the night. There had been a drop-off in his production. Fatigue hung around his neck and cramped it, above his eyes in headaches. He was self-conscious about the attitude of slack that had crept into his duties. His coworkers assessed that all of this was simply a byproduct of his newborn, but Barry was mystified. It couldn't be that simple.

He felt like he was losing both the drive and ambition to get out of Ford. The foundry was supposed to be a stop along the way, a means to an end. He had planned to be gone years ago. Had he finally resigned himself to being a union man? Was that it? A Ford employee? A procurement clerk? He still went to class on Saturdays, 8 a.m. until 2. He only had a couple more semesters before he got his Associates in computers. He'd been wondering lately what this all meant.

The early '80s had been hard on Detroit. Except for the Tigers, there wasn't much brightness. After last season, it looked like even the recent world champs were headed for the shitter. Jobs like Barry's were under fire, but at least they were unionized. Mechanization and outsourcing had killed some skill sets, databases and inventory systems snuffed others. A round of contract talks approached, and no one, from plant managers down to the lowest committeemen, could muster much hope.

Hank, the man twice Barry's age, tapped Barry's knee with a clipboard holding triplicates.

"You get that, Bear?"

"Sure," Barry lied. He took the clipboard from Hank, but did not go out to begin the procurement inspections. Instead, he went to his desk as the pow-wow broke up. The word *wife* popped into his head, so he called.

"Hey," he said as she picked up on the first ring.

"Hey," she said back.

"Snow bad?"

"Kind of. Pretty, though. What's up?"

"Nothing. Just thought I'd call."

"I'm fine."

"Okay. Don't shovel. I'll do it when I get home."

"You know Burns. He loves you. He'll be over here like clockwork with the snowblower around 9:00. Guaranteed."

"I think Burns loves you, not me."

"Either-or, he'll probably beat you to the punch."

"Okay, baby. Well, I just wanted to check in."

"Be careful driving tonight. Oh! Bunny, I'm going to move Kara's crib into our room tonight."

"Just wait and I'll do it when I get home."

"Shush. I'm fine. I can do it. I've been cleared to lift things, jackass."

"Well," Barry said, "watch your back."

"You watch yours," Sera replied.

"Lates," Barry said.

"Lates," Sera replied.

He drifted for a moment, then set his inner-ear plugs and headed to the floor. Barry was splitting Johnson's work with Brown, as Johnson had lost some fingers last week when he decided to help out some guys with a winching chain. Johnson was still on medical and was sure to milk it. Barry donned his headphone-sized ear protectors over the inner-ear plugs. The world slipped into a light, constant humming as he walked down flight after flight of metal fire escape stairs.

Barry walked through the foundry with his clipboard making a series of check marks on procurement triplicates. He went to Johnson's areas and did the same. Minutes stretched into hours. This was Barry's shift. Later, he returned to the loft and ate a meat loaf sandwich. He spent the rest of the evening sorting and filing, miserable work.

* * *

Barry joined the long line waiting to punch out at the main. He mashed his time card into the old clock slot when he reached it. The stamp crashed down with mechanical crispness born of another generation. They did not build things like that time clock anymore. His card was stamped on the last Friday of the two-week register: *10:16 p.m.*

Barry passed through the metal detectors and the Pinkerton security that manned them. Normally, this twisted his guts, made him feel like stealing just to spite the fuckers. But aside from the tools that everyone had already stolen three sets of, what was there to take from this place? Raw brake drums? Frame parts? Axle castings?

He stopped at the bay of pay phones to call Sera, but he could not get through, busy both times. He sat in the booth watching coworkers trudge by. It seemed they'd been set upon by a blackness deeper than the film that coated them. They traipsed after a shift, as if the ingots that stuck to their coveralls each weighed a ton. Barry tried the call several more times, but gave up after a few minutes as the last of the foot traffic had passed. He made for the exit and wrestled with the soft dread of new fatherhood. He wondered if something had happened. Was everything okay?

It had snowed fourteen inches in all. No tricky drifting as the wind had died, just a snow laid heavy, flake upon flake. Someone had shoveled the walk leading from the main to the lot, but typical union, they'd done a half-ass job. It was unsalted and slick to each footfall. Barry ran and slid on the sidewalk leaving furrows as he went—running and sliding, running and sliding. He thought of the Hawaiian Islands and surfboards.

To everyone's surprise, the snow crews had hit the foundry's lot. But it must have been hours ago as there remained about six inches of snow. Vehicles spun and churned like slot cars trying to lock in a rut which would guide them out. Barry slowed to a shuffle and took some long, powerful strokes to mimic a speed skater, but he couldn't get enough glide in his gait to do it right. He switched again to a careful walk, after almost falling, then tilted his head and stuck out his tongue.

The flakes that struck his face were hefty, cottony straggler types. One landed electric on his tongue and sent a shiver to his pelvis. The ones that touched his face cleaned a little of the carbon from his skin. Barry stopped at the lot's main road to put on his gloves and pea cap. He heard a compressed air burst from far off. It sounded like a rocket had ignited. He was always captivated at night by the view of smokestacks all around shooting orange pollutant fire into the skies, strangely beautiful, as he imagined combat might be. The air burst dissipated with a hiss. Barry could hear what sounded like the approach of geese.

They came on quick, out of nothing. A line stretched across his entire field of view. Three great V formations approached, squawking and honking as they made adjustments in the echelon. Barry watched them approach. The geese grew silent falling into final ranks. A few honks and replies as they passed overhead, but mostly just the silence of birds in flight. They disappeared quick into the night.

An air horn blast startled Barry. A freight truck slid, its tires locked above the snow. Barry put his arm out instinctively to brace for the blow. The truck groaned to a stop with its grill touching Barry's outstretched hand. It was mildly warm from diesel heat, wet and gritty to the touch. He could feel the truck nudging slightly forward against his palm. The stack pipe exhaust caps tapped in a syncopated rhythm. Barry stepped backwards and apologetically raised his hand. Barry had lost track of how many times a day he felt like this, a complete and utter dunce.

The driver gave him a pistol point, forefinger and thumb. He moved his thumb a couple of times to indicate shots Barry had just dodged. The back tires of the rig spun and dug for traction. The trailer moaned a long sigh of metal fatigue as the rig caught

and dragged it—cold and overloaded with axle castings—out toward the main road.

Barry reached his car and heard a solitary squawking from
the sky. A straggler from the flight was trying to catch up. A
small, fleeting fear washed over Barry, like he'd forgotten something on his desk. The goose flew intently south into the empty
sky. It made no sound as another compressed air burst began.
The goose disappeared into a low canopy of cloud cover which
was illuminated in orange from the various pipe flames and the
piss-poor Rouge lighting. Barry was filled with a great desire to be
home. It felt acidic here in the parking lot, a grand doom settling
over the foundry, the district, the city, the world.

The Lincoln fired up on first crank. An anomaly. Barry let
it warm while he cleared its layer of covering snow. The car
normally didn't start and go straight to its high idle, usually it
fluttered and knocked at start-up like the weak heart of an old
man being resuscitated. But the car seemed brand new as Barry
cleaned it with a whisk broom and scraper. He could remember
his father bringing this car home in '73, tickled pink that he finally owned a Lincoln.

There were no cars where Barry was parked. He got in and
gassed the Mk V a few times, then he dropped it in drive and
kicked it. The snow tires shot a long rooster tail into the rearview. The lot was slick, icy underneath, but utterly desolate except
for a skeleton third shift. The only other vehicle in the outskirts
was Vernon Reed's Buick Regal, broken and cinderblocked since
summer when he transferred to midnights. Barry got crazy: reck-
less donuts, power slides, spins induced by oversteer. He considered this a fine end to the shift.

He took the main road out from the foundry, and caught
himself smiling in the rearview as he went. The year's first blizzard put a slowness over the city, like a hex had been cast on Detroit. There was an utter lack of urgency in anyone not driving a
salt truck. The few other people that had to be out were mostly

other shift workers headed home, trudging along purposefully, sliding to stops, spinning at starts.

Perfect, this fraction of time. To Barry it placed him in a free zone, a brief space, a world outside the one of responsibility that seemed born with his daughter like her twin. He wondered if he was just making a big deal out of all of this. He wondered if things were okay with the phone being busy and all. He wondered if he should even be entertaining the thought of stopping by the Shamrock for a beer. Did it make him a bad person? A rotten husband? A drunk? But without much more thought, Barry announced to his father's plastic hula girl—always a freakish sight, but especially against a snowy backdrop—that he was stopping for a quick beer and a shot. He would call home from there.

Just like he promised, Barry order a beer and a Beam back. He showed Hal, the owner and a regular acquaintance, obligatory baby pictures. Barry accepted a second, congratulatory shot from Hal. It was the good stuff—single batch bourbon—stuff he didn't share with the patrons. Barry got a dollar's worth of quarters for the juke box which sat sad and quiet in the corner, like it was serving out a punishment. But as a plow truck scraped by the bar's front window, Barry got a guilty feeling. After a moment, he pocketed the coins and checked his watch. Almost 12:00; too late to ring the phone. He cashed out, said good night, left a nice tip, then cursed himself for stopping on an evening such as this. He felt sure Sera would be freaked as he angled the Lincoln back to the drag.

He thought back to a time right before the two of them got married. They were dating and had stopped at Micky D's after pricing air compressors from Sears.

"You want kids?" she asked as she popped a chicken nugget into her mouth.

"Yeah. Absolutely—kids. But not, like, until I'm finished with school and have a good job. I mean, anything but the foundry, really. But yeah, definitely, kids. Definitely with you."

They craned across the bench seat of his truck for a kiss that tasted of hot mustard and fryer oil while driving up the Lodge. Only five years back, but Barry reckoned the past in dog years. It seemed like he'd uttered those words more than thirty years ago.

The salt trucks and plows had hit the main thoroughfares, but the Lincoln was rear wheel and open differential. It made even slightly slippery a chore. Barry now drove carefully on the remnant ice. He cursed himself for losing track of time, for stopping at the bar. It was just after midnight. Why didn't he just call from there? He could see the low, full moon through patchy clouds and breaks in the sky. He turned off the radio and tried to concentrate on the road, but not the moon. It was bigger than him, and it sat just above his hood like a deluxe option his father had ordered for the vehicle when it rolled off the line. Barry sat back in the bucket seat as he got a good, clear view. He was iffy, and prepared to ask the moon for answers, but stopped short as the dead rock looked back stupid, offering nothing but luminescence.

He pulled onto Avalon from Van Born and noticed the streetlamps were out. The block was dark, then the next, and the next. No house lights, just the beams from the Lincoln cutting a path Barry could drive in his sleep. He moved through the old streets and turned into the cleaned and salted drive. Mr. Burns had indeed come by and ran the snowblower over everything. That old man and his snowblower. Sera must have shoveled the steps and porch.

The porch light was off and Barry knew he was in trouble, as the light was always left on. The house was colder than normal. On the kitchen table, a large candle sat on an old stone plate. The three wicks flicked with the drafts from outdoors. A note lay on the clean Formica table top near the candle.

> *Honey,*
> *Electricity went out about 10*
> *Leftover plate in the oven*

*Should still be warm*
*Milk in fridge*
*Kara is in our room tonite*

*Love,*

*S.*

Barry ate quietly, by the light of the candle: a plate of cold roast beef, dab of brown gravy, cold redskin potatoes with onions, milk from the carton still cold in the fridge.

He soaked the dishes in water; carried the candle into the downstairs bathroom, where he showered. He checked his watch on the way up to bed: 12:55.

The bedroom seemed warmer to Barry, yet utterly dark without the glow of the digital clock. His calm child slept in her crib, and his wife, soundly in their bed. The two of them breathed soft and patterned in unison as he did everything not to wake them. The quilt his mother-in-law had made by hand had emerged from its seasonal retreat. Barry pulled himself so softly into bed. His wife spoke in half-sleep as she stirred to face away from him.

"I was worried," she mumbled. A long second passed, then another. "Couldn't stay awake though," she said. A moment drifted by and Sera asked with a sleepy concern, "What time is it, baby?"

"It's not too late," Barry whispered as he pulled up next to her. "Eleven-thirty." He repeated, "Not too late," and mimicked her shape while nuzzling in search of what was still good in the world. He listened for some time expecting something, anything, but heard only the tiny signs of patterned life engulfing the small, dark room.

# NIGHT COMING

BY DESIREE COOPER

*Palmer Woods*

W*hy doesn't the key fit?*
Nikki hesitated for a second in the early dusk, wondering if she was at the right house—whether the hundred-year-old, rambling Tudor was really where she lived. She put down her briefcase, and looking around nervously, laid her black leather purse down beside it so that she could try the key with both hands.

Nikki had left work early hoping to avoid just this kind of meeting between herself, a locked door, and sundown. The spiral topiaries flanking her front door stood mute. She flinched as a squirrel darted across the damp cedar mulch.

"Damn!" she said out loud, jiggling the key impatiently in the swollen lock. "Damnit all!"

It was stupid, she knew, but suddenly she wanted to cry. Maybe it was the tension that had built up during the desperate rush home to meet Jason, only to see that he hadn't made it there yet, the house disappearing into blackness, the porch cold and unlit.

Maybe it was because she didn't really want to go with him to the Diaspora Ball after all. They went to the benefit for African American art at the museum every year. She was tired, feeling nauseous. Couldn't they skip it, just this once?

Stemming easy tears, she gathered her things and clomped to the back of the house, her sleek pumps crushing the brittle leaves in her wake. The motion-sensitive lights along the side of the house blinked on, holding her startled in their beams.

Entering the backyard, Nikki scanned it quickly: the brick barbeque pit, the teak outdoor furniture, the star-white mums offering a last bloom before frost.

No one was there.

*Of course no one's back here,* she thought, sniffling courageously. *This neighborhood is safe.*

It was as if the house had been waiting for those magic words, for her hands to turn the key with patience, for her clammy palm to push open the door, for her feet to tread cautiously into the warmth of the kitchen.

"Whew," Nikki blew, immediately flipping on the light and locking the door behind her. Putting the briefcase down, she kicked off her pumps and rolled down her panty hose, which, of late, seemed to be even more confining.

Hungrily, she opened the refrigerator. It was typical of DINKS—couples with double income, no kids. Leftover Chinese, a bottle of Fat Bastard Chardonnay, fruit-on-the-bottom yogurt, Diet Coke.

Nikki eyed the wine but thought the better of it, slamming the door. Instead, she took out a box of Cheerios from the pantry and munched to quell her nervous stomach.

*Just a few handfuls,* she promised herself, glancing at the clock. *Jason will be home soon and we'll eat dinner at the party.*

She dialed him on his cell, but got his voicemail. Shrugging, she picked up her purse and briefcase and went to the front of the house to turn on the lights.

5:30 p.m. It wasn't like Jason to be late without letting her know where he was—especially these days. Nikki paced before the leaded glass windows of the living room, her mind racing.

*Maybe there's been an accident,* she thought. *Maybe he'll never walk again. Maybe he's . . .*

"He's just running late," she said out loud, her voice echoing around the vaulted ceiling. She tried Jason's cell again. No answer.

Making her way across the marble foyer to the den, she turned on the lights in each room as she passed. The quivers returned to unsettle her stomach. Her muscles drew taut like a cat's. Placing her briefcase on the coffee table, Nikki plopped on the leather sofa. She tried to concentrate on the paperwork she'd brought home, but stopped after only few minutes. It was futile. The words had no meaning. She felt like an actress, improvising busyness for some invisible audience.

Every once in a while, Nikki touched the back of her neck where her short black hair lay in soft curls against her chai tea skin. Had she imagined that swift puff of air—a stranger's warm breath?

She thought about Jason's bottle of wine chilling in the refrigerator and was tempted to dash back through the empty house to take a sip. Instead, she picked up the remote, turning on the design channel. But soon she found her attention shifting from the flat-screen TV to the neighborhood security truck outside, its yellow patrol lights splitting the night.

"You'll love it in Detroit," Jason had said about his hometown.

That was five years ago, only weeks after they'd graduated from Emory's business school. Nikki remembered the wide grin on Jason's handsome chestnut face as he'd flapped open his offer letter from General Motors. She'd thrown her arms around him, her heart clutching. Her mediocre grades had left her without similar options.

Nikki's mother had cried when she'd found out her baby girl was moving from Atlanta to Detroit, of all places. Nikki had cried, too, as she'd followed Jason to the Motor City, red-eyed and rudderless.

The newlyweds had sublet a loft in the Cass Corridor next to Wayne State University that first summer. Jason had convinced her that it would be a hip place to live, a place where the hookers coexisted with organic bakeries and socialist bookstores.

For Nikki, Detroit had been her first real adventure. Raised by a black middle-class Atlanta family, she'd walked on the debutante stage at sixteen and graduated from Spelman University at twenty with a marketing degree—the third woman in her family to attend the historically black women's college. She'd applied to Emory to assuage her parents, who'd kept asking, "What are you going to do now?" Her performance at Emory was lackluster, reflecting both her ambivalence to business school and her waning interest in marketing. But when she'd met Jason Sykes, a well-heeled Detroiter who had a way with numbers and women, she decided that her investment in graduate school would pay off in one way that she hadn't predicted. She married him after their first year.

She'd been immediately seduced by the side of Detroit that never made newspaper headlines. There was the large, tight-knit black upper class, with their galas and vacations on Martha's Vineyard. In addition, there were the unbelievably long July days when the sun didn't set until after 9 p.m. During her first summer, the city seemed to be in permanent celebration with endless concerts, happy hours, ethnic foods, and festivals.

*Maybe Jason was right,* Nikki had thought. *Detroit just gets a bad rap.*

But being from Atlanta, she had no way of knowing that she was experiencing only a seasonal euphoria. As summer turned to fall, a paralyzing darkness encroached upon the city. By December, it seemed to cut the afternoons in two. Nikki found herself leaving the house in the morning and coming home at night without ever seeing the sun. For months on end, the drag of winter circled from gray to black, then back again.

Thankfully, she'd landed a position as a private banker with a suburban boutique bank that first fall. The high-powered job helped rescue her mood.

Their second year, they'd bought in the exclusive Palmer Woods, the same integrated, ritzy neighborhood where Jason had grown up. Despite her privileged upbringing, Nikki had a hard time comprehending the wealth that the stately homes represented.

"The Archbishop of the Detroit Archdiocese lived there," Jason had said, pointing to a sprawling estate that looked more like a castle than a house. "Then one of the Pistons moved in—can you believe it? And that's the old Fisher mansion."

Fisher, she realized, as in Alfred Fisher, the auto baron. As in one of the many car moguls who blossomed in Detroit in the early twentieth century. Jason was full of stories like that, stories that made her think of the neighborhood of stone mansions, carriage houses, and English gardens as something out of a fairy tale.

"During World War II," he said, "people had to wall off entire sections of their homes to save energy. Neighborhood patrols went around at night and knocked on people's doors if any light was showing through the windows. Some people filled their attics with sand in case the roof caught on fire." When Nikki looked at him quizzically, he added, "Air raids."

Their own house had only three owners, the last of whom had sealed the drafty milk chute and turned the maid's quarters into an exercise room. But it was the back staircase—the one that went from the maid's room to the kitchen—that had given Nikki pause.

"Why would we need that nowadays?" she'd asked as they considered putting down an offer.

Jason had looked at her and shrugged. "I don't know. A secret escape route?"

It had been just a joke, but many nights since, Nikki had been lying awake imagining herself scampering down the back stairs, away from an intruder. Or worse, an intruder creeping up the hidden staircase to where they lay sleeping.

Nikki had quickly filled the den, dining room, and master bedroom with furniture from mail order catalogs—the working couple barely had time for grocery shopping, much less interior decorating. They left the rest of the sprawling Tudor echoing and empty. On weekends, she and Jason spent Sundays trolling for antiques to accent the other rooms in the century-old house.

But deep down, Nikki worried that escape would be harder when weighed down with useless things.

Outside, a car pulled up in the driveway, the headlights forming prison shadows through the blinds.

*Jason!* Nikki thought. But before she could get up, the car backed out, then headed in the opposite direction down the winding, elm-lined street.

She sighed heavily, pushing aside her briefcase, hating herself for being so clingy. She'd rushed out of her suburban office at 5:00 so that she could beat the Friday afternoon traffic and meet Jason at home. She was always tired these days, and had hoped they'd have a couple hours to unwind before getting to the Diaspora Ball by 8:00.

Now it was nearly 6:30, according to the dull green read-out on the cable box. *I guess I should get ready*, she sighed.

Her footfalls made the refinished wood stairs creak. She laughed at herself for wondering—if only for a second—whether the sounds were coming from someone else lurking inside the old house.

She went into the bathroom, with its white pedestal sink and claw-footed tub. Running the hot water, she slowly took off her navy-blue knitted suit. She couldn't help but notice the slight bulge of her stomach, which made her self-conscious even though it was easily hidden beneath her straight-cut jackets.

She hated being vulnerable in the bathtub with only the sounds of the settling house to keep her company. She thought about turning on the television in the master bedroom, or putting on some Miles Davis, but what if someone tried to break in and she couldn't hear?

*Jason will be home soon*, she thought.

The warm water was like a baptism. She breathed in the lavender aroma of the suds, and let her shoulders relax. Sometimes
she could be so silly, she knew.

When had she become a woman afraid to stay alone in her
own house?

It was the news. The constant stories of car jackings and mur-
ders. The endless stream of black men in mug shots, or bent low
with their hands cuffed, getting into the back of police cruisers.

No, it wasn't just the news, it was the way the different social
classes bumped up against each other in Detroit. In Atlanta, this
house—all 5,000 square feet of it—wouldn't come with a neighborhood, but with horses and a long, gravel driveway. And even
if it came with neighbors, it wouldn't come with poor ones.

Nikki added more hot water to her bath and closed her eyes.
She remembered her first Halloween in Palmer Woods. How
she'd gone and bought three bags of candy, even though she'd
seen very few children in the neighborhood.

That Halloween had been particularly cold, and she'd wondered how the children were going to show off their angel wings
and Superman capes if they were bundled up like Eskimos. She'd
just come home from work and barely had a bowl of soup before
the doorbell rang.

She'd put on her witch's hat and run to the door, expecting
to see tiny tots hollering, "Trick or Treat!" Instead, there were
adults and teenagers, most with only a half-cocked attempt at a
costume—the stark white face paint of the "Dead Presidents," or
a terrifying Freddy Krueger mask—holding out a pillowcase for
candy. They came in droves all night, kids tumbling out of buses
and church vans, and the hungry adults vying with them for the
best candy.

The enormity of it had shocked and depressed her. As she
opened the door, some of them peeked inside. "You have a nice
house," they'd said and she'd blushed, Marie Antoinette doling
out her little pieces of cake.

Within an hour after sunset, she'd given away all of her candy and had started combing the kitchen for bags of chips, apples, anything. She'd finally closed the door and turned off all of the lights, trembling. And still, the footsteps came.

This was Detroit. A city where there was no place to hide.

"Nikki? Nikki!"

Suddenly came her husband's voice on the stairs—the front stairs—his keys jangling in his hand. Nikki felt a wash of relief. "I'm in the tub getting ready. Where were you?"

"On an international conference call, couldn't get away to call you. Sorry."

Just like that, there he was grinning in the doorway, his teal silk tie setting off his russet complexion.

"Is that what you're wearing?" he asked, his eyes lingering on the bubbles glistening against her amber skin.

In his presence, the noises of the house silenced themselves. Her fears shriveled.

"Stop playing," she said. "Get dressed."

There's no such thing as *a little bit pregnant.*

Nikki was surprised at how true the old adage was, how completely pregnancy had changed everything, though she was only nine weeks and barely showing. Even now, as Jason helped her into her plush, vintage Mouton coat, she felt a tip in the balance between them, something she hadn't known in their five-year marriage.

"Careful," he said, as he tucked her into the Cadillac.

Nikki noticed how her own senses had become heightened, almost feral. As they walked up the marble steps to the Detroit Institute of Arts, the cold spotlight of the moon caused her to squint. She could almost hear the clacking of the brittle limbs overhead as the autumn wind tossed the branches. Jason's cologne—the bottle she'd bought him on her last business trip to New York—was suddenly overpowering. She thought, too, that she could sense something uneasy in the way he guided her by the elbow into the Diaspora Ball.

No, she thought. It was her own insecurity. The long-coming surprise of a baby after two years of trying. The kind of doubts that a child can raise in even the most prepared couples.

Jason had been less than accepting when Nikki had presented him with the blue plus sign on the plastic stick. Maybe he'd been going along with her quest for a child because he'd come to believe that they'd never conceive. But the positive pregnancy test had called his bluff.

Suddenly, he'd been full of reasons why they shouldn't have a baby: He traveled too much; they didn't have enough savings; in Detroit, they'd have to commit to twelve years of private school, not to mention a nanny.

Nikki had listened to his rational arguments and smiled. At least he was thinking like a father, even if he wasn't sure he wanted to be one. Maybe what both of them needed was time to get used to the idea.

Since then, the baby had floated in the silent sea between them.

"Julie!" came Jason's greeting as he planted the customary kiss on an acquaintance's cheek. "Julie, you remember my wife? Nikki . . ."

Nikki smiled and offered a limp handshake. There was an effort at conversation—the Pistons, the mayoral election, the coming auto show—then on to another couple. Sipping club soda with a lime twist, Nikki soon found herself wandering away from Jason's salesman-like energy. She needed to breathe.

She found herself where she always ended up whenever she visited the art institute, even when she came there for Thursday night jazz or Sunday Brunch with Bach.

The N'konde, a nail figure from the Congo.

It was like no other artifact in the African collection. Standing nearly four feet tall and carved out of ebony, its features were oddly un-African—a jutting chin, sharp nose, and bony cheeks. Against the palette of the smooth, smoky wood were the figure's half-moon eyes, as white and dazed as a mummy's. Nikki hadn't noticed the cowrie shell belly button before. Suddenly it seemed to gape open rawly, like the figure had just been yanked from an umbilical cord.

What always drew her to the N'konde was its torso, jabbed and jammed with rusted nails, screws, and blades. According to the placard, when two parties reached an agreement, they'd drive a nail into its body to seal the oath. If anyone broke the promise, the N'konde's spirit would punish him.

This N'Konde's body was a garment of promises, spikes sticking horribly from its chest, belly, shoulders, and even its chin. The figure's mouth was partially open in a punctured surprise, its jagged teeth guarding a deeper darkness.

Nikki gazed at it in horrified fascination, wondering how the parties had decided where to impale the figure to seal a deal. What were they doing now, their contracts hijacked to this glass case, their promises forgotten and unaccounted for?

The din of the party nearly evaporated as Nikki stood there, entranced. The figure seemed to want to tell her something. She was suddenly aware of the low-grade nausea that was her constant companion. Her head started to swim.

Then came the sound—a man's familiar laughter echoing in the empty exhibit hall.

"What *else* do you want me to do to you?"

Low murmurs. A woman's muffled giggles.

Nikki thought she had heard that same sexy bass in her own ear many times. "Jason?" she whispered, as the N'konde stared, eyes hard white.

Her heart began to pound. Spinning around, she saw no one nearby. Wobbling, she wondered if she'd dreamed the voices. She fought to tamp the bile gathering at her throat. Heading into the crowd, she hoped to make an escape. She was nearly to the door when someone grabbed her arm.

"Nikki? I didn't know you were here!"

It was her sorority sister, Terry Hines, dressed, as always, in shades of pink and green.

"Hey, Terry," Nikki managed foggily.

"Girl, are you okay?"

Nikki blinked twice. *Try to get it together.* "I—I'm pregnant."

As soon as it left her lips, she regretted the slip. Detroit was a small, big town. People were constantly cross-pollinating. Gossip took root quickly.

"WHAT???" Terry shrieked, her garnet lips shimmering against her dark honey skin. Then, lowering her voice conspiratorially, she asked, "How far along are you? Do you need to sit down?"

Before she could answer, Jason was at her side. "There you are," he said, exasperated. "I was wondering where you'd wandered off to!" He sidled up to her, lovingly planting a kiss on her cheek.

"My God, Jason, Nikki just told me!" gushed Terry, not catching the look of foreboding in Nikki's eyes.

Jason glanced from Terry's exuberant face to Nikki's miserable one, sizing up the awkward pause.

"The baby?" Terry prompted.

Jason was taken aback, but tried to conceal it. "OH!" he said, smiling uneasily. "Yeah! Imagine me—a dad!"

"We're not really telling people yet," Nikki said. "It's still early, you know . . ."

Terry's eyes grew large and she covered her mouth as if to cap a secret. "Of course," she said. "But I just know that everything will be fine."

"I'd better get you home," Jason said. "You look a little pale."

Nikki nodded, letting him lead her toward the door, his hand firm around her waist. Her body went limp against his, seeking forgiveness.

Outside, the night air had turned frosty, the flat moon giving the ground its luster.

"It slipped," Nikki said finally, as they waited for their car.

Jason nodded, but said nothing.

While they rode home, she glared at the sights along Woodward, the strange people with their nightshade business, shivering in the cold. She was tired, her bones heavy.

Jason noticed her trembling and turned up the heat. The fan only blew the freezing air harder and she reached up to close the vents. She could feel his eyes on her, but he said nothing to lighten the mood. The moon, yellowing as it rose, followed them home.

His silence humiliated her, and she wondered how he'd managed so quickly to turn the tables. Wasn't it he who'd just backed another woman against a display case and fondled her? Wasn't it he who'd suddenly been unable to come home on time like he used to, who always left her waiting, who wouldn't return her calls?

He pulled the Cadillac into their driveway, got out of the car, and walked around to her side to let her out. On the porch, he was about to put the keys in the lock, but instead he turned and looked at her.

"I don't want a baby," he said.

He stared at her, his eyes accusing her of ruining everything. But she stared back, her feet planted and steady, the queasiness fading into resolve.

"I do," she said back, the shivering now ceasing. "I do."

He lowered his eyes. For a long moment, he didn't speak. "It's cold out here," he said finally. "Let's talk inside."

He leaned to put the key in the door, but like a dark invitation, it swung open by itself. His eyes shot her a question: "Didn't you lock the door?" But it was too late.

Inside the house, the night moved.

# PART III

SILENCE OF THE CITY

# THE COFFEE BREAK

BY Melissa Preddy

*Grandmont-Rosedale*

O*h, miss!"*
*"Miss!"*
*"Waitress, could we get some service down here?"*

More cream, more ketchup. Tuna on toast, ham on rye, two slices of cherry pie. I slapped down one heavy white crockery plate after another like a blackjack dealer at a full table, my lace-up oxfords treading sideways, crablike, on the Coke-sticky linoleum floor behind the counter.

Welcome to the lunchtime shift at Cunningham's.

Clinking cutlery and the snapping of streamers attached to the store's giant fans created a background hum that sometimes made me strain to take in the orders for egg salad, iced tea, and Vernors.

It was August 1 of a sizzling summer and no one was ordering the patty melt.

Payday, no less. Which meant that every stool would be occupied for at least two hours straight, as the drugstore's flush-with-cash shoppers hovered like vultures and those seated pretended not to see waiting patrons' reflections fidgeting in the big ad-plastered mirrors that hid the kitchen from view.

Finally, around 2 o'clock or so, the counter was mostly clear and the pockets of my celery-green apron—our uniforms matched the tile on the store's façade—drooped with their welcome load of nickels, dimes, and the occasional quarter. I packed a tumbler with crushed ice, topped it off with water, and sipped.

Grabbing a copy of *Photoplay* from under the counter, I fanned myself for a minute before glancing at the bleached-blond starlet on the cover. That's when it dawned on me: It was two days now since Marjorie had been in for her customary coffee and cigarette. We had been kicking around some ideas for Saturday— maybe go to a show, maybe even ride downtown to check out the fall fashions just appearing in Hudson's showrooms.

I peered through the window, trying to catch a glimpse of her in the storefront manicure booth at Kay's Beauty Nook across the street, but the bustling sidewalk crowd blocked my view.

One of the redeeming features of this job—aside from the tips, which really were pretty good if you were fast on your feet like me and not above a little flirting with the guys and fawning over the women—was the movie screen–like view of this busy shopping district where Grand River sliced through Greenfield Road at a forty-five-degree angle.

Triangle-shaped Cunningham's jutted out into the intersection and the wide windows on both sides of my counter gave me a better view than Jimmy Stewart had in last year's Hitchcock hit, *Rear Window*.

Buses chugged up and disgorged patrons for the beauty parlor, the funeral parlor, dress shops and dentists, bakers and shoemakers and hardware merchants.

Not Detroit's most posh neighborhood, this westside district was far from the worst, either—just a solid Main Street–style shopping center about seven miles down Grand River from the city's skyscrapers.

Montgomery Wards' cupola, revolving door, and ritzy awnings lent the neighborhood a bit of big-city flair, while across the street Federal's and Woolworth's appealed to the budget trade.

The busy intersection pulsed with secretaries and factory workers, housewives from the nearby neighborhoods, teachers and students from the schools down the block. On a clear day you could almost see the Penobscot building, but a lot of my customers felt no need to trek downtown. It was all right here.

I'd come to Detroit a couple of years ago to nurse a sickly cousin. She was long gone, but I was still behind this counter—mostly 9 to 6, sometimes the late shift. With that wide-angle view I could spot the regulars on their predictable rounds, like the players in my own private movie.

The daily drama unfolded with the breakfast trade.

There was Mrs. Boyd, the raven-haired pet shop lady, who showed up promptly at 9:15 every weekday for her poached egg, wheat toast, and tea. Woe betide the cook if her yolk was broken.

Today, she was exchanging small talk with Mr. Giles, the head floorwalker on Wards' second floor. While awaiting his daily oatmeal and cream, he'd snatch a napkin from the chrome dispenser and polish the walk-to-work perspiration from his steel-rimmed spectacles. I often maneuvered to seat them side-by-side, envisioning a romance between the animal-loving widow and the courtly merchant, but so far my meddling had only spawned dry comparisons of inventory ledgers.

The neighborhood beat cop, Mick—short for the less pronounceable Michlewandoski—took his usual turn through the store and then stopped to exchange news with the security guard from the bank across the street. Mick's report was usually pretty tame—a broken window, a bit of shoplifting—and I had the impression he liked it that way. As always, the guard was late and wolfing his ham and eggs in order to take up his post by 9:30.

Missing today was Carl Strachan, who managed the Thom McAn shoe store down the street and stopped in most mornings for a BLT. Blessed with the leading-man looks of John Gavin and a healthy helping of offhand boyish charm, he capitalized on both and the result was possibly the liveliest love life west of Woodward. Most of us single women who lived and worked around the intersection had been lured once or twice by the salesman's spiel.

Carl, as he constantly bragged, kept a boat docked down in Wyandotte. While a sail on the breezy, cool Detroit River sounded like heaven, I could never quite bring myself to accept. There was something sly about the way he knelt in the shoe store, turning what should have been a two-minute fitting into a stealthy caress of my nyloned feet and ankles. Girls who did set sail with Carl said he dropped the Cary Grant act once they were beyond swimming distance from shore, and made it clear he expected a lot more than a goodnight kiss for his troubles. Some were dismayed at his brutish insistence and their own vulnerability out on the choppy waters. Others had the night of their lives on the blankets in Carl's floating love nest. Myself, I didn't fancy becoming just another notch on his mast.

There were plenty of other curiosities among my customers, but you get the general idea. And the passersby on the street, whose names I never knew, rounded out the cast.

There was the sultry brunette who spoke only Russian but showed up twice a week to Kay's for her shampoo and set; the gaggle of gossips who never failed to check out the weekly dress sales at Lerner's and Three Sisters; the harried-looking mothers dragging red-faced kids up the narrow stairway to the dentist's chair.

Gingham-dressed cleaning women emerged each morning from Woolworth's with a fresh supply of Bon Ami and ammonia; efficient church ladies bustled in and out of Holy Cross Lutheran. Veiled mourners trudged up the steps at Bishop's. Brylcreemed delivery boys jostled doting grannies who clutched string-tied cardboard cake boxes from Ralph's Bakery.

Weekdays around 4 o'clock, you could set your watch by the cluster of tool-and-die men who wiped greasy fingers on bandanas as they pushed their way into Leonard's Bar & Grill for thirty-cent bottles of Stroh's and bloody-rare ground rounds.

And Tuesday through Saturday, there was Marjorie's Doris Day–platinum bob bent over a customer's bright talons in the window at Kay's.

\* \* \*

"Okay if I take my break now?" I asked the cook. He nodded, so I stepped around the counter and pushed through the glass doors onto the simmering sidewalk.

Inside the salon it was even steamier, the hair dryers fighting a losing battle with the humidity. Kay was doing a manicure on a longtime client at Marjorie's station. She was clearly rusty, fumbling in exasperation with the unfamiliar tools and supplies.

"Is Marjie sick or something?" I asked.

Kay wielded her emery board laboriously, not looking up. "This is the second day she's missed without calling. I don't know if she's sick, but I can tell you one thing: She's fired."

"Such a sweet little thing," chirped the customer, a mousey little woman I'd mentally dubbed Peachy due to her perennial choice of lipstick and nail polish hues. "It's hard to believe she would just run off on you. Hope she's okay."

I looked around the room but the other operators, taking their cue from Kay, continued their work in silence.

"If anyone hears from her, please let me know," I said. "You know where to find me."

Back inside Cunningham's, I leaned against the ledge in the phone booth and leafed through the directory. Marjorie and I were after-work buddies, just shopping and the movies, that sort of thing. But I knew she lived a bit south, off Plymouth Road somewhere, with her parents and younger sister.

Here it was—*John Sklar, 9980 Asbury Park, VErmont 5-2537.*

I wrote the number on the back of an order slip but didn't dial the phone. A brisk rap on the open booth door startled me and there was the drugstore boss and pharmacist, Mr. Smith, frowning and jerking his head toward the far end of the counter. Some of my best tippers were taking their customary seats.

There were a handful of the neighborhood's bigwigs, including the banker, the undertaker, the pastor, and the dentist—their daily get-together was a years-long tradition. Smith joined them as usual on their afternoon break.

It had been a busy day for them too. Payday check-cashers swamped Mr. Littmann's corner bank. Families were taking advantage of the summer break to get teeth pulled and cavities filled, Dr. Foster said. And of course there was never any shortage of work for Mr. Bishop, especially in this kind of heat wave.

In a nod to the weather, they wanted iced tea instead of coffee—though Dr. Foster, with an exaggerated look around to make sure no clients were watching, switched his order to a large Coke.

I obliged him with appreciative laughter, hoping it didn't sound too fake, and pocketed their dollar bonus. Then as usual I drifted away and they drew closer, talking business deals or gossip in lower tones.

The others looked more frazzled by the heat than amused. Mr. Bishop tamped his pack of Chesterfields on the counter and then lit up, exhaling the smoke with an exasperated sigh. Banker Littmann wiped his brow and then painstakingly refolded his handkerchief. Reverend Gruenwald looked miserable, plastered inside his black suit and tight collar.

When my relief finally arrived at 6:00, I went down the wide, worn oak stairs to the staff rooms in the basement. Alone in the ladies', I shrugged out of my damp Dacron uniform, peeled off the white stockings, and drenched a stack of pleated brown paper towels, wiping my sweaty skin from forehead to ankles. I redid my French twist and slipped into the full-skirted cotton dress in my locker, then wiggled bare, sore feet into flat sandals. Toting my soiled clothing in a paper sack, I crossed Greenfield and slowly strolled around the corner. No one familiar was in sight and it took just a minute to slip down an alley and up the wooden stairs to the apartment above Leonard's.

Jerry, one of the bartenders, was waiting with a bottle of Canadian Club and a bucket of ice. Smiling, he pulled his necktie off over his head and began to unbutton his shirt.

* * *

Later, while he dozed beneath the ceiling fan, I stepped into my slip and perched on the arm of a chair near the wide-open west window. Miles distant, probably over the infamous DeHoCo—Detroit House of Corrections—prison in rural Plymouth, black clouds swelled with the weathercasters' promised thunderstorm heading our way.

It was near dusk and people were happily milling the streets, enjoying a respite with ice cream, window shopping at shuttered boutiques.

The door at Leonard's swung open at rhythmic intervals, letting out blasts of "Little Darlin'" and other juke box hits.

One girl drew my attention, as she walked slowly away from the intersection. Despite the heat and the twilight, she wore a dark green chiffon scarf tied beneath her chin, and cat's-eye sunglasses. If her step had been more chipper, I'd have thought she were a starstruck teenager attempting the Hollywood look, but her pace was slow and her chin hung low.

My curiosity was answered when she turned the corner and headed up the steps to Bishop's.

I shuddered and sipped my tepid whiskey. What a night to have gloomy dealings with the undertaker, in contrast to the midsummer carnival atmosphere of the business district. As I watched, the front door of the sprawling brick Victorian opened and she slipped into the dark foyer. You'd think they could turn a few lamps on.

By contrast, the white blinds at the windows of the funeral home's rear quarters—a recent addition to the original house—were lit up like a hospital operating theater. In a way, that's what it was. The embalming room.

How often I'd grimaced lately, trying to tune out Bishop as he boasted with relish to his cronies, between bites of oozing cherry pie, about the envious modernity of his facilities. As I watched the shadows moving behind the shades, I recalled his loving description of the gadgets and techniques he used on the dead. Littmann, who'd lent him the money, seemed fascinated by the inner workings of the mortuary, and Dr. Foster asked lots of questions, with the air of one scientist quizzing another. The reverend always looked a little queasy, though.

The thunder had moved closer when Jerry stretched and dressed and joined me at the window with a fresh drink. I told him about Marjie.

"Yeah, I heard," he said. "Lennie told me the cops were asking around, but no dice. She's probably just shacked up with some guy you never heard of."

"I don't know," I said. "Her parents keep her on a pretty tight rein. She went out with Carl a few times, but who hasn't? And I know she has a thing for that guy Steven, the pressman for the *News*. That's about it."

"Well, she ain't with him," Jerry said, tightening the knot of his tie. "He's downstairs right now—or was. Want to come see for yourself? I got to get back."

I wasn't in the mood to strike up a chat with the shy, dapper workman who sipped many an afternoon milkshake at my counter. His job was wrestling the giant rolls of paper onto the presses, and disposing of the heavy hollow cardboard cores. Aside from Steve's surprisingly savvy clothes sense, I thought him dull, but Marjie had chosen to interpret him as the strong, silent type. She'd taken to delaying her late break to coincide with his, and for a time he seemed awkwardly flattered by her sparkly admiration.

"But Jer, do me a favor. If that Steven is still down there, ask him what he knows about Marjie, okay?"

He sighed elaborately but I knew he'd come through.

When the coast was clear I hurried down the alley and headed home. Abruptly the storm began and I dashed down Bishop's driveway. Cutting through the yard beside the funeral parlor would shave a block off my rainy walk.

Hurrying past the portico, I was surprised to see Mr. Smith and the pastor huddled there. About to hail them, I was caught in the headlights of a Lincoln Town Car as it swung into the driveway at a fast clip. Littmann was behind the wheel and I jumped sideways to get out of his way.

Smith was obviously startled to see me.

"What are you doing here at this hour?" he asked irritably.

"Better get on home and out of this weather," the reverend added more kindly.

Littmann just gave me a nod as he hustled by and the trio stomped the rain off their shoes before crowding through the funeral home's side door.

Next day, no Marjorie.

After lunch I forced myself to dial the phone and was connected with Mrs. Sklar. Yes, she said, it had been three days now since Marjie had been home. No, there had been no arguments. Yes, the police had been called. No girls matching her daughter's description had turned up in hospitals or, God forbid, the morgue.

"What do you think has happened?" I asked gently.

"Her sister thinks she might have eloped," said Mrs. Sklar, but fear eclipsed hope in her voice. "We didn't think she knew any boys that well. Did she?"

I told her the truth—that maybe sometimes when she was supposed to be out with the girls, Marjie dated a couple guys around the intersection. But as far as I knew it was all very casual—a hot fudge sundae at Sanders, a burger at the Fairlane bowling alley, a couple of drinks at Leonard's.

"She's a nice girl," I assured the older woman. "That's why I'm kind of worried about her."

Mrs. Sklar, at first reticent, now poured out information in an anxious rush. Marjie had been quiet and absentminded for weeks. The police had learned she'd drained most of her savings out of the bank. Her sister had startled her in the room they shared, trying out the look of a sheer lace veil over her white-blond hair. As best they could tell, one small bag and a few garments were missing from her room.

"But she didn't take her grandma's pearl cross," Mrs. Sklar burst out. "Ever since she was a little girl, she planned to wear that cross on her wedding day. It's still in her jewelry box. And her best nylon stockings, that she was saving for good, are here. None of it makes sense . . . Where is my baby?"

I promised to keep asking around.

Hungry despite the heat, I helped myself to an egg salad sandwich, an iced tea, and a newspaper. On an inside page the headline *Reward* caught my eye. It seems that Miss Irene Ballard, twenty-four, hadn't been home to Dearborn's 5030 Curtis Street in more than a week.

The bespectacled dry cleaner's assistant had boarded the Greenfield Avenue bus, headed for the Grand River shopping district, the article said. She hadn't been seen since. None of her clothing was missing, but her bank account had been drained.

The ponytailed blonde had a serious expression behind tortoiseshell frames in the blurry newspaper photo. The princess collar of her white blouse was buttoned to the throat. She looked vaguely familiar. In fact, I'd swear she'd been in the pharmacy lately. I recalled my envy of those shiny blond locks, which obviously hadn't come from a bottle.

Looking up, I could see Mr. Smith puttering in his mezzanine-level dispensary and realized that his cronies hadn't been in yet for their usual break. In fact, my next customer was Jerry, stopping by for bottle of aspirin and a Coke before starting his shift behind the bar.

"Hey, I got some news for you," he said. "You said that girl's name was Marjie, the one who's missing?"

I nodded.

"Well, I was wrong last night," he said. "The woman the

cops were looking for is Angie, not Marjie. Angela something—worked a few blocks down at Novak's Bar. So I guess we got two missing girls in the neighborhood, eh?"

"Three if you count this one," I said, pointing to the folded newspaper.

We looked at one another, perplexed.

"It's kind of like last winter, remember?" Jerry said. "Those two sisters from over on Lyndon—what was that, February, March? They never turned up, did they?"

It rang a bell. Pretty brunettes, so they got some write-ups in the crime blotter. The family lived a block or two behind Ward's. Something about one girl gone and then her older sister disappearing a few days later. But I wanted the scoop on Marjie.

"What about Steven?" I asked.

"He claims he wined and dined her a couple of times—even sprang for Chinese at Victor Lim's downtown—but that was about it. Says he doesn't know where she skipped to, and acts like he doesn't care."

Jerry washed down two tablets with the last of his cola and swiveled off the chrome-trimmed stool.

"You coming up tonight?"

"I think so," I said. When he left I stood there for a moment, absently tearing up the cotton puff from his aspirin bottle, then made up my mind. Had a word with the cook and headed for the back of the drugstore.

Up a half flight of steps was the pharmacy, Smith's domain. I knocked and pushed open the door. Surrounded by the bottles and boxes of his trade, he was grinding away using a mortar and pestle. "Yes?"

"Mr. Smith, I'm not feeling well. It's a pretty slow afternoon at the counter—Bill says he wouldn't mind serving. Would it be okay if I took off early today?"

He obviously wasn't happy but there wasn't much he could

say. Then he cleared his throat and asked, "Oh, by the way, what were you doing over at Bishop's last night?"

Taken aback, I explained that the driveway was my usual shortcut. "I couldn't help but notice the pastor and Mr. Littmann there too," I added. "And I see they aren't here today. Did someone in the neighborhood pass away?"

"No, no," the pharmacist said, "just one of our regular committee meetings last night—Chamber of Commerce business, you know. Mr. Bishop is kind enough to host us from time to time."

"That's nice," I said dutifully. Then I showed him the folded newspaper page.

"Wasn't this girl in here a week or so ago?" I asked. "Don't you recognize her?"

My boss glanced at the paper and shrugged. "Not offhand," he said. "I don't memorize every face that walks through the door."

"Oh, I know," I said. "It's just that she's the third girl in the neighborhood to go missing. I thought if we could help police with a clue—if she'd been ill or picking up a prescription . . . ?"

At that Smith stopped grinding and looked up, eyebrows raised. "I suggest you leave the detective work to the professionals. And weren't you saying you didn't feel well?"

I took the hint and left. As I passed Bishop's, a funeral procession wheeled out of the mortuary lot. The undertaker himself stood at attention, hand over heart, until the black-curtained hearse was out of sight. Then he relaxed and, whistling, marched up the steps of his elegant home.

That night, I swished sore feet in a dishpan of ice water at Jerry's and told him about my afternoon.

Right after leaving the drugstore, I'd strolled over to Lyndon Street, where two-story wooden frame houses were cooled by the shade of tall elms. Some elderly porch-sitters directed me to the Toltecci residence, home of Grace and Theresa, the missing high school girls.

Their mother let me into the dim front room. The girls had been gone since early March. First Grace, sixteen, had failed to return home from what she called a movie date with her school friends. Soon it was learned no such plans existed.

Theresa—pronounced *Tree-sa*—was relentless in searching for her sister, grilling friends and acquaintances, showing Grace's photo around the shopping district, trying to retrace her sister's trail. All she learned was that Grace had been urgently seeking work in the shopping center, filling out applications at the dime store, the ice cream shops, the tea rooms—any place that might hire a high schooler for washing-up chores and the like.

Naïvely, the younger girl had even stopped at the bank and asked to apply for a loan.

The family was stumped. Grace had always been content with her dollar-a-week allowance and the wages from a few baby-sitting jobs. What could she need so much money for?

Later that ghastly week, Mrs. Toltecci said, Theresa too had failed to come home. The police did the best they could—Mick kept going door to door for blocks around, even on his days off—but no leads turned up. No bodies either, which left the grieving parents in a wretched limbo, balanced between hope and despair.

Leaving her, I took the long way around to Thom McAn's.

"Missed you this morning," I said as Carl shoehorned a pale-pink pump onto my left foot. "Heat got your appetite?"

The salesman shrugged. "Guess so. How does that one feel?"

I got up and walked around the store, modeling the shoes and watching his expression in the tilted mirrors.

"I'll bet you're heading out on your boat tonight," I said. "Any chance of me tagging along? Marjie said it was fabulous."

His answer was a raised-eyebrows stare.

"Wasn't she out with you last week?" I pressed, smiling. "I could've sworn she said you two had a date. Or am I thinking of Angie, that girl from down at Novak's? You dated them both, didn't you?"

"Not lately," he dodged, deadpan. "And sorry, but I'm not sailing tonight. How are the shoes? Shall I wrap them?"

"It's funny, them both being missing," I said as he wrote up the order. "And that girl from Curtis Street. They say she was headed this way."

His long lashes flickered. "Missing? I didn't know. How awful for their families." With that automatic smile, he handed over my receipt and the crisp brown bag. "See you around."

Dismissed, I ambled along the sidewalk, trying to think. Five girls—that I knew of—vanished in the last five months. Nice girls, who worked, lived at home with their parents, and weren't engaged or going steady. And no corpses had turned up.

Ronnie, one of Marjie's pals from the salon, was coming toward me.

"Any news?" she said. "Mick the cop was in again asking questions. At least no unclaimed bodies match hers—so far—he said." Ronnie was holding out for the elopement theory, though like me she couldn't imagine who the groom was. And deep down we both doubted Marjie would do that to her mother.

"But I did see her going over to Holy Cross a few times," Ronnie added as the light changed and she stepped off the curb. "I don't know why, but it seemed like she was always running across Grand River to the church lately."

A devout Polish Catholic seeking solace in a Lutheran chapel? That was a new one on me.

Jerry said the bar was buzzing today with talk of the missing women. Mick had alerted the precinct's detectives and two gray-suited, crew-cut guys had been canvassing the intersection.

"Are they starting to doubt it's coincidence?" the bartender said. "Outwardly they're saying it's just routine. But Mick told me they've got a clerk going back through records, looking for similar cases over the past few years. Especially where no bodies have turned up. The thing is, none of these girls had anything in common. Think about it."

Some of them knew Carl, I said. "I could see him shoving a girl out of a sailboat if she started to be a nuisance. We know he dated Angie and Marjie; for all we know Grace could've fallen for him too. Or that girl from Dearborn—she shopped around here. I am positive it was her in the drugstore. Maybe she bought shoes around here too."

We went back and forth. Steve could probably stuff corpses into those heavy newsprint tubes, for that matter, Jerry said. But it was doubtful he'd crossed paths with the younger girls.

It was the money that puzzled me. Mick told Jerry that all of the older girls had gone missing with several hundred dollars on them. Grace had seemed in a big hurry to earn some money. And Theresa had vanished trying to find out why. Was someone touting a get-rich-quick scheme? Or offering "modeling" contracts to pretty young women?

Jerry went to refill our gin but his paring knife slipped on the lime rind and deeply gashed his fingertip. We both froze for a minute, watching the thick dark blood well out and drip on the corrugated drain board. He fished out his handkerchief and I folded it around some ice and pressed it on the cut. Within moments a bright red stain seeped across the bleached white cotton.

The heat and the gin made me light-headed at the sight. My thoughts swirled.

Blood. Money. Missing women. Shadowy silhouettes on blazing white blinds.

The ice burned the palm of my hand and my stomach churned.

I knew.

"Jesus, you gonna stand there and let me bleed to death?" Jerry teased. "Run down to the kitchen, okay? They've got bandages and gauze and all that in a locker on the wall."

Bleed to death. That's what my friend had done. And all the girls before her.

I felt my pockets for change and ran downstairs. The barroom was smoky and congenial. Someone shoved the quarter tray forward and pool balls clattered down their chute.

The phone booth was empty. I put my icy-cold finger over the 0 and turned the dial.

*"Oh, miss. Could we get some more butter here, please?"*

It was nice to be the one being waited on for a change. I savored another bite of my Delmonico and added a little more chive-flecked sour cream to the baked potato.

Mick was picking up the tab. He knew I'd turned down the Ballard reward and insisted on treating me and Jerry to a white-tablecloth dinner a few miles down the avenue at Carl's Chop House.

I leaned back in the curved red-leather booth and sipped my wine. What I really wanted was more details. Mick wasn't supposed to talk much since the trials hadn't started yet, but we promised to be discreet.

"Of course, we all thought you were goofy at first," he repeated for perhaps the tenth time. "Why would well-off guys like them get involved in that kind of scheme? Then we thought about the money potential and, well, it seemed worth asking around."

Buddy, a longtime waitress at Novak's, was the first to crack. Seated at one of the tavern's red-checkered tables, she told detectives she'd been in trouble once too, and she told them who had recognized the symptoms and offered to help her out of it. When Angie had the same problem, she sent her to the kindly dentist at the intersection.

Then, Mick said, one of Irene Ballard's girlfriends told a similar tale. She said it was well known up and down Greenfield that Mr. Smith could help you out of a fix.

And Marjie, who had apparently succumbed to Steve after all in the backseat of his '49 Ford, heard from a girl at Federal's that the Reverend Gruenwald was understanding about these matters.

Grace, of course, applied for a bank loan and got a different kind of assistance there.

"And Theresa?" Jerry asked.

"She found out what was going on," Mick said, forking up some dessert. "A lot of girls around the intersection knew about Bishop's. They kept it quiet because, well, because of a there-but-for-the-grace-of-God-go-I kind of thing. When we realized the volume they were doing, it was obvious the money—a girl or two a week at $400 apiece—made it worth the risk."

Shaking my head with chagrin, I said, "I thought I knew everything that went on around there, and I never suspected a bit."

If only Marjie had told me.

I imagined the terror of those veiled girls being led past the plush parlors of the funeral home through the service door and into the cold, clinical embalming room. The heavy chemical odors. The sinks and the drains. Being ordered to disrobe and to climb upon the same table where hundreds of corpses had been shed of their lifeblood. The curt orders and the pain and fright when one's own red fluid started to flow.

Jerry squeezed my hand and smiled. Mick was talking again.

It might never have come to light, he said, if it weren't for some newfangled equipment Bishop installed. I cringed as I recalled his boasting and Foster's animated questions; obviously embalming gear wasn't all he was buying with Littmann's generous bank loan.

"Don't forget, most of the girls made it out okay," Mick added. "Between them, Bishop and Foster had the anatomical know-how; the other three supplied the patients. The vast majority of women were in and out with no problems."

Then things started going sour. Grace wasn't the first but

she was the closest. Theresa, who shared a room with her sister and had noticed her bouts of nausea, figured out the scheme and confronted the undertaker.

"She had a couple of hypo marks on her arm and neck," Mick said. "It wouldn't take much embalming fluid to put her out. And of course he had the perfect setup for hiding unwanted corpses."

Detectives yearned to dig up every casket Bishop had closed for the past couple of years, to find out how many carried an extra occupant. They had found Theresa in with an elderly woman way over at Mt. Olivet, and poor Marjie stuffed beside a middle-aged man right up the avenue in Grand Lawn.

But Bishop's mortuary helper, Stan, realizing he could face a murder rap or ten, was likely to turn state's evidence, Mick said.

"At least it'll help us narrow things down," said the cop, waving to the waitress for the check. "But there are going to be a lot of gravediggers busy between now and the trial."

The scandal was keeping me hopping too. In the weeks since the news broke, complete with grainy newspaper photos of the manacled businessmen, Grand River and Greenfield had become a regular tourist attraction.

The new pharmacist, a white-tuniced Wayne State grad, was appalled but had to admit it was great for business. Everyone wanted to see Bishop's lair, light a candle at Holy Cross, and stop for Coke or a tube of toothpaste at Cunningham's infamous drugstore.

Gawkers edged out the regulars at my counter, prying for details between bites of tuna or grilled cheese. I obliged as best I could and my uniform pockets bulged with extra-big tips from grateful curiosity-seekers. But I tried not to glance out the window to my right, where Marjie's storefront booth was dim and empty.

A lot of my quarter tips found their way out to St. Hedwig's Cemetery in the form of a wreath of pink roses, which I carried one day to my friend's shiny new gravestone. I sat for a while and talked to her about the usual—the fall fashion's at Hudson's, and the new show Jerry was taking me to one night, and how nice it was to get a break from the heat. Somewhere down there she was lying still, wearing her grandmother's pearl cross and the new nylon stockings she was saving for good.

# SNOW ANGEL

BY E.J. OLSEN

*Grand Circus Park*

In late December, Mrs. Rose Erwell passed away slightly ahead of schedule. She'd been diagnosed with Stage IV bone cancer back in August, and the only thing they could do for her was increase the painkiller dosage in the IV drip every week. Palliative care, it's called, and it usually means keeping the patient too stoned to care about the terrible pain. The way her doctor told it later, Mrs. Erwell's condition "had not yet progressed to its terminus," and she was scheduled for a few more months of suffering before the motor shut down. He backed it up with a bunch of statistics.

In the previous three months, seven terminally ill people in Detroit died before they were supposed to. Being of sound mind and failing body, these seven folks elected not to wait for their respective conditions to reach the ultimate conclusion and ended their lives with very strong narcotics. Not street poison, but clean, prescription-grade pharmaceuticals. End of suffering. They simply floated away on a pink cloud of dope. In all seven cases, the friends and relations of the patient were sympathetic to the decedent's wishes, but ultimately cleared of any wrongdoing. In all seven cases, the cause of death was a combination of drugs other than what was prescribed for the patient. In all seven, the last visitor these people had was a man who wore a Roman collar; a man who called himself Father David.

We were double-parked at Downtown Coney Island. My partner, Tucker, was outside in the unmarked while I was accepting an illegal bribe from the proprietor in the form of lunch.

Gus Manos loved to see cops in his joint. All that blue was good insurance. In the sixty-odd years he'd been open he'd never been robbed. An absolute miracle in Detroit. An ancient, grease-spattered Philco was tuned to WJR, and it told us that the Pistons dropped another game to Cleveland. Gus shook his head and shrugged. I shrugged back, and thanked him for the food. As I reached for the door, my partner's immense frame blocked out the dull winter daylight.

Tucker was a man of few words. He was tall and wide, like a human vehicle. He wore his hair very short, but it didn't look paramilitary like so many of the rookies these days. He was quick and light on his feet, and in all the time I'd ridden with him, I never heard him curse or even raise his voice. In fact, he hardly talked at all. It was kind of like working with the Buddha.

He held up his cell. "Priest."

Tucker drove. We hit I-375 and had the Coneys gone by the time we took the McNichols exit. The address was on Dequindre above Seven Mile. The neighborhood was mostly ranches. Aside from the bars on all the windows and doors, it could have been a suburb anywhere. Not so remarkable if it wasn't a pocket surrounded by the urban prairie that was reclaiming the city. The areas just a few blocks west of Mrs. Erwell's trim little beige home were filled with pheasant and possum, most of the homes long since demolished or fallen in. All that was left was a grid of streets, sidewalks, and light poles squaring off fields of weeds as tall as a man. It was spooky to see how fast all traces of us disappear.

We pulled up behind the van marked WAYNE COUNTY CORONER and headed up the walk. The infamous Jack Kevorkian certainly had his detractors back in his day, but the "right-to-die" pathologist also had his supporters. Tucker and I met one in the person of Mrs. Nora Combs, sister of Mrs. Erwell. She stood in the doorway with her arms folded and cranked up before were we halfway to the door.

"My sister was ill and sufferin'. No earthly reason to make a lovely human being go through all that pain. No earthly reason."

We stepped onto the porch and flipped our badges.

"I *knew* you were police. Why else would a white man and a . . ." she looked Tucker up and down, "*dumptruck* be coming to visit Rose?"

The corner of Tucker's mouth tightened. I'd worked with him long enough to know that this passed for a smile. I gestured at Tucker, then myself.

"Sergeant Tucker, Sergeant—"

She waved me off. "Come on. They're back this way." She disappeared inside the house.

We followed and stepped into a neat living room. A floral-patterned couch with matching recliner faced the picture window. Both pieces wore plastic slipcovers and looked showroom new. In the corner opposite the recliner a wooden TV table held an old nineteen-inch Zenith complete with rabbit ears. We heard Ms. Combs's voice calling us from a hallway off the living room and headed that way.

Two guys from the coroner's office stood murmuring in the corner of a bedroom. They nodded when we walked in. A huge four-post bed dominated the room. The wood was dark and polished to a proud shine. In the center of the bed, a tiny brown woman lay under an enormous antique quilt. Thin wisps of gray hair fanned out on the pillow beneath her head. Her mouth was pulled in slightly at the corners, as if she were smiling at some pleasant memory. Mrs. Rose Erwell looked for all the world to be asleep.

There was a small nightstand beside the bed, and it was filled with prescription drug bottles. The coroner guys were watching me now. I looked at them and raised my eyebrows. The one in charge, a gray brush cut named Marty, flipped though his notebook.

"Decedent is one Rose Mary Erwell, age seventy-nine."

Flip. "Chondrosarcoma, advanced. Treatment was basically pain management at this point. Mrs. Erwell wasn't responding particularly well to either the treatment or her ultimate prognosis. Her primary care guy," more flipping, "a Doctor Bainbridge . . . recommended antidepressants." Marty looked serious. "Patients facing end-of-life conditions sometimes have problems with depression."

Tucker rolled his eyes.

I said, "Please tell me no one is surprised that the terminally ill don't go out singing and tap-dancing."

Marty smirked and shoved the notebook in his shirt pocket. "Cause of death was likely an overdose of something strong, like the others, but we'll need the autopsy to confirm."

I pointed to the bottles on the nightstand. "Could it have been this stuff?"

Marty shrugged. "It could have been. Any of her pain meds would've stopped a rhino. But the home nurse . . ." he pulled out the notebook again, "Shauna Collins, company is General Hospice . . . says all the heavy stuff is accounted for. Right down to the pill. The lab guys were here and they dusted everything. Said the only prints on the bottles belonged to the decedent and the nurse."

"Where did the lab guys go?"

"Had another stop. Said to call them if you need details, otherwise their report will be ready tomorrow."

I nodded. "Thanks."

They zipped up Mrs. Erwell and carted her to the van outside.

We poked around for a minute, then I looked at Tucker.

"Where's the nurse?"

Tucker shrugged.

We caught Marty before he pulled away. Nurse Collins had called her company to report the death and they'd sent out a car to pick her up.

"The guy behind the wheel said he was her supervisor. Said she'd already given you guys a statement, and gotten your okay to take her in for a company deposition. Some internal procedure thing."

I didn't say anything.

Marty looked stricken. "Oh shit. I bought a line, didn't I?"

Tucker tried not to appear exasperated.

I gave Marty a sympathetic smile. He felt bad because he should know better. "Don't worry about it. They're doing corporate CYA, but this will cost them." I waved him on.

Tucker called in and sent a couple of squad cars over to collect the nurse and her supervisor. General Hospice wouldn't like that, but interfering with a police investigation is serious. You step on the playing field, you're in play.

Ms. Combs was crying softly when Tucker gently touched her shoulder. She shook her head and pulled away. "All right. Ask me the damn questions." Mrs. Combs was angry about being questioned, but she told the truth like all the others. She was not present when her sister died (doctor appointment). She had not met the priest yet (planned to do so), as his visits began only recently (last two weeks). She only knew that the priest had been "recommended" by someone whose identity Mrs. Erwell would not divulge to her sister. After eight of these, it was sounding like a script. But not fiction; the thing was set up so the relatives didn't get their hands dirty, and therefore couldn't be charged as accessories. An act of kindness for those left behind to deal with the mess. It almost made me feel warm inside.

We thanked Mrs. Combs and walked out to the car. As we pulled away, I could see her in the rearview, holding herself on the front porch and frowning in the cold gray afternoon. Another old woman whose world had just gotten smaller by one. I looked away from the mirror and drove.

It turned out that General Hospice had a compelling reason to try and sequester Shauna Collins: She was not actually a nurse. Instead of hiring actual RNs or licensed hospice workers, General Hospice recruited former retail workers through a company website and sent them out to medicate their terminal clients. Armed with three days training and a cheap cell phone, Shauna was to follow the medication schedule provided by the company. If things got dicey, she was to call in to the actual trained medical personnel at headquarters. For this, she was paid ten dollars an hour; no benefits. Not surprisingly, General Hospice was making record profits. In the end, a whole bunch of GH executives were arrested at their beautiful homes in Bloomfield Hills and Grosse Pointe.

You should have seen their faces.

We spent the morning of the next day in the police headquarters. I pushed paper around my desk for a while, then Tucker and I grabbed an unmarked and headed out to question Mrs. Erwell's neighbors. Outside, the sky was the color of a fading bruise.

"Snow coming," said Tucker.

The cell phone chirped just as we were headed for the 375 entrance ramp. There was a homicide over off Gratiot, on the city's near east side. Since we were the closest detective car we picked up the slack. I made the siren whoop a couple of times while Tucker cut off a bunch of gesturing commuters. We hit the grill lights and rocketed out Gratiot.

Gratiot was the old artery out to the east side and its storefronts were sturdy monuments to the durability of the past, even as they died slowly in the present. Ugly signs defaced the old buildings, offering nothing more than pagers, liquor, or the sucker bet of the Lotto. Former neighborhood banks anchored major intersections, but now they were charismatic churches or strange shadow-economy shops that seemed to fade in and out with the seasons. Some of the places had been empty for most of my tour of duty. And that's further back than I want to think about.

We turned north on Joseph Campau street. Most of the

homes in this neighborhood were over a hundred years old. They sagged, slowly sinking into the ground, exposed wood graying in the cold wind coming off the river. Many were simply gone; replaced by vacant lots, trees, and the tall weeds known locally as "ghetto palms," their fronds brown until spring. Driveways went nowhere, broken sidewalks marked off irrelevant property lines, light poles supported winter-dead creepers. In the summertime, the vegetation would make this urban neighborhood appear rural. Detroit was slowly reverting to the landscape that the French settlers knew, and I wondered how long it would be before the residents began farming again.

It started to snow. Thick flakes floated down, and I knew a blizzard was coming without being told. You grow up in Michigan, you get to know these things. Two cruisers were parked outside a two-story wood frame that was sloughing off the dark green paint of forty years ago. Three uniforms, all women, stood chatting next to one of the cruisers. They stopped talking as we walked up.

Tucker and I flipped our badges.

"What's up?"

A uniform by the name of Biggs spoke up. She was pretty, with big brown eyes and freckles across her nose and cheeks. Her hair was pulled into tight braids under the uniform cap. She was all business.

"The call came in as a 187. A Gerald Holloway. But a neighbor who apparently knew Mr. Holloway stopped us on the way in and told us it was not a homicide but a suicide."

Tucker's eyebrows rose. "The neighbor still around?"

Officer Biggs gestured to an old woman standing on the porch of a ramshackle house across the street. She wore an ankle-length down coat which she clutched at her throat as she stamped her feet in the cold.

"Her name is Helen Bates and she said she was the one who checked up on Mr. Holloway. Apparently, he didn't have anyone else."

"You said she checked up on him. Was he sick?" I asked.

Biggs nodded. "Cancer. He was going downhill and she basically played nurse for him. She said he was in a lot of pain."

"Why did she say it was a suicide?" I asked.

"Mrs. Bates said it wasn't his time yet. Said he was suffering, but apparently not close to passing yet. She said she'd buried three siblings and she knew what cancer looked like. That's a quote."

Tucker shot me a glance.

I said, "The neighbor mention anything about a visitor?"

Biggs got a look. "Matter of fact, she did. There was this priest who's been stopping by for the past couple of weeks . . ."

It was identical to the other eight cases—nine now, counting Mr. Holloway. But we'd never had two in one week before. I wondered if the good Father was beginning to enjoy his work.

A telephone pole next to our car was covered with the carcasses of a dozen or so stuffed animals, gray and wet and dead after a long time outdoors. Stapled above the limp bunnies and puppies was a faded scrap of cardboard. I stepped closer. The cardboard still had a couple of flecks of glitter stuck to the edges, and the washed-out magic marker lettering was faded, but legible.

*We miss you, Ty!*

Sometimes I hate this fucking city.

The Cathedral of the Most Blessed Sacrament was the mother church of the Archdiocese of Detroit, a classic gothic fortress that rose above Woodward. We found Archbishop Wojciechowski in the sanctuary of the cathedral. He was wearing an Adidas tracksuit and giving direction through hand gestures to a pair of guys buffing the marble inlaid floor surrounding the altar. The sound of the buffing machine bounced around the hard surfaces of the cathedral interior and he waved us to a door behind the sanctuary. After a couple of turns backstage, we stepped into a spacious, comfortable office. The Archbishop closed the door and gestured to a couple of plush chairs. He sat behind an enormous desk that looked enough like mahogany to be the real thing. The sound of the floor buffer was a distant memory.

Archbishop Wojciechowski's face said he was expecting us, so we got right to it. I started to explain that we were simply following up on every possible lead, and he waved me off.

"No explanation necessary, detective. The church will do whatever it can to assist the police in stopping these terrible crimes. I assume you're going to ask if one of the priests of the Archdiocese might be responsible?"

"It's my job."

The Archbishop leaned back and made a steeple with his hands, I kid you not. He smiled wearily and explained that the Vatican was very clear on what he called "culture-of-life issues." Suicide, assisted or not, was a big no-no. And no one who called himself a priest would take part in such a sinful act if he wanted to remain a part of the One True Church.

As soon as the moral high ground had been staked out, Archbishop Wojciechowski said he would instruct all clergy in the Archdiocese to make themselves available to answer our questions.

"My secretary will get you a list of contacts."

On the way out, Tucker caught me dipping into the holy water font. I hadn't even realized I was doing it. I took one last look at the castle and walked to the car.

The snow had intensified while we were talking to the Archbishop, and there was already a couple of inches covering Woodward. Cars had their headlights on and traffic had slowed to a slippery crawl. I sat in the unmarked while Tucker cleared the snow off the windows with a long brush. He's very conscientious about that sort of thing. I would have used my coat sleeve.

The call from 1300 came in just as Tucker slid the car into traffic.

"This is Detective Stan Greenway. We got a pair of lowlifes down here telling a story you might want to hear."

"Yeah? What's up?"

"We grabbed 'em runnin' shorties around the Brewster-Douglas. Whole lotta rock. They were smartasses until they found out the kids aren't taking the brunt of it. Distribution, minors involvement, large-quantity possession. They had a change of heart and started talking about a certain at-large clergyman."

"No kidding? What are their names?"

He paused. "You remember the Williams twins?"

The Twins. Ronnie and Lonnie. Legend had it that the identical Williams brothers got their criminal start in the old Young Boys, Inc. gang while still attending Birney Elementary. YBI was the brainchild of some west side thugs who used school-aged children to push heroin and coke. The kids were too young to do any serious time if they got caught, and YBI frustrated the department for a long time. At its peak, YBI was the largest drug ring in Detroit, providing nearly forty percent of the city's supply.

When YBI finally went down, their rivals Pony Down (named for the popular gym shoe) moved in. War broke out and the homicide rate shot up, but the Twins read the writing and defected to Pony Down. YBI strongholds like the Herman Gardens and Brewster-Douglas projects went to the Ponies and they enjoyed top-dog status for a while.

Pony Down was busted up by the Feds in '85 and the Twins again managed to dance away without being tied to anything serious. They were now in their late thirties, a little older and slower. Prison would be harder for them.

We hit the lights and skidded down Woodward.

The Motorola was going a mile a minute like it always does when winter weather comes down hard. Traffic patrols shifting to accidents. The commuters get pissed when they can't do their normal eighty miles an hour and start bashing into each other. I turned the radio down and concentrated on helping Tucker see through snow that fell sideways.

1300 Beaubien Street, Detroit Police Headquarters, is a grim citadel that sits on the edge of Greektown's ethnic theme park. The building is old and crumbling, and sometimes I think the only thing holding it together is sweat and tears and fear. The collective pain and trauma of thousands of cops, thugs, and victims seeped into the walls like some kind of bad shellac.

We grabbed a space in the lot across the street and half-skied to the door. Inside, we shook our coats, stamped the slush from our feet. The interview room was painted an awful shade of government green that died back in the '60s. Ronnie and Lonnie sat behind the table opposite the one-way glass. They were cuffed together, and a long chain ran from the cuffs to a steel loop set in the floor. At first glance, Ronnie and Lonnie were a pair of working Joes; jeans and thermal Ts under flannel shirts. Both wore heavy work boots and grubby ball caps on their heads. The days of the flashy tracksuits and pristine sneakers were gone. The Twins, like dealers all over the city, had learned to dress to blend in. Detroit kids laughed at the sharp-dressed, colors-wearing thugs in places like L.A. Called them "targets." The new uniform of the day was no uniform at all.

The Williams brothers raised their heads as Tucker and I walked in. Greenway spoke to them.

"Tell the detectives what you said earlier, about the priest."

Either Ronnie or Lonnie said, "We know who he is."

I said, "Which one are you?"

"Lonnie."

"Okay, Lonnie. Who is he?"

Lonnie looked at Ronnie, then back at me. "His name is David Wilkins. Ronnie and I know him from the old days."

"He run with Pony Down?"

"Yeah, later on. He's younger than us. This dude Ray-Ray

brought him in when he was just a shorty. He was Ray-Ray's cousin."

"Ray-Ray?" asked Greenway.

"Ray Bonaventure. He's dead. Got sent up in '86. Some cracker busted his head in Jackson."

"Okay, tell us about David Wilkins," I said.

"Not much to tell. Ray-Ray brought him in because he didn't have nothin' else. His dad was long gone, and his moms was real sick. She couldn't work or nothin', so David had to Pony up to get some money."

"So why do you think this David Wilkins is the priest?" Greenway asked.

"It was the thing with his moms." Lonnie looked at the floor. "She had the cancer real bad. Real bad. And David couldn't get nobody to do nothin' for her. They'd give her some pills and shit, but never enough. David said she was hurtin' real bad."

"Didn't she see a doctor?" I asked.

"Yeah, but it was the free clinic, you know? They tried to help her with assistance and shit, but it wasn't enough to get her the right medicines."

Ronnie added, "Or *enough* medicine. She needed more pain pills but she just couldn't afford 'em. At first, David would tell us how she would be screamin' sometimes cuz it hurt so bad. But after a while, he stopped talkin' about it. He got real quiet."

Lonnie said, "Way we heard it, took a *long* time for her to die. She was sufferin'."

"The way you *heard it?*" asked Greenway.

"Yeah, cuz by that time David had stopped comin' around. We just didn't see him no more. We heard he was on the bottle, on the weed, on the pipe, every damn thing. Can't blame him after that shit with his moms. We thought he was gonna show up DOA."

"But he didn't?"

"Naw," said Ronnie. "He showed back up at our crib."

After the seasons had changed a couple of times, David appeared on the Twins' doorstep one day. He was clear-eyed, clean and sober. The Twins described his demeanor as friendly, quiet, and serious. After some small talk, he told them he wanted drugs. "Not that street shit," he'd said. He gave them a list; heavy stuff, major-league painkillers and narcotics. Large quantities. They negotiated a price and a pickup time and he left.

"Okay," I said, "so where can we find David Wilkins?"

Ronnie surprised me. "Downtown. He's staying at that old theater building on, what is it, Bagley . . . ?"

He looked at his brother, who nodded and said: "United Artists."

"Yeah, that's it. He's staying there."

"He's staying in the United Artists Theater or the office building?"

"The office building. At the top."

I was skeptical. "At the *top* of the building? And what about the security guard?"

Ronnie and Lonnie traded smiles. "He *is* the security guard. Some dude out in Bloomfield Hills hired him. He's got a cot and space heater up there."

I looked at Tucker, then Greenway, who shrugged. We all went out.

Greenway spoke first. "I know it seems too neat, but the other stuff they've been giving us has been straight. I think they're serious about not doing the hard time."

Tucker said. "I think so too. I bet they're thinking about some of their old crew who got sent up back in the day. They played both sides, you know. YBI, then Pony Down. Could be that they know they wouldn't get a very warm welcome inside."

"Does anyone?" asked Greenway.

He had a point.

It was still mid-afternoon, but the heavy snowfall made it seem like dusk already. The commute had become a nightmare; businesses were closing early and sending their people home. The streets were fast clogging with snow and cars spun out in every intersection we passed. It was going to be a long rush hour.

The old United Artists building stood eighteen stories above Bagley Street on a flatiron-shaped plot. The narrow end of the flatiron faced Park Avenue, with Grand Circus Park just across the street. At one time, the area was the city's theater district and Detroiters could stroll to any number of ornate movie palaces. The Fox and the State were rescued from the wrecking ball and refurbished, and the Gem had to be moved from its original location to be saved. Most of the other old theaters were either gone or falling to ruin.

Like many of the vacant towers in downtown, the UA had been invaded by all types over the years. Squatters, bottle bums, and under-medicated street psychotics all left clues to their maladies in the nests they vacated. Recently, the monoliths had become destinations for self-styled urban explorers and curious suburbanites. They posted photos of the crumbling towers on websites, attracting more and more to come and visit the Urban Failure Amusement Park. The police insisted that the building owners seal off the entrances and provide security to keep the junkies or thrill-seekers out, and the owners mostly complied. It seemed that David Wilkins had found a way to exploit this situation and hide in plain sight.

We pulled up on the Bagley side and tracked through the virgin snow that drifted under the old marquee. Most of the doors to the theater lobby were covered with painted plywood and sealed, but the owner had installed a steel security door to allow access to the building when necessary. Tucker tried the door, but it was locked. He pulled a small leather zip-pouch from his coat pocket. Lock picks. I stepped back from the door and looked up and down the street. We had the block to ourselves. I raised my eyes to the building façade and scanned the windows. Nothing.

Tucker popped the lock. We slowly opened the door, and a backwash of foul air hit us. The smells of mold, mildew, building rot, and piss swirled around and it occurred to me that breathing the air might be hazardous to our pulmonary health. Tucker pulled a small but powerful flashlight from his pocket and we stepped inside.

The once-beautiful theater lobby was a disaster of standing water, shredded plaster, and piles of rubble. Something, maybe a rat or feral cat, splashed into a corner and disappeared through a tear in the plaster. We gave the lobby a pass and looked for the entrance to the office tower. After fumbling along dank hallways, we found a stairwell off an elevator lobby that stretched far upward into the musty air. Tucker shined his light. Dust and God knew what else floated through the beams. The stairs were piled with bottles, clothing, fast-food wrappers, and assorted trash. We chose our steps with care and started up. It would be almost impossible to stay quiet as we crunched our way up, and the noise would probably alert any residents to our presence. All we could do was try to minimize our footfalls and maybe the bird wouldn't flush until we were close enough to grab him.

About five floors up, the garbage thinned and we stopped to listen to the building. Silence. We kept climbing. At floor ten, we stopped again. Still no sounds from the floors above. At fifteen, we stepped out into an office corridor that didn't look much different from the day its last occupant packed up back in '75. Marble panels lined the hallway and dark hardwood trim detailed the offices. One of the rooms was piled high with battered steel desks. We searched the whole floor and found nothing but empty offices and dust.

We climbed to the sixteenth floor and into an eerie red glow. A blood-red hand was painted on the window of the elevator lobby, and it cast the room in crimson light. A few years back, the UA became a favorite for local graffiti taggers and street artists. These guerilla Picassos were inspired to cover the building's windows with unusual and brightly colored images. The UA became a kind of modern folk art symbol. Too bad for art. A powerful local real estate developer acquired the UA for some unspecified future venture and immediately set about "cleaning up" the windows. Either they had missed a couple of windows, or the artists were coming back.

We moved down the hallway. Tucker was ahead of me and he stopped by a blue-colored doorway. He waved me over and nodded in at what had been an office. An attempt had been made to clean the window, but a light aqua tint persisted and the room washed in soft blue light. A bed was laid against one wall, and there were several pairs of shoes lined up along the bottom of a bookcase filled with hardcovers, paperbacks, and magazines, all shelved as neatly as a library. On the other side of the bed was another set of shelves that held toiletries and john paper. A fine coating of dust covered everything and it looked as though the occupant hadn't been home for a long time. A *Free Press* next to the bed was dated July 2000. We moved on.

The seventeenth floor was empty. All of the hallway and office walls had been removed, the entire level stripped down to the thin concrete support columns. Snow fell past the naked windows in the dimming afternoon light. We moved carefully through the huge empty room, the columns breaking up our sight lines. Tucker suddenly stopped and nodded toward the far corner. There was a doorway to another stairwell, a twin to the one we'd climbed. I glanced back at my partner, who looked impatient. He nodded at the corner again, at something beyond this other stairwell. Off in the shadows, I could just make out the flat panel of a hardwood-trimmed wall. As we got closer, I could see a darkened doorway with an open transom. One of the level's old offices had been left intact. Tucker and I knew this was where we would find David Wilkins.

We came up on either side of the old room, guns drawn, flashlights out. There was no door in the frame and nothing to stop us from moving in quickly, guns covering opposite ends of the interior. Nobody home.

An old army cot and space heater stood at one end, just as Lonnie had said. A couple of milk crates had been turned over to make a table for a hot plate, and a battered old pot hung from a nail in the wall. Empty soup cans and paper waste filled a tiger-striped trashcan that said *Bless You Boys!* on the side. Opposite the room from the cot was a stack of cardboard cartons.

Tucker pulled up the flaps of the topmost box and looked inside. I stood with my back to the doorjamb so I had a clear view of both Tucker and the empty floor beyond. Tucker held up quart-sized containers filled with tablets, capsules. The names were dull in the flashlight beam, but I made out *Dilaudid*, *Percocet*, and several other Schedule I and II drugs. It was the mother lode.

I was about to say something smart, when we heard a scrape coming from the stairwell just outside the office. We froze. The scrape came again, then became footsteps pounding up the flight. We flew out of the room guns first. The pounding crossed the floor above us. We took the stairs two at a time.

As with the level below, the eighteenth floor was stripped bare. Even the windows had been removed. Dimming light leaked in from the holes that once held windows and snow flurries drifted across the concrete floor. Through the window openings we could see the façades of other empty buildings, their edges softened in the falling snow and the late afternoon dusk.

We were running for the footfalls echoing in the opposite stairwell when we heard the *boom* of what sounded like a heavy door.

"The roof," said Tucker between breaths.

Across the floor and up the first flight, we paused at the landing to listen. There was only the silence of the falling snow. The roof door stood partially open sending a thin shaft of light into the upper flight. Through the gap, we could see footprints trailing away in the thick snow. Tucker crept up the stairs and spread his large hand against the steel door. He looked back at me. I nodded and raised my gun. Tucker slowly pushed open the door.

We could see the entire rooftop. It looked like a frosted cake with all the snow. Tucker stepped though the doorway and for a moment the stairwell went dark. Then he was out, moving deliberately, his head fixed straight ahead. I followed, ranging off to his right. The flurries were coming thicker now, but I could still see my partner. And beyond him, David Wilkins, the priest.

Wilkins stood at the eastern edge of the roof. His back was to us and his long black coat hung nearly to the snow. He was framed on both sides by the empty towers that surrounded Grand Circus Park, and in the distance we could see the orange glow from the new baseball and football stadiums.

"David." My voice was only a hoarse whisper and that surprised me. Or maybe the thickening snow ate the sound. Tucker stood about ten yards to my left. He was looking at me, his eyebrows raised. My mouth was dry and I swallowed to get some spit going.

Tucker turned his head and said, "David Wilkins," in a clear voice that carried over the rooftop.

When I remember the moment, I am struck by the silence. The vacant towers around us seemed to bear witness through their dark windows. Streetlights glowed from far below, and the falling snowflakes softened the hard edges and planes of the concrete that surrounded us. Wilkins seemed to cant forward, then disappeared over the edge. I looked up into the sky, into the snow. There was a flapping sound as his coat caught the wind on the way down.

It sounded like wings.

# THE NIGHT WATCHMAN IS ASLEEP

BY JOE BOLAND

*Downtown*

M itchell, the other night watchman at the Guardian Building, was a moonlighting cop. The night Stoner started, Mitchell gave him the once-over—height and build, age, haircut—and decided that Stoner must be a moonlighting cop too.

Stoner let him think what he wanted.

"You from the Northwest District?" Mitchell asked.

"I'm from Downriver," Stoner said.

"Well *sheeit*," Mitchell said, putting a twang into it.

Mitchell was an enormous black man, and Stoner wasn't certain if he was trying to be funny. When Stoner didn't laugh, Mitchell said, "Don't wanna double in your own bunk, huh? That's smart, rook. I'm from Farmington Hills. You from Taylor-*tucky*? Wyan-*tucky*?"

"Beautiful Brownstown," Stoner said.

Mitchell seemed to decide that Stoner wasn't going to be trouble.

"Oh no," he laughed. "You in beautiful Brownstown *now*."

Stoner was from Wyandotte, twenty miles south of Detroit. His family and most of his neighbors were originally from Tennessee, not Kentucky. He'd really only been to the city a few dozen times before, for Tigers or Red Wings games, or to check out the casinos when they first opened. His idea of the city came from the news, and from the bad word-of-mouth he heard every day. As far as he could tell, Detroit hadn't changed much in his lifetime. It was no longer the nation's murder capital, but it didn't seem like a city on the rebound either. He always thought of it as dirty and abandoned-looking, and a couple new buildings and stadiums downtown didn't do enough to change his impression: You were still only a block or two away from being surrounded by black people who hated you.

He had never been in the Guardian Building before, an office highrise two blocks from the Detroit River with a tiled façade the color of light coffee and a lobby like a cathedral. Stoner had to admit it was beautiful.

Mitchell walked him through the building. At first Stoner was apprehensive, wondering if the tour was going to be an excuse for Mitchell to talk cop-shop with him, but Mitchell only seemed interested in talking on his cell phone, which rang every few minutes. Half an hour after their shift began, Mitchell put a hand over the mouthpiece and said, "Listen—you got this, right?"

Stoner nodded. "I got it."

"Just do like the flashlight stiffs on your beat," Mitchell said, backing away. "You know. Pretend you a cop."

Stoner's second cousin, Hawkins, had gotten him the job. After work, Stoner waited for him at the bus stop near the corner of Woodward and Larned, on the west end of the Guardian's block. Hawkins guarded a bank building on West Grand Boulevard in the New Center area, ten minutes north of downtown. Stoner stood around for twenty-five minutes, staring at the statues along Woodward—Joe Louis's fist, the crouching naked man who was supposed to be the Spirit of Detroit—before Hawkins pulled up.

Hawkins's Grand Marquis Brougham—white-on-white, rust-shot, passenger-side mirror hanging down, driver-side mirror missing—might have been one of the cars jamming Hawkins's family's driveway, or up on cinder blocks in their side yard, back when Stoner and Hawkins were kids.

He handed Stoner a warm tallboy in a paper bag. "How was your first night, sweetie?"

"This about the time you'll be getting down here, man?"

Hawkins laughed. "Don't worry about it, bitch. Nobody's gonna fuck with you, not in this uniform." He made a right onto Jefferson Avenue, taking the Lodge to I-75 South. "I thought you were a cop myself."

Stoner decided to let it go. He didn't like standing around a bus stop, but the alternative was waiting inside the building for Hawkins to pull up to one of the entrances and honk the car horn. He didn't want Mitchell or the guards who relieved the both of them or the neighborhood patrolmen to know that he didn't have a car of his own.

It was the Motor City, for Christ's sake. What kind of a man didn't have a car?

It was a temporary situation—he'd get his truck running again soon enough—but there was no need to make it worse by pissing off Hawkins.

Stoner didn't really know him anymore.

"I think you're gonna like it," Hawkins said. "And remember, this is just getting a foot in the door."

Hawkins was talking about his big plan again: to start his own security company. "There's gonna be more call for security work than ever. First we get in the hotels Detroit's building. Then you get contracts with the bigwigs who come to stay in the hotels. When they're looking for a bodyguard to travel with them when they fly to China and shit, they're gonna say: *Get in touch with the people at the Book Cadillac, the Pontchartrain, their security force was the bomb.*"

Hawkins was the only night watchman at his building. Stoner pictured him pacing the empty building alone, hiding his beer from the janitor, reading every inch of the *Free Press* or the *News*, listening to the radio through the night, dreaming his dream of founding a world-class security company.

They were friends in childhood, then drifted apart—helped along by Stoner's mother, who dismissed Hawkins's family as "country." He barely remembered Hawkins in high school: a solitary figure, starting to get heavy, reading *Soldier of Fortune* magazine when he thought no one was looking.

Stoner felt a sudden emptiness thinking about it. He took a long swallow of his beer.

"Yeah, I'd like to get Mitchell on board too," Hawkins said.

"Oh yeah? You talk to him about it?"

"No, dude, but he'd be great. It would be cool to get a cop on board, especially at the beginning. It'd help, too, to have a brother, you know, help us get situated in Detroit." Hawkins lit a cigarette. "And Mitchell's from Oakland County, too, up there with the richies, so he knows how to talk to people."

"He thinks *I'm* a cop," Stoner said. He filled Hawkins in, repeating the conversation he'd had with Mitchell, at Hawkins's insistence, word for word.

"And you played along?" Hawkins laughed. "Well, I hear the man's getting married soon, going over wedding shit all the time. His brain's probably fried. You're gonna hafta set him straight—not now, but sometime."

Mitchell introduced Stoner to the neighborhood patrolmen as a cop too.

Red and McSmith, both high-yellow black men in their forties, stood with their fists on their hips, regarding Stoner dubiously, as Mitchell said, "Stoner's on the job, down in Brownstown."

"That so?" Red said.

"We're going to the Lafayette," McSmith said. "You want a Coney dog, Mitchell?"

That night Stoner told Hawkins he wanted to come clean before it was too late. "They didn't buy it."

"It's too late," Hawkins said. "Listen, if push comes to shove, tell everybody you're a dispatcher."

"What if they quiz me? *What's a seven twenty-one?*"

Hawkins was certain it wouldn't happen.

Two nights later, Red and McSmith pulled up next to Hawkins's Grand Marquis at the bus stop as Stoner was walking up to the car.

Stoner tensed. He could see that Hawkins already had an open beer between his legs, and was reaching down to grab a beer for Stoner out of a bag on the floor of the front seat.

They had already settled into a pattern, driving around the city after work, drinking beer in the early morning hours, Hawkins giving Stoner uninformative tours of various sights Stoner didn't even want to see in daylight, putting off heading for the freeway home just a bit longer each day.

With the mirror on his side of the car missing, Hawkins hadn't noticed the cops. McSmith was resting an arm on the open window in the passenger seat of the patrol car, noting the absence of the mirror, and hearing the country music that Stoner noticed was, regrettably, coming out of the stereo.

"Hey!" Stoner called, trying to draw everyone's attention.

"Hey, rookie," McSmith said, without looking in his direction.

Hawkins sat up and looked at the cops and killed the radio. He slowly placed his hands at 10 and 2 on the steering wheel, a gesture meant to be ironic and hostile, lost on no one.

"Stoner, this your car?"

"It's mine," Hawkins said, looking out the windshield.

"You need to do something about the mirrors, my man."

"And the body," Red said, leaning over.

"Yeah," McSmith laughed. "Looks like a junkyard toilet. Stoner, see your buddy gets some mirrors, y'hear?" They pulled away.

Stoner got in the Grand Marquis.

"Fucking assholes," Hawkins said.

"Man, don't fuck around with those guys."

"Fucking Dee-troit po-lice. Bunch of thugs. They just love

to fuck with white people. The only time they go into the neighborhoods where their own people are killing each other over crack is when they need to make some quick cash."

Stoner had seen the stories in the *News* and the *Free Press* lately, and Hawkins had filled him in with details that hadn't made the newspapers. Detroit residents reporting shakedowns by cops—or people claiming to be cops. The mayor's personal security detail—made up entirely of cops who'd been on the football team with him in high school—escorting visiting rap stars to after-hours clubs. A stripper who'd performed at a party at the mayoral residence, Manoogian Manor, turning up in a dumpster.

To Hawkins the stories were gospel truth. They explained why he'd been rebuffed whenever he tried to talk to any of the cops up in the New Center about coming on board, becoming a partner in his security company venture.

"They don't want to get in bed with Whitey. Might knock 'em out of line for that cushy job at the motor pool, or sitting in a car outside the Manoogian on permanent overtime. Might fuck up their payments from the union in the next round of layoffs or the next strike. That's their whole ambition, dude."

Stoner knew that trouble was coming, but he wasn't certain what to do. The money that was, in his mind, earmarked for his truck repairs kept going to Hawkins, for gasoline and beer. What was he going to do, not give his cousin gas money? He knew he should turn down the beer, make some noise about heading home when Hawkins started driving around aimlessly at night, make excuses when they pulled into their usual final stop, the bar down by the Ford plant in Wyandotte that never seemed to close. There had to be an easy way to get Hawkins to take him home after work. Stoner needed to separate himself—start drinking less, stop sleeping through all the daylight hours, fix his truck—without crushing his cousin's spirit any further.

He just didn't know how to do it.

\* \* \*

A few nights later, the Grand Marquis Brougham was already idling at the bus stop when Stoner arrived, the patrol car sitting behind it, Red in the passenger seat this time. McSmith was behind the wheel, writing Hawkins a ticket.

Red watched Stoner walk toward the patrol car. "Hey, rookie."

"We were gonna take care of that this weekend," Stoner said, hoping this was about the mirrors.

"Know what I was gonna do this weekend?" McSmith asked, without looking up from his writing. "Titty-fuck Pamela Anderson." Red laughed and shook his head. "Now I hear that Kid Rock gone and marry her."

"We don't see a lot of daylight during the week," Stoner said, thinking of his dead truck. "You know how it is."

McSmith didn't look up. "Woulda, coulda, shoulda."

"How about one break?"

Red shrugged. "He's already writing, Stoner."

"His money's kind of tight, man."

McSmith handed over the ticket. "Then pay it for him, rookie."

"Just go slow," Stoner said to Hawkins back in the car.

Hawkins pulled up to the light. His face and neck had turned bright red. He made the right onto Jefferson.

"It never fails. Give 'em a badge, they bust on a honky." Hawkins tipped his beer.

The cops gave a short burst on their siren, a single *whoop*. Stoner looked back: The patrol car was right behind the Grand Marquis.

Hawkins spilled his beer down the front of his uniform. "Fuck!"

"Just be cool," Stoner said.

Hawkins pulled to the curb. McSmith appeared at Hawkins's window.

"I don't know about Brownstown," he said, with a certain the-atrical relish, "but here in Detroit? We *frown* on open intoxicants."

Stoner's door opened. "Come out here, Stoner," Red said.

Stoner climbed out of the car and followed Red to the mid-dle of the sidewalk. They turned and watched Hawkins hand the rumpled grocery bag filled with beer out his window.

"Your buddy on the job?" Red asked.

"No."

Red shrugged. "Army buddy?"

"Kid I grew up with," Stoner said.

"Well," Red said. His voice had become gentle. He nodded back in Hawkins's direction, inviting Stoner to follow his gaze and contemplate the battered car and the sullen young fat man in the soiled uniform. "You're all grown up now. Right?"

*He's my cousin*, Stoner wanted to say.

He knew it was too late.

For a cop, Red didn't seem like a bad guy, and being black, he might have understood about family; and he seemed to be making Stoner some kind of offer—square your shoulders, join the club.

Stoner had blown him off, though, and dissed his cousin in the bargain. It was too late to take any of it back.

"They're just fuckers, all of them," Hawkins said, back be-hind the wheel. "I hope they choke on that beer."

"I thought you wanted to *be* a cop," Stoner said.

"*What?*"

"Didn't you want to *be* a cop? I thought I remember you say—"

"*When?*"

"I don't know—high school?"

"Oh hell, that's possible."

They drove in silence.

"No, wait. *Kill* a cop. I said I wanted to *kill* a cop," Hawkins said, deadpan, then laughed at his own joke.

Stoner didn't join him.

The laughter broke into a cough. Hawkins cleared his

throat. "Bunch of short-sighted motherfuckers. This is what I keep running into. I'm looking for a partner—not even a *real* partner. *You're* my real partner. I need a cop to liaison with the cops. I need a cop like a car dealership needs a washed-up Lions receiver. These idiots would rather take their pissant pensions and drink themselves to death in the La-Z-Boy. They'd rather play their little games, take their penny-ante scores. Like there's anything special in pushing people around with your uniform. You wanna see how special it makes you feel? We could get out at the next intersection."

Stoner had a bad feeling: He knew exactly what Hawkins was getting at.

"I'm serious. You look like a cop to me."

"That's just the uniforms, in the dark."

"That's what I'm saying." Hawkins dragged on his smoke. "I think we oughta take a little walk around, see what we can do."

"Man, what are you talking about?"

"We wouldn't have to be *good* cops, dude," he said, grinning now. "That's what I'm talking about."

Hawkins had turned the wrong way leaving downtown. He looked lost, but seemed too angry to care. Stoner was looking for the freeway, any freeway, spotting a section of one now and then, like a man in a desert might see water. The on-ramp was nowhere in sight.

They were driving west on Rosa Parks Boulevard, a two-lane artery through some bleak residential neighborhoods. Hawkins looked left and right, and spotted a boarded-up corner party store up ahead, covered in tags. It was the only thing they'd seen that passed for a landmark. Hawkins turned up the street, pulled to the curb, and killed the headlights. "Come on," he said, shutting off the engine and taking the key out of the ignition. He picked his uniform cap off the dashboard, stepped out of the car, and closed the door.

Stoner got out of the car. Standing up, he felt shaky, and

realized how crazy the scene with Red and McSmith had made him feel; sitting in the car since then had only made it worse.

Hawkins was pulling on rain gear: a poncho, a bonnet for his cap, both gray. The gear covered up the security company insignia on the uniform, and left his holster and badge to the imagination.

Stoner was amazed: At that moment, Hawkins looked just like a cop.

He followed him up the center of the dark street.

"Just keep talking," Hawkins said. "Normal voice. Have a conversation, like you're not afraid of anything, and you won't be."

Stoner looked in the broken front window of the first house on his right as they walked past. Moonlight shone right through from a window in the rear. He told himself they were all empty— it was a carnival attraction, the haunted street—and that he was calm and ready.

It wasn't working.

Hawkins asked him how the Tigers had done the night before, knowing Stoner read the sports section during his lunch break.

Stoner laughed. The fact that Hawkins cared nothing about sports made his prompt to start talking seem even more ridiculous. But he launched into what he could remember of the newspaper account of Jeremy Bonderman's fourth-inning meltdown on the mound, and Hawkins feigned interest, and soon Stoner noticed his pulse had stopped racing.

He was beginning to feel pretty good when a figure came from the shadows and slanted across the street up ahead of them.

"PO-LICE," Hawkins yelled. "HOLD UP!"

The man stopped and looked back, then turned away from the sight of Hawkins barreling toward him and took a couple of loping steps, without gaining any ground, before Hawkins crashed into his back and sprawled him over the hood of a Lincoln Zephyr.

"Hold up, hold up," the man sputtered. He was lifting his arms straight above his head, like a diver. Hawkins was doubled over on top of him, catching his breath.

"Hands on the hood," Stoner said. "Please."

He looked around. The shouts, the whistle of Hawkins's uniform as his thighs collided during the sprint, the tackle into the car had all sounded to Stoner like gunfire in the quiet. But no lights had come on anywhere in the block. When he glanced back, Hawkins was holding a small, wet-looking wad of money in front of the man's hollow eyes.

"Where you headed with *this*, huh?" Hawkins said, panting. When he'd gotten his wind back, he pushed off the hood of the car, then grabbed the man's arm and spun him around. "Go on."

"My aunt's. My aunt's house." The man stood there, hugging himself. Stoner could see he was waiting, halfheartedly, for his money back.

"Go on now," Hawkins said, making a shooing motion.

The man stood a second longer, his lips working like he might cry, then he turned and walked up the street.

"Jesus Christ," Stoner said.

"Did you see his hands?" Hawkins asked, holding up his own to look at them. "His fingertips were black, like, down to the second knuckle. Must be he's one of them cutting the copper wire out of the streetlights and shit."

"Fuck you!" the man shouted back at them.

Stoner jumped. The man had stopped at the end of the block, but once he'd gotten their attention, he turned away and continued walking.

Hawkins laughed.

"Let's get out of here," Stoner said.

"Yeah," Hawkins replied. "Come on, let's get a beer."

Back in the car, Stoner drank a beer in two swallows while Hawkins started the engine and drove away. He grabbed another beer, and Hawkins pulled a pint of whiskey from beneath the driver's seat. Hawkins took a swallow and handed it to Stoner, then flipped the wad of cash at him. "Looks like about twenty bucks. Count it."

It was a five and thirteen ones. "Eighteen."

"Is that all?"

The elusive on-ramp appeared suddenly on their right, and Hawkins aimed the car down it.

Stoner peered over at him. Disheveled, still winded, he looked near collapse, like he'd been up for days, yet he still seemed angry, full of determination.

For his part, Stoner felt like he'd been in a fight that ended before he was able to throw a punch.

"The problem," Hawkins said, "is that these people don't have a lot of money, because they spend whatever they can get on drugs."

They exited the freeway and drove through Greektown, finding their way to Jefferson Avenue. Soon they were heading alongside the Detroit River, a mile east of the Renaissance Center; on their right, gated communities with their own shopping centers; across Jefferson, empty lots and liquor stores, hand-painted sandwichboards advertising bait.

"Did you see the artist's drawings in the paper, the plans?" Hawkins got a cigarette going. "This is all gonna be part of the new riverfront, and here there's gonna be office and retail and residential all together, like retail on the ground floor, offices and condos upstairs. *This* is where we need to put the office. I'm telling you, man, we've got to act now. The Super Bowl. The All-Star Game. Terrorists coming over from Canada. There's big money to be made."

Stoner looked out over the river. He had to admit it was a nice view. "What's the plan?" he asked.

The crack house sat in weeds and gravel on a street off Grand River and the Jeffries. Wet trash lined the curb between the parked cars. Several newer cars and SUVs were standing, engines idling, and silhouettes moved through the dark between the vehicles. Voices, low and harsh, carried through the night air. Then someone turned up the walk to the front door of the house.

Hawkins stepped away from the window. "Here comes another," he called.

*Not so loud,* thought Stoner, standing in the kitchen. He looked down at the man in the chair, haphazardly bound with bungee cords and duct tape, and caught the guy reading the irritation on his face. *He'll try to play us against each other.* Stoner took a step toward the chair.

"You ain't po-lice," the man said, just before Stoner forced the gag back into his mouth.

Now Stoner was truly exasperated.

"You think?"

He backed up against the wall and waited. The weight of his Maglite was dragging it slowly down out of his fist. When there was no sound from the front room for too long, he edged around the corner and stage whispered, "What's up?"

Hawkins was back at the window, his hair standing on end. Stoner glanced around the room: Hawkins's uniform cap lay upside down on an arm of the ratty sofa.

"I think he saw me."

"He see the cap?"

"I think so. He turned back."

"Ah, fuck."

"Easy," Hawkins said. "They may've just remembered they never saw the other dude come out."

"Let's go now."

"And do what?"

They'd searched the house, but found only forty dollars, and no drugs at all. The man in the kitchen wasn't talking.

"You're right," Stoner said. "Let's stick to the plan. If we knock out all the runners, maybe the rich white suburbanites will hop out of their SUVs and come to the door themselves to get robbed."

"Chill the fuck out."

Stoner left Hawkins at the front door and went to the bedroom to check on the first guy who'd knocked on the door, the one Hawkins had hit on the head repeatedly with his Maglite. He found the man on the bed where they'd left him. He was sitting up, alert enough to mutter something about swelling, and to call Stoner a fucking cracker. He was a kid, really. He didn't look good. His eyes kept trying to close.

"Shut up," Stoner told him.

"Gimme back my money, you prick." The kid sounded disgusted; then, suddenly, he slumped back against the wall and his chin dropped to his chest.

Stoner moved closer, but couldn't bring himself to reach in and check for a pulse. He stood over the kid until he was satisfied that the kid's chest was actually rising and falling in the dark, that he wasn't just willing himself to see it happen.

Hawkins called his name from the front of the house, again too loudly.

He was moving toward Hawkins's voice when something started banging against the outside of the front door.

Hawkins stood at the peephole with his palms flat against the door. Stoner put his hand on Hawkins's shoulder, and Hawkins took one step sideways, not moving his palms, as if he were bracing the door.

"Just pulled up," Hawkins said.

Stoner ducked between Hawkins's arms and put his eye to the peephole, just as the man on the porch began to speak. He ducked again, instinctively, at the sound of the guy's voice, then slowly lined his eye up with the peephole and looked out.

The man stood with his hands clasped behind his neck and his feet apart, in the stance of someone about to be handcuffed, but he was alone. The black cat between his feet, once Stoner's eyes adjusted, became an oily-looking gym bag.

"What the point havin' a cell you don't answer it?" the man said.

"Fuck's he talking about?" Hawkins hissed into Stoner's ear.

"This some *unnecessary bullshit*," the man continued, his head back, addressing the night sky.

Stoner could just make out a dark SUV behind him at the curb. "See if anybody's in that truck," he whispered to Hawkins.

Crouched by the window, Hawkins shook his head.

Stoner reached for the deadbolt with his left hand, grasped the doorknob with his right.

Hawkins scrambled around to the other side of the doorway, hefted his Maglite over his head.

"Tell him to bring it in," Stoner said.

"BRING IT IN!"

Stoner yanked the door open.

The man on the porch did not step inside.

When three seconds had passed, Stoner and Hawkins collided in the doorway.

"Oh, *hell* no," the man on the porch said. His hands were dropping from behind his neck. He seemed to be caught between kicking the bag and reaching to grab it when Stoner swung the Maglite into the side of his head.

They met at the Ford plant bar the next afternoon. Hawkins was talking to the pretty bartender as she worked a rag over the top of the bar.

"Hey, Stoner, tell Kiley what part of Detroit you work in."

"The Central Business District."

The bartender laughed convulsively, held the back of her wrist to her mouth, trying to stop.

"See? What I tell ya?" When she moved away to draw a beer

for Stoner, Hawkins leaned toward him and said, "We gotta go back."

"*Where?*"

"What? *Come on.* Thanks, Kiley." Hawkins picked up both of their glasses and started walking toward a booth.

"Eddie, did you see the newspaper?" Stoner's own voice sounded crazy to him, almost as crazy as Hawkins did.

"Yeah, I saw it. One of those crackheads had the decency to call an ambulance like you told them."

"And?"

Hawkins sat down. "And—everybody's in Detroit Receiving with a headache?"

"And the fucking FBI is in town investigating the police department."

"That just means the dickheads the bagman was looking for are gonna be laying low." Hawkins drummed the tabletop, grinning widely. "Fucking three grand, dude!"

Stoner sat down, shaking his head. "Think about it, man. Even the cops who're total jackoffs have got to be thinking about finding the guys who took down that house, before Internal Affairs tries to pin it on *them.*"

Hawkins nodded. "They're closing ranks. But that's what always happens when some shit hits the news. I've been doing this for three years, remember."

"Doing *what* for three years?"

"*Been a security man* three years."

"They gotta be looking at the patrolmen," Stoner said, thinking aloud, "because who else is gonna go to the trouble for a few hundred bucks?"

"We did better than that."

"They don't know how much we got. We took three thousand off the guys they're looking for. And those guys have got to be looking for us."

He waved the folded *Detroit News* he was still carrying.

"And now the FBI is watching everybody," Stoner added.

"They're looking for dirty cops, not for us."

"They're looking for *dickhead* cops. They have no idea that they're looking for cops as dirty as the cops we ripped off."

"Still—they're looking for dirty cops, so the dirty cops will lay low."

"Yeah, well, that's also pretty good incentive for the good cops to find us, don't you think?"

"That's why we have to act fast. We have time for one more score, while they're still all bumpin' dicks."

"Man, what are you talking about? You want to shake down another house?"

"I want another gym bag."

Stoner looked into his cousin's crazy eyes and laughed. "Dumb luck, man."

"We need two months' rent. Stationery and business cards. I'm telling you, dude, we've got to act now. The Super Bowl. The All-Star Game. Terrorists coming over from Canada. There's big money to be made."

Stoner thought about the money again.

He'd already set aside a grand from the bag—a third of the take, less than a full share. That was money enough to fix his truck, or make a down payment on another used car. His cousin could keep the rest, and five hundred of Stoner's share, and put it toward the business. He'd help him tonight, because he could see there was no way Hawkins wasn't going, but that would be the end of it.

"There's no way we can know about another house that's paying off those cops. What do you want to do, stake out the entire fucking supermarket?"

"No, dude. We don't have time. We gotta do the same house."

They went that night.

They turned off Grand River Avenue onto Fullerton and moved in a grid, staying at least two blocks away from the street the house was on. Hawkins drove slowly, with the headlights off and the windows rolled down. They both sat leaning forward, watching and listening.

Stoner thought it was a good strategy, but it was hard to see much: The houses were set too close together, the spaces between filled with overgrown shrubs and bedsprings.

Finally he saw yellow police tape poking through the backyards. "Stop," he told Hawkins, pointing.

Hawkins put the car in park and killed the engine, right in the middle of the street. "That's not the house," he said finally.

"It's not, is it?"

"Nope," Hawkins said. "Wrong side of the street. Too far down."

"Think something else happened?"

"What do you think?"

"I think they moved them to this house, here, then called the cops."

"There must've been something in that house. I mean, we didn't find shit. But there was some shit in there they did not want to give up, or there was too much of it to move."

"I think they're still in business, at the other house."

"Man, those guys didn't seem together enough for this." Hawkins sounded scared.

Stoner shook his head. "Let's get out of here."

"I think you're right," Hawkins said.

"Let's try someplace else. Let's try southwest Detroit. Along Michigan Avenue somewhere." Stoner held his wristwatch up to his face, but without any working streetlights, it was too dark to read it. "What time is it?"

Hawkins poked a finger at the dashboard radio, as if he'd forgotten the ignition was off and was trying to summon the digital clock.

"Let's just go," Stoner said.

Hawkins turned the key in the ignition, and country music, badly distorted at full volume, blasted out of the speakers and pinned them back in their seats.

They both shrieked like girls. Their hands collided, trying to turn the radio off.

"Jesus Christ!"

They looked at each other and laughed in the sudden quiet, true partners at last.

"Man," Hawkins said, listening, "not even a dog barking."

"Guess we didn't wake anybody up."

"I wonder why they don't like dogs."

They came to the end of the block, and a dark four-door with its headlights off slammed into their front end, spinning the Grand Marquis ninety degrees.

Four broad-shouldered men, moving the way cops moved, scrambled out of the car. They said nothing Stoner could hear. They were dressed nothing like cops. The car looked nothing like a cop car: It looked like one of the cars jamming the Hawkins family's driveway, or up on cinder blocks in their side yard, back when Stoner and Hawkins were kids.

The man who'd gotten out of the driver's seat shot Hawkins in the chest, twice.

Stoner opened his door and fell to the ground. There was nowhere to go. He crawled underneath the Grand Marquis.

"Oh no," a voice said, chiding, "no-no."

Stoner felt hands close around his ankles.

"Cover this bitch!"

Stoner was dragged backward. His shirt bunched up under his armpits. He got a hand up to grab at the underside of the car, but whatever he managed to close his palm around immediately burned him, and he let go. He was in the open. They dropped his ankles. He tried to turn onto his back. Someone planted a boot between his shoulder blades.

"Got a wallet," one of them called from the other side of the car. "Got ID."

Someone patted Stoner down, put fingers in his back pocket. His wallet came out.

"Got his too." The boot lifted off his back. "ID, got it."

"Where's the bag?"

They kicked him in the ribs. It took his breath away.

"It at his house, your house?"

"Mine," Stoner managed to say.

Was there any chance they might not shoot if they thought he really was a cop? What had he said to Mitchell?

"I'm from Downriver," he said, but this time it sounded like a plea.

"Fucking cracker," the man said, and shot Stoner in the back of the head.

# OUR EYES COULDN'T STOP OPENING

BY MEGAN ABBOTT

*Alter Road*

She always wanted to go and there was no stopping her once she got it in her head. Her voice was like a pressure in the car, Joni's mother's Buick, its spongy burgundy seats and the smell forever of L'Air du Temps.

Joni was game for it and I guess we all were, we liked Keri, you see, we admired her soft and dangerous ways. So lovely with her slippery brown hair lashed with bright highlights (all summer spent at the Woods Pool squeezing lemons into her scalp), so lovely with her darted skirts, ironed jeans, slick Goody barrettes. She was Harper Woods but, you see, she transcended that, so we let her slide, we let her hang with us, even let her lead us sometimes, times like this. Her mother put every dime of her Hutzel Hospital nurse's salary into her daughter's clothes, kept Keri looking Grosse Pointe and Keri could pass, pass well enough to snare with her pearl-pink nails, fingers spread, a prime towheaded, lacrosse-playing Grosse Pointe South boy, Kirk Deegan, hair as blond as an Easter chick and crisp shirts with thin sherbet-colored stripes and slick loafers, ankles bare with the fuzz of downy boy hair. Oh my, did she hit the jackpot with him. Play her cards right, she could ride him anywhere she wanted to go.

None of us, not even anyone we knew, was supposed to cross Alter Road, even get near Alter Road, it was like dropping off the face of the earth. Worse even than that. The things that happened when you slipped across that burning strip of asphalt, the girl a few years older than us—someone's cousin, you didn't know her—who crossed over, ended up all the way over on Connor, they found her three days later in a field, gangbanged into a coma at some crack house and dumped for dead, no, no, it was three weeks later and someone saw her taking the pipe and turning tricks in Cass Corridor. No, no, it was worse, far worse . . . and then it'd go to whispers, awful whispering, what could be worse, you wondered, and you could always wonder something even worse.

But there Keri would be, nestled in the backseat, glossy lips shining in the dark car, fists on the back of the passenger seat, saying, *Let's go, let's go. C'mon. What's here, there's nothing here. Let's go.*

How many nights, after all, could be spent sloshing long spoons in our peanut butter cup sundaes at Friendly's, watching boys play hockey at Community Ice, huddling down in seats at Woods Theater, popcorn sticky on our fingers, lips, driving around trying to find parties, any parties, where new boys would be, boys we'd never met, but our boys, they all wore their letter jackets and all had the same slant in their hair, straight across the forehead, sharp as ice, and the same conversation and the same five words before your mouth around beer can begging for the chance to not talk, to let the full-mouthed rush of music flood out all the talk and let the beer do its work so this boy in front of you might seem everything he wasn't and more—how many nights of that, I ask you?

So when Keri said, *Let's go,* maybe we let ourselves unsnide our tones, let our tilted-neck looks loosen a bit, unroll our eyes, curl into her quiet urging and *go, go, go.*

When he was around, Joni's brother, he'd buy us beer, wine coolers, and she'd hide them in the hedgerow underneath her bedroom window until we needed them. But he was at Hillsdale most of the time, trying to get credits enough to graduate and start working at Prudential for his dad. So there was Bronco's, right off the Outer Drive exit, and you could buy anything you wanted there, long as you were willing to drop twelve dollars for a four-pack of big-mouth Mickey's, or a tall 40 of Old Style, the tang of it lingering in your mouth all night.

Bronco's, it was a kick, the street so empty and the fluorescent burst of its sign rising like a beacon, a shooting star as you came up the long slope on I-94. Sometimes it made your heart beat, stomach wiggle, vibrate, flip, like when the manager—a big-bellied white guy with a greasy lower lip—made Keri go in the back with him, behind the twitchy curtain. But he only wanted to turn her around, only wanted to run his fingers studded with fat gold over her chest and backside, and what did any of us care? It was worth the extra bottle of Boone's Farm Strawberry Hill he'd dropped in our paper bag. Hell, you always pay a price, don't you? Like Keri said, from the dark of the backseat, how different was it from letting the Blue Devils football starters under your bra so you'd get into the seniors' party on Lakeshore where the parents had laid out for six cases of champagne before heading to Aruba for the weekend? How different from that? Very different, we said, but we knew it wasn't.

And it wasn't only Bronco's. Bronco's was just how it started. Next, it was leaving a party on Windmill Pointe, hotted up on beer and cigarettes and feeling our legs bristling tight in our jeans and Keri saying, *Let's go that way, yes, that way,* and before we knew it, we'd tripped the fence.

Goddamn, Alter Road a memory.

We pitched over the shortest curl of a bridge, over a sludgy canal not twelve feet across, and there we were. But it wasn't like over by Bronco's. It was just as deserted, but it didn't look like a scarred patch of city at all. The smell of the water and trailers backed up onto the canal, abandoned trailers, one after another, rutted through with shimmering rust, quivering under streetlamps, narrow roads filled with rotting boats teetering on wheels, mobile homes with windows broken out, streets so narrow it was like being on the track of a funhouse ride and then, suddenly, all the tightness giving way to big, empty expanses of forlorn, overgrown fields, like some kind of prairie. Never saw anything like it, who of us had? And our breath going fast in the car because we'd found something we'd never seen before. And it was like our eyes couldn't stop opening.

We'd let the gas pedal surge, vibrate, take us past sixty, seventy on the side streets, take the corners hard, let the tires skid, what did we care? There was no one here. There was no one on the streets. All you could see was shivering piles of trash, one-eyed cats darting. What did it matter? There was no one left. I tell you, it was ours.

But Keri, she kept finding new streets and her voice, soft and lulling, the Grosse Pointe drawl, bored-sounding even when excited, hot under the eyes, all that. She'd say—and who were we to decline?—she'd say, *Turn left, turn left, Joni, there, Joni, there,* and we'd find ourselves further in, further in, down the river, the slick brew of the canals long past now, and trembling houses cooing to us as the wind gasped through their swelling crevices, their glassless windows, their dark glory. That's the thing Keri showed us. She showed us that.

*It's beautiful,* she said without even saying it.

If we'd all been speaking out loud, we'd have never had the guts to say it.

And eventually, we saw people.

First, a stray cluster of figures, young men, walking together. A man alone, singing softly, we could hear, our windows open, radio off, we wanted to hear. Do you see? We wanted to hear. He was singing about a lady in a gold dress.

A woman, middle-aged, clapping her hands at her dog, calling him toward her, the dog limping toward her, howling, wistful.

But mostly small fits of young men standing around, tossing cigarette embers glowing into the street.

At first, Joni'd pick up speed whenever she saw them, chattering high-pitched and breathless, about how they'd try to jack her mother's car and take it to a chop shop—there's hundreds of them all over the city, there are—and in twenty minutes her mother's burgundy Buick Regal would be stripped to a metal skeleton. *That's how it works*, she'd say. *That's what they do.*

None of us said anything. We felt the car hop over a pothole, our stomachs lifting, like on the Gemini at Cedar Pointe.

Then, Keri: *This time, Joni, go slow. Come on, Joni. Let's see what they're doing. Let's see.* And Joni would teeth chatter at us about white girls raped in empty fields till they bled to death, and we let her say it because she needed to say it, had to get it out, and maybe we had to hear it, but we knew she'd go slower, and she did.

And then we'd be long past Alter, past Chalmers even, into that hissing whisper that was, to us, Detroit. Detroit. Say it. Hard in your mouth like a shard of glass. Glittering between your teeth and who could tell you it wasn't terrifying and beautiful all at once?

His voice was low and rippled and yeah, I'll say it, his skin was dark as black velvet, with a blue glow under the streetlamp, and he was talking to his friends from the sidewalk and we could almost hear them and God we wanted to and there was Keri and she had her hands curled around the edges of the top of the car door, window down, and he was looking at her like he knew her, and how could he? He didn't, but he couldn't miss that long spray of hair tumbling out the window as she craned to get a better look, to hear, to get meaning.

"You lost, honey?" is what he said, and it was like glass shattering, or something stretched tight for a thousand miles suddenly letting loose, releasing, releasing.

"Yes," was all she managed to whisper back before Joni had dropped her foot down on the gas hard and we all charged away, our hearts hammering . . .

. . . and Keri still saying, *Yes, yes, yes* . . .

You have to understand, we didn't know anything. We didn't know anything at all about conditions, history, the meanings of things. We didn't know anything. We were seeing castles in ruin like out of some dark fairy tale, but with an edge of wantonness, like all the best fairy tales.

Keri, by the lockers Monday a.m., doors clattering, pencils rolling down polished halls, she leans toward me, cheek pressed on the inside of my locker door, swinging it, rocking it. She says, *Remember when Joni drove the car real slow and let us get our eyeful and he looked at me and in his eyes I could see he knew more than any of us, more than all the teachers at school, all the parents too, he knew more in that flashing second than all the rest of everyone, all of them sleeping through forever in this place, this marble-walled place. In his eyes, what I could see was he was someone more than I could ever be.*

Keri, she tells us, first date with Kirk Deegan, he resplendent in Blue Devils jacket and puka shell necklace from a December trip to Sanibel Island, he winds his way from his hulking colonial on Rivard to her faded one-story in Harper Woods, can smell the pizza grease from the deli on the corner and he won't come inside. No, he stands one foot on the bottom porch step, Ray-Bans propped, and says, "Nah, where would I fit?"

I should've seen it coming because who wanted to keep doing the same thing, which was fun at first, but where could it go, in the end? You couldn't get out of the car. It was for kicks and you did it until the kicks stopped. This time, it worked like this: Joni started dating a De La Salle boy and he had a car anyway and evenings were now for him and I was starting up tennis and there were new parties and Keri, we saw her more like a long-haired flitter in the corner of our eye. We barely saw her at all. She was there in the Homecoming Court, glowing in her floral dress, smiling brightly, waving at everyone and standing ramrod straight, face perfect and still. Face so frozen for all the flashing cameras, for all the cheering faces, for all of us, for everybody.

It was her last of everything that year. It was her last. You could kind of see it then, couldn't you? It was there somehow, making everything more special, more like *something*, at least.

Later, at the dance, willowing around Kirk Deegan, he tow-ering over her with that bright wedge of hair, the blackwatch plaid vest and tie, that slit-eyed cool, he who never let another boy come near, even touch her shoulder, even move close. What boy ever kept me so tight at hand? What boy? I ask you. He loved her that much, everyone said it. He loved her that much.

Sidling up to me in study hall, eyes fluttering, red, Keri's voice tired, slipping into my ear. *How was the party?* she's asking. *Was Stacey mad I didn't go?* I just smiled because of course Stacey was mad, because Keri was supposed to come and bring Kirk, because if Kirk came, so would Matt Tomlin, and she was angling for Matt Tomlin, was so ready for him she could barely stand it.

Where'd you guys go? I asked. And she gave me a flicker of a smile and she didn't say anything. And I said, Did you and Kirk . . . and she shook her head fast.

*I didn't see him. It wasn't that.*

And she told me Kirk was too wasted to go anywhere, show-ing off some old Scotch of his father's and then drinking three inches of it, passing out on the leather armchair like some old guy. So she took his Audi and went for a drive and before she knew it she was long past Alter Road, long past everything. Even the Jefferson plant, the Waterworks. She said she drove all around in his car and saw things and ended up getting lost down by some abandoned railroad.

She was crazy to be doing it and I told her so and she nodded like she agreed, but I could tell by the way she looked off in the other direction that she didn't agree at all and that all she'd real-ized was that she wouldn't bother telling me about it anymore. But she didn't stop going. You could feel her rippling in her own pleasure over it. Like she was someone special who got to do things no one else did.

*I met some people a few weeks ago,* she said. *They invited me to a party at this big old house, I don't even know where. You could see the big Chrysler plant. That was all you could see. The house, it had turrets like a castle. Like a castle in a fairy tale. I remember I wanted to go to the top and stand in the turret like a lost princess and look out on the river, waving a long handkerchief like I was waiting for a lover to come back from the sea.*

I didn't know what she was talking about. I never heard anyone talk like this. I think it was the most I ever heard her talk and it didn't make any more sense than Trig class to me.

*The house was empty,* she said. *The floors were part broken through. My foot slid between the boards and this boy, he had to lift me out and he was laughing. They were playing music and speakers were all over the house, one set up on an old banister thick as a tree trunk and everyone dancing and beer and Wild Irish Rose, wine so red like bloodshot eyes and smoking, getting high, and the whole place alive and I danced, one of them danced with me, so dark and with a diamond in his ear and he said he'd take me to Fox Creek, near the trailers, and we'd shoot old gas tanks, and I said I would, and he sang in my ear and I could feel it through my whole body, like in lab when Mr. Muskaluk ran that current through me in front of the class, like that, like that. It was this. I could do anything, no one cared. I could do anything and no one stopped me.*

"What did you do, Keri?" I asked, my voice sounded funny to me. Sounded fast and gasping. "What did you do?"

*Anything,* she whispered, voice breathless and dirty. *Anything.*

Did I have time for that, for that kind of trashiness? Don't you see, Joni said, she's Harper Woods. She may look Grosse Pointe, she may have one on her arm. But that's a flash, a trick of the eye. Deep down, she's five blocks from the freeway. It all comes back. You can fight it, but it comes back.

So we dropped her and it was just as well because lots of things were happening, with boys' hockey starting and everyone's parents taking trips to Florida and so there were more parties and there was the thing with the sophomore girl and the senior boy and the police and things like that that everyone talked about. Other stuff happened too—I'd dropped out of tennis and then dropped back in—there was a boy for me with a brush of brown hair and the long, adam-appled neck of a star basketball player, which he was, and I took him to Sadie Hawkins's dance and he took me to parties and to parents' beds in upstairs rooms at parties and slid his tongue fast into my dry mouth and his hands fumbling everywhere, and his car, it smelled like him, Polo and new sneakers and Stroh's, and when it was over and I smelled those things, which you could smell on a dozen boys a day, it was him all over again, but then before I knew it, it was gone. He was gone, yeah, but the feeling that went with it too. Just like that.

*Please, please can you drop me somewhere?* Keri said, and we were in the school parking lot and her eyes rung wide and fingers gripped the top of the car door.

Okay, I said and even barely seeing her for months, a quick hello in the hallways, a flash in the locker room, me on my way in, she on her way out. To Kirk's? I asked.

She said no. She said no and shook her head, gaze drifting off to the far end of the parking lot. Further than that. Further than that.

And then I knew and I told her it was my father's car and if I got a scratch, he'd never buy me the Fiero come graduation and she promised it would be okay and I said yes. Against everything, I said yes.

So she was next to me and the sky was orange, then red as the sun dropped behind the Yacht Club, its gleaming white bell tower soaring—when I was a kid I thought it was Disneyland—I was going to take her. I felt somehow I had to.

Where are we going? I'd say, and she'd chew her gum and

look out the window, fingers touching, breath smoking the glass. She was humming a song and I didn't know it. It wasn't a song any of us would know, a song we sang along with on WHYT, a song we all shouted out together in cars. It was something else all together. Plaintive and funny and I thought suddenly: Who does she think she is in my father's car singing songs I don't know in her white Tretorns and her pleated shirt and hair brushed to silk, whirling gold hoops hanging from her ears? And she thinks she can just go wherever she wants, do things in other places, touch more than the surface of things, and then keep it all inside her and never let anyone see in. Never let any of us.

*You can drop me here*, she was saying. We were at the foot of Windmill Pointe.

You just want me to leave you here? I asked, looking around, seeing not a soul. In Grosse Pointe, especially these its most gleamy stretches, the streets were always empty, like plastic pieces from a railroad set.

*Yes*, she said, and waved as she began walking toward the water, toward the glittering lighthouse.

Wait, Keri, I said, opening my door so she could hear me. Where are you going?

And she half turned and maybe she smiled, maybe she even said something, but the wind took it away.

When I saw her in school, I asked her. I said, Where did you go? What were you doing there? She was putting on her lipgloss and shaking her hair out. I watched her eyes in the mirror magnet on the inside of her locker door. I thought maybe I'd see something, see something in there.

She watched me back, eyes rimmed with pale green liner, and I knew she had to tell someone, didn't she? What did it count to run off the rails if you didn't tell a soul? I looked at her with the most simpering face I could manage to make her see she could tell me, she could tell me.

But she didn't now, did she? And that was the last time, see? It was the last of that flittering girl.

"Her cousin's letting her drive her Nova, you should see it," Joni was telling me. "I saw her in it. Do you think she's taking it there? Next thing you know, we'll be driving down Jefferson to go see the Red Wings game and she'll be rolling with some black guys." Joni was telling me this as we squeezed together on the long sofa at a party, beers in hand, Joni's face sweaty and flushed, bangs matted to foreheads, chests heaving lightly.

I said I didn't think she went at all anymore. I told Joni she wasn't going at all. I didn't want her to know. It was something between us. And, truth told, if she'd asked me, I'd've gone with her still. But she didn't ask me, did she?

It was in the aching frost of February and I was coming out of a party on Beaconsfield and I saw her drive by. I saw the blue Nova and I saw her at the wheel and I saw which way she was headed and maybe my head was a little clogged from the beers, but I couldn't help it and I was in my dad's car and I headed toward Alter Road. She was long gone, but I kept driving and I thought maybe I'd see the car again, especially once I hit the ghostly pitch over the bridge at Alter and Korte Street. How many beers was it, I thought I could hear the squeal of her tires. The only sound at all, other than the occasional sludge of water against the creaking docks over the canal, were those tires. I thought it had to be her and I stopped my car, rolled down my windows, couldn't hear anything so figured she stopped. Did she stop? I edged past the side streets and ended up back at that shell of a trailer court, those aluminum and wood carcasses, like plundered ships washed to shore. And that was when I thought I saw her, darting around the bowed trees, darting along like some kind of wood nymph in a magic forest, and yet it was this.

I could admit, if I let myself, there was a beauty in it, if you squinted, tilted your head. If you could squeeze out ideas of the kind of beauty you can rest in your palm, fasten around your neck, never have an unease about, a slip of cashmere, one fine pearl, a beauty everyone would understand and feel safe with. But I wouldn't really do that, not for more than a second, and Keri, she would. It was like this place she'd found was Broadway, Hollywood, Shangri-La, and she would make it hers.

I parked my car and got out, the wind running in off the lake and charging at me, but I went anyway. That beer foaming my head, I just kept going. Who was going to stop me? I was going to see, see the thing through. I wasn't going to tell, but I was going to see it for myself.

Wading through the golden rod, studded with scrap metal, with shredded firecrackers, flossy crimps of insulation foam, there I was. The trailers all edged in rust like frills peaking from under a dress, but as you got closer, it wasn't so dainty and there was a feel in the air of awfulness. All of it, it reminded me of places you're not supposed to be, they're just not for you, like when we went to that house, when we were in Girl Scouts, to deliver the Christmas presents to the family on Mt. Elliott, and everyone told us, Just watch, they'll have a big TV and a VCR and they'll be lying around collecting welfare with tons of kids running around, and that wasn't what happened at all, and re-member how the baby wouldn't stop shaking and the look in the mother's eyes like she'd long ago stopped being surprised at anything, and the plastic on the windows and the leaking refrig-erator, we weren't supposed to be there at all, now, were we?

This, it was like that, but different, because this had that lostness but then too in place of sad there was this hard current of nastiness and dirtiness and badness, sweaty, gun-oil, mattress-spring coil throbbing, stains spreading. My eyes skating over the abandoned trailers and thinking of the things happening behind the bulging screens, the pitted aluminum. The sky so black and the vague sound of music and the feeling of teetering into something and then it getting inside you, feeding off you, making you its own.

There was a laugh then and it struck me hard right through the swirling muzz in my head, but it was warm, rippling, and it broke up some of the nastiness for me, but not enough.

Coming from one of the trailers, a faded red one with a rolling top, like a curling tongue. There was something glowing inside and there was music.

I felt my ankle twist on a bottle curved deep into the earth. I could hear the music, a thud-thud, bass tickling me, promising things, and I walked closer, I just did.

I walked closer like I could, like I was allowed, even as this was no place for me. That tickling laugh kept rolling itself out, felt like long fingers uncoiling just shy of me, just shy of my body, hot and itchy under my coat, aching for the cold wind ripping off the water and instead this runny canal, a ditch swelling.

And then there it was.

Soft, high, sweet, Keri's own laugh.

Like when we watched a funny movie or when we watched Joni make cross-eyes or when we danced in our bedrooms, singing, singing until we thought our lungs would burst.

But then turning, turning like a dial and the laugh got lower, throatier, and I could feel it prickling under my skin, then sinking through me, down my legs, along the twitching pain in my ankle, straight into the ground.

Reaching under my feet.

And in my head, I could see her face and she's lying on a stripped mattress, hair spread out beneath, a windmill, and she's laughing and twisting and squirming, her head tilting back, neck arching, and who knew what was happening, what was happening to draw that throaty laugh from her, pump that bursting flush into her cheeks, face, God, Keri, God, all kinds of dark hands on her, she at the center of some awful white-girl gangbang. All those hands touching her white white-girl skin. These are the things I thought, I won't claim otherwise.

I was standing ten seconds, a minute, who knew, the cold snaking around me but not touching. I could've stood forever, twenty feet from that trailer, watching. But then. But then. The sound.

A hinge struck and I could hear and there it was, I could see they weren't in the trailer but on the other side of it and there I was, back to the mangled sheet metal, sidling around, and that's when I saw the bonfire that made the glow and I hid behind the tinsely branches of a half-fallen tree and I watched and I saw everything, or figured I did.

There were two black guys and a white guy and there was a tall black girl with a dark jacket on and I could see it had gold print struck in it and then I saw it was a letter jacket, Keri's letter jacket from volleyball, and the girl was climbing on the picnic table and that was where Keri was and she was dancing. She was dancing to the music from the radio they'd brought and one of the black guys, Keri was saying something to him as she danced, and he was laughing and watching her and I could tell he was the one she was with, you could see it in his eyes and hers, it was vibrating between them.

*She was there in the Homecoming Court, resplendent in her floral dress, smiling brightly, waving at everyone and standing ramrod straight, face perfect and still.*

And the black girl joined Keri and the girl had a can of beer and so did Keri and the guys, they were shouting and they were lightly rocking the table, and the white guy was tipping a bottle of something into his mouth and singing about how some girl was his twilight zone, his Al Capone, and I could smell the pot and a lot was going on like at any party and it seemed like maybe more, but I was watching Keri and Keri's face, it was lit from the fire and it was a crazy orange flaring up her cheeks and she was wearing her long cashmere muffler from Jacobson's, coiled around her neck, flapping tight in the wind, and she was dancing and the fire lit her hair and I could see her face and it was like I'd never seen it before and never would again because things made sense even if they didn't because there was something there that I felt twenty years too young to understand, no, not too young, because I couldn't understand it because she was fathoms deep and I would be driving along Kercheval in fifteen minutes, driving to my family's three-bedroom colonial and tucking myself in and hoping the boy would call and thinking about the next party and here was Keri and she was fathoms deep and I was . . .

I couldn't have known, watching her there, watching her dancing and looking like that, feeling that way, that she would be gone by finals, by junior prom even. I never said a word about what I saw and I never told her to watch out either, even though, the way I was, I could only see it as she was going for broke and it could turn out any number of ways but most of them bad. But even if I had tried to warn her, to hold her back, it wouldn't have mattered because I would've told her to watch out for the wrong things, the wrong places. I couldn't have known, watching her there, that two weeks later she'd be driving a drunken Kirk Deegan home late after a postgame party, driving him in his Audi and coming into the Deegan garage too close to the wall and shearing off the sideview mirror. I couldn't have known Kirk Deegan would get so mad and push her so hard against the garage wall and her head hitting that pipe and then turning and hitting the edge of the shovel hanging and what must have been a sickening crack and her falling and her dying and her dying there on the floor of his garage. Her dying on the floor of his garage and him there, too dumbstruck to call the police, an ambulance, his parents, anyone, for a half hour while she was there, hair spread on the cement floor like a windmill and then gone forever. I couldn't have known that. But one way or another I did.

# HONESTY ABOVE ALL ELSE

BY DORENE O'BRIEN

*Corktown*

I've never told anyone this story, and I'm only telling you now because Mrs. O'Leary is dead. You don't need to know my name—what's it matter? I grew up in Corktown, live in the same Carpenter Gothic on Church that my great-grandparents lived in. Against all odds, Corktown has survived—bravery, gentrification, the luck of the Irish? But back in '99 when it happened, everything was going to hell. You couldn't count on things anymore the way the Carmodys and the McNallys could count on trains to plow into Michigan Grand Central to the south and scatter tourists onto the doorsteps of Limerick's Pub and the Lager House, or Tiger Stadium to the north to draw crowds like ants to spilled sugar. The Tigers were a magnet for suburbanites, who'd line their Cadillacs and Cutlasses up and down Michigan Avenue, the money bursting the seams in their pockets. My family inherited a parking lot on Trumbull, but that well ran dry when after a century of major league ball in our neighborhood the Tigers just trotted off, leaving behind a sad and hulking mess that nobody wants. The stadium's still there, eight years later, a painful reminder of a better life, though out of loyalty or homage it's the only abandoned building on Michigan that isn't carved up, burned out, or sprayed with *State Boyz* and *Plato* tags.

Listen, I'm not going to get nostalgic; I'm not going to bend your ear about the heyday when bleacher creatures and CEOs focused on the same thing—warm hot dogs, cold beer, and a Major League pennant—or how Michigan Avenue suddenly popped bright when the outfield lights snapped on. I could see them from my bedroom window; I could hear the crack of the bat and I always pretended it was Kaline or Horton, the guys my father said were heroes, giving the opposing team pure hell. Why am I telling you this? Because people's low-level fear after the depot closed turned into full-on panic when Tiger Stadium shut down, when Corktown's seemingly sturdy bookends fell, crushing us under their collective weight. People grew sad when they realized they could no longer describe the boundaries of their city as anything within a one-mile radius of the pitcher's mound, and they grew hopeless when they watched Reedy's and the Gold Dollar get nailed up tight, graffiti-splattered boards covering multi-paned antique windows crafted by their Irish ancestors nearly two hundred years before. People change when they watch their heritage being obliterated, when they walk past vacant buildings every day, when they feel the luster fading from their lives. They do desperate things. I'm not making excuses for Mrs. O'Leary, who had the best intentions, after all; I'm just telling you how it was.

When our Trumbull lot closed I was out of a job, which was bittersweet for my father, who didn't care for his twenty-two-year-old daughter collecting money in parking lots but who could also cast his eyes across the cars and calculate the night's take in mere seconds. For a while I just kicked around Detroit, thinking with my associates degree in Business Administration I might get a part-time office job in the Fisher Building, hopefully near the top floors so I could watch the peregrine falcons loop and dive into the chaos below. What did they see from their skytop perches? Not the smoke from the Seven Sisters; those stacks had been detonated three years before in '96. I wondered what the falcons thought of the sixteen-story dust cloud that turned their daytime sky dark for three full minutes after the Hudson's Building on Woodward was imploded two years later. Then I realized that what they thought mattered about as much as what I did.

Jefferson Avenue looked so much brighter than Michigan Avenue as I traipsed along in my mid-heeled shoes, resumé tucked into the small briefcase my father used on insurance calls. Why was I relieved when told I was overqualified for the receptionist's job at the ad agency in the Ren Cen, when DuMouchelles said they'd prefer to hire someone with knowledge of Royal Doulton pottery, when the dental office in the Fisher Building never called back? My father said I'd been ruined for indoor work, that working outside even in inclement weather beats the hell out of typing letters in the nicest office. He was right. At night I'd sometimes walk to the lot for old times' sake, past the Corktown houses with their crumbling Queen Anne turrets, Georgian Revival roof lines, Greek columns—what were the city planners thinking? Things that were once charming became irritating. The antique buildings felt old and lifeless, the formerly vibrant skyline a jagged silhouette in the pre-night dusk, the family-owned bars a haven for punk and goth wannabes, their pink rubber miniskirts and chain-draped leather dresses hiked up for the jump onto handmade mahogany barstools. The bars that were trying to weather the economic storm—LJ's, Casey's Pub, the Parabox—did it by offering dirt-cheap drink specials, and kids sporting neck corsets, rhinestone sunglasses, and platform boots studded with more straps and buckles than a straitjacket, would sweep through Corktown for a quick buzz before moving on to the night's real adventure at St. Andrew's or City Club. They wrapped their tattooed hands around the brass bar rail, slipped their studded tongues into the tall pilsner glasses, and we felt violated. They were the dark infiltration of the outside world. Part of me understood—I was young, I went to college with kids like this, I saw their need to be provocative—but the timing was just bad. Everything was falling apart, and they seemed to be leading the charge. Well, Mike Ilitch and Dennis Archer led the charge, and the painted and hole-punched kids, like entitled vultures, picked at the carrion in their wake.

My loyalty to Corktown and the fact that the intermittent

classes I was taking at Wayne State weren't going to pay for themselves led me to O'Leary's Tearoom at Brooklyn and Porter, where I took a job waiting tables and reading tarot cards in the afternoons for rich ladies from West Bloomfield or Northville who had nothing better to do than to seek out the novelty of a town that they were too dim or too dismissive to see was drowning before their eyes. They lifted the homemade shortbread to their lips with soft, tanned hands and tapped manicured nails against off-white china cups as they sipped Irish Breakfast tea while waiting their turn at the tarot table. Mrs. O'Leary was the true psychic, though, had worked hard to teach me the cards herself, but she never ever read for these women. She served their scones and muffins with a smile, poured their tea while exchanging pleasantries, but later she would say what small, sad lives they lived, that she couldn't read for them because she'd have to tell the truth. *Honesty above all else* was her motto, and the motto of her mother and her mother's mother, ad infinitum, traveling in the minds and sensibilities of the O'Leary women from across the Atlantic, remaining intact all the way from County Cork. The words, in Gaelic, had been carved into a wooden plaque and hung over the front door of the tearoom. Locals can handle it, she said, the Irish are strong, practical, resilient. But if she told these women the truth, they'd never come back, and then where would we be? That's why I read for them. It wasn't that I didn't believe in the truth, I just wasn't a good enough psychic to see it. What I saw clearly were the women's designer clothes and leather shoes, their diamond-studded watches and sharp haircuts, and their lives didn't look small to me, but, as I said, I was never able to see the things that Mrs. O'Leary did. Telling this story now makes me miss everything: the weed-smothered Trumbull lot, Tiger Stadium glowing like an earthbound constellation, the tearoom with its lace doilies and antique spoons, Mrs. O'Leary with her black tooth and her visions of misery.

She did not see good things in Detroit's future; she said she dreamed of flood waters gushing over the banks of the Detroit River, a tidal wave as tall as Cobo Hall consuming Grand Circus Park, then fanning eastward to smother Greektown and westward to our very doors, water rising to overtake the front steps of Corktown's crumbling worker's cottages. She stared at the window, and it was as if she could see the nightmare being projected there. "Begorra," she said, fingering the Celtic cross over her breast, her eyes far, far away, "there was a torrent on Porter, and we were in it, you and me, the tearoom gone, my china cups bobbing around like corks." After noticing my horrified expression she smiled. "Ah!" she said. "Just a silly dream. It's this casino stuff's got me thinking too much."

Despite the fact that citizens had twice voted against it, the mayor had just granted a license to MGM to build a casino in Detroit, and Mrs. O'Leary said she'd be damned to hell and roasted crisp before she sat back and let them build.

"They're all crooked," she'd said, the *Free Press* and *Detroit Monthly* spread across the table before her. "Politicians steal our money and give it to these greed mongers. This one's mother died, this one's wife's having an affair. What do they care as long as they can build their casino? Come here and look at what they're doing to your city." She made me read about the latest political graft or look at the smug grin of a socialite newly arrived on Detroit's small glamour circuit. "Look at that," she'd say, poking her chubby finger into the face of the offender, her tone bursting with rancor. Sometimes I'd see her pull out the White Pages, address an envelope in her looping cursive, and drop her business card inside, and I'd wonder who was on the receiving end of her selective advertising. But she wrote many letters: to her family back in Cork, to the newspapers, to watchdog groups, to the mayor's office. Though I was young, my future not necessarily tied to Corktown, even I understood her anger over its recent state, her worry over the fate of her business. Mrs. O'Leary, for her part, was convinced that if the MGM people knew how desperate the people of Detroit were—*Who's going to put fifty dollars down on a blackjack table? They'll come in and rob the place, that's what they'll do!*—they would thank the mayor kindly and be on their way.

"Go read their tarot," I said. "Tell them they'll be sorry."

"You can laugh," she countered, "but these businessmen wouldn't bring their families here if they knew how dangerous it was. They wouldn't want to open a casino if something happened to stop them. And this is a place where bad things happen." I laughed at her naïveté, for I wasn't too young to know that there's no stopping the push of capitalism. Actually, the casino was just the latest impediment in her drive to save Detroit: She was working to have Archer impeached, the new Tiger Stadium—she would not say the words "Comerica Park"—boycotted, and Mike Ilitch run out on a rail.

This is the history of the story I'm trying to tell you, the thing that happened in the tearoom, the thing that I can tell you now that Mrs. O'Leary is dead. All that fear and sadness drove Mrs. O'Leary to do what she did, but who's to say that under similar pressure you wouldn't have done the same thing?

It should not surprise you, then, that he appeared before us on a desperate night, for there were many desperate nights in Corktown after the close of the '99 season. Perhaps I should have taken as portents what I dismissed simply as the manifestations of a dying city as I walked to work that day: a man running down Trumbull with a pair of crutches under his arm, a woman pushing a baby stroller full of empty bottles, a car without a passenger door cruising slowly up Leverette. That night the sleet was driving down, little needles piercing the gray snow below, and even though the tart smell of cabbage was making me queasy, the drone of the rain and the six-block walk home kept me there long after I should have left, flipping cards in a Hearts and Spades game against my employer. We were on display at Mrs. O'Leary's favorite linen-covered table in the front window of the tearoom, which always made me feel like a target at night, but Mrs. O'Leary seemed oblivious to the paranoia of a fearful mind. Is it an indictment of Mrs. O'Leary's psychic ability to say that when the doorbell chimed we both gasped? Why? Because we hadn't expected anyone, of course; we couldn't imagine anyone strolling around in the knifelike torrent. But there he was.

The man who stood before us looked as if he'd just walked out of a movie—chiseled features, dripping trench coat, brown fedora. We stared at him, and Mrs. O'Leary said, "I'll get the tea."

"That's all right," he said. "I don't need any tea."

"Yes you do," she said. "Sit down."

The man—he couldn't have known, the cards weren't out—sat at the tarot table, far from the dark front windows. "My car broke down on Bagley," he said as Mrs. O'Leary placed a teacup before him, and by the way she smiled, showing only the lower left corner of her blackened tooth, I knew she didn't believe him. Though she had a stockpot of food warming in the kitchen, she never offered him any—do you see what I mean about the way she knew things?

The man took a small sip of his tea and smiled. Later I'd learn that she'd put two fingers of Ballantine's in his cup, that she knew he needed it, and you didn't have to be a psychic to see that he was thankful. Mrs. O'Leary nodded at me, as if we'd earlier set up a system of communication that would tell me exactly what to do, but my psychic abilities, as usual, failed. Though she'd been teaching me the tarot for two months, I still struggled. I knew the meaning of the cards—I'd memorized them as easily as I'd mentally charted who owned each car in the Trumbull lot—but when I had to transplant their meanings into the lives of the people who sat before me, their fear and exhilaration always seemed to short circuit my intuition. She nodded again, then turned to the man, who had removed his hat to reveal a thick head of red-blond hair, and said, "Why don't you have your tarot read while you wait?"

He looked at her expectantly, as if that is precisely why he'd come, as if she'd read his mind. I recall thinking that I had read his mind too, just then, that my skills had kicked in, that my intuitive antennae were finally picking up signals from the psychic airwaves around me. I was suddenly convinced that he had come to us deliberately, desperately, and I knew then that I would be the one to save this poor soul, this gorgeous man. Is arrogance not the downfall of the fool? Before Mrs. O'Leary could stand up, I had stationed myself across from him and pulled the tarot pack from its green silk pouch. That she believed me incapable of doing any real harm seemed clear when she poured herself three fingers of Ballantine's and embarked on a game of solitaire at the small table where she had been winning all night. Perhaps that was yet another missed sign?

"All right, then," I said to the man before turning on the tape recorder. "For five dollars you can buy a cassette of the reading." This was something the rich ladies loved, for they'd often repeat the same questions, their recall apparently faulty.

Mrs. O'Leary, her back to us, sighed heavily and shook her head, and the man stared at me like I was insane. He then shrugged and draped his wet coat over a vacant chair beside us, and I imagined I could smell the taunting rain and bitter smoke in its folds, fear seeping into my nostrils like ammonia. I started turning cards immediately after he'd cut them, eager, too eager, I see now, to test my newfound skills.

The first card was the two of Wands, a lone, lost man with his back turned, the card of mortification. This card meant that the man before me had received news, bad news. Next came the Empress, crowned in stars and robed in gold, signaling his involvement with a strong, wealthy woman, but isn't that common amongst handsome men? At any rate, I turned the third card, a reversed Ace of Pentacles, a gargantuan hand clutching an oversized coin and symbolizing the dark side of wealth.

"You've had some bad luck," I said, hoping for some type of acknowledgment from him, but he was like a stone.

I turned more cards: The four of Cups, an inconsolable man, then the two of Pentacles: fear, obstacles, romantic entanglement.

"There is a woman," I said. "She is raven-haired. She is powerful. She is tormented." Of course, I didn't know for certain that the woman in charge of his troubles was raven-haired—only Mrs. O'Leary would know *that*—but I think it was a safe bet that a woman was at the root of his unhappiness, for my father had always said a woman is at the root of most men's unhappiness, and I pretty much had a one-in-four shot at getting hair color right.

The man's tension was wreaking havoc on my psychic radar, and it shut down entirely when he whispered his first question: "Is she going to kill me?"

The women from Grosse Pointe and Bingham Farms never asked questions like this. They wanted to know if their husbands would be promoted, if their sons would get into Yale, if they would be safe under the scalpel during plastic surgery. I turned the seven of Cups, which is merely a dark child. "Not yet," I said. "Maybe never."

Next came the eight of Cups, the child growing.

"But she's thinking about it." How else can one read that sequence? Mrs. O'Leary, God rest her soul, was no help at all, staring into the abyss framed by the window and humming "Danny Boy" while thumbing the handle on her Prince Albert china cup.

The reversed Queen of Swords was next. It had to be the woman, right?

"She's here," I tapped the card, recalling the textbook definition in the *Pictorial Key to the Tarot*. "This queen has intentions that, in the reversed position, can not be exercised."

The man looked from me to the card and back again, frowning.

"She's upside down," I said. "Immobilized. Her sword is useless in this position."

He tilted his head. "I see," he said, absently running his fingers along the belt of the trench coat beside us before downing his remaining tea. What did he see? I wondered, and I had to stop myself from asking.

I then turned the King of Swords, handsome, troubled, the least wealthy of the four kings.

"This is you," I said. Who else could it be?

"And?"

And I was blank. Nothing. "And you're in some kind of trouble." It was an idiotic thing to say—you didn't need a tarot pack to figure that out—but it was also safe. Was I in over my head? Should I have summoned Mrs. O'Leary out of what I thought was her liquor-induced complacency, admitted to having nothing more than a good memory for the cards, ended the reading right there? Certainly, but there's no use in posing those questions now (though on the blackest nights I often do).

I turned the six of Pentacles, prosperity, followed by the Knight of Pentacles, more prosperity, and then I sat there staring at the cards as if the characters on them would speak, waiting for something to happen. Then it did.

"This Knight of Pentacles," Mrs. O'Leary murmured from across the room, "is your queen's husband. A dangerous man."

"But he's not a king," the man argued.

I stared at the cards, the King of Swords lying beside the Queen of Swords on the table. "You're her king," she answered, "without a kingdom."

I remained silent and next turned the ten of Swords. Let me make it clear that no one told me to do that. No one told me to turn another card, but I did.

"What is it?"

"Nothing," I said.

"He's on the ground with swords in his back. That doesn't look like nothing."

Mrs. O'Leary put her head down then. At the time it meant little to me, but now, before I take my sleeping pills, before I ask myself why I didn't walk out of the tearoom and not look back, before I blame the closing of the stadium for what transpired, the vision of Mrs. O'Leary folding her head forward, as if in prayer, haunts me. The man knew, even if he didn't know for certain, what even I could see: This was the card of horrific death.

"Tell me," he said.

"It's bad." I stared at him. "I see the raven-haired woman." And I did. Was it the night? Was it the sudden appearance of this troubled man in this troubled neighborhood with his questions of death that triggered a vision more clear than if she'd been standing before me in the flesh? I saw her, or I called her up from some deep place of knowing: a thick bowl of black hair sprouting from a sharp widow's peak, blunt red talons, a smile like a blade in her teeth. "It's bad," I repeated.

"Yes," he said, leaning back in his chair and setting his chin like a man about to take a punch. He stared at the cards intently, almost as if he could read them, and said, "It's bad."

My heart constricted, and I understood for the first time the true depth of Mrs. O'Leary's burden: How could she channel all this pain and heartache? No wonder she drank Ballantine's, no wonder her tooth had rotted from the toxic news that had washed over it each time she read a tarot. My head was pounding, and I had to remind myself to breathe. "Maybe this is enough for now," I said.

The man nodded at the deck in my hand, and as I slowly turned the next card, an upside-down knight wielding a large gray sword, Mrs. O'Leary said, "The reversed Knight of Swords spells doom. Do you want another card?"

The man nodded again, and it was then that I realized how little he'd spoken.

"Are you certain you want another card?" Mrs. O'Leary was staring at the plaque above the door looking like misery propped up in a chair. She could not have seen the cards from where she sat, even with her glasses on, but as I turned the most feared card in the tarot, the skeleton coming to claim on his white horse, she said, "Death may not be imminent, but it is present."

"I know," he sighed. "I know."

Next came the six of Swords, the symbol of painful journey, and I dared not recite the definition of the card as it appeared in this sequence: "Your death will be violent." But I didn't have to, because Mrs. O'Leary did.

Mrs. O'Leary was never comfortable telling clients that tarot readings are for entertainment purposes only, that they are not to be considered financial, legal, or psychological counseling, but we always did. And that's what she told the detectives who showed up at O'Leary's three days after the skeleton slipped the tape into the pocket of his trench coat and threw a fifty on the table.

"I heard on the news," she said. "But I can't help you."

"Well, you can't claim client privilege," said the elderly detective in a cheap suit as he pulled the tape from his briefcase and slid it across the table. "Who's the other voice on the tape? Doesn't sound like you."

"It's mine," she said, "there's no one else here does tarot. It's a cheap tape, bad quality."

Through a crack in the saloon doors that opened onto the kitchen I watched the detectives exchange looks.

"It was just a wee bit of fun," said Mrs. O'Leary with badly played nonchalance. "He came in to get out of the weather."

"Well, it doesn't sound very funny to me," said the detective with the acid trip necktie. "Does it sound funny to you?" he asked Cheap Suit, who shook his head.

"See that? Neither of us finds it funny. Maybe we lack a sense of humor, but for some reason we just don't find murder funny."

When I saw Mrs. O'Leary crumple to the chair before enlisting the exaggerated brogue she engaged only under the most stressful circumstances, I wanted to rush out of the kitchen and take the blame for something horrible, something I didn't yet fully understand, for a death I could have prevented. But I didn't.

"Sounds to me like Mr. Donegan felt he was going to be killed," said Necktie. "Now, how do you suppose he came to that conclusion?"

"Aye, he knew it when he walked in."

"You sure didn't help matters."

"I'm not here to change the course of fate," said Mrs. O'Leary.

"Did you discuss anything you didn't get on this tape?"

"No."

"Are you sure?"

"As me great-grandmother used to say, 'He wasn't the talkin' sort.'"

"Well his trap's sure zipped now," said Cheap Suit.

"We found this in his coat pocket," said Necktie as he held up a small white business card. "Where do you suppose he got it?"

"Me cards are there on the table," said Mrs. O'Leary, nodding. "Who's to say?"

Necktie then unfolded the front-page *Free Press* article describing the murder of Victoria Lanni, the wife of MGM casino CEO Terrance Lanni, with a tiny corner photograph of her very handsome killer, Bruce Donegan.

"Maybe," he said, "this will jar your memory."

She stared at the photograph, then touched it. "Nothing," she said.

"So he thought Mrs. Lanni was gonna kill him," said Cheap Suit as he wiped his eye with a yellowed handkerchief. "Why do ya think she'd do a thing like that?"

Mrs. O'Leary shrugged.

The detectives glanced at each other. "You never saw him killing her?" said Necktie, and I felt Mrs. O'Leary staring at me through the thick wooden door, her voice softening to a whisper.

"I just saw death," she said.

"Strangulation?" said Necktie. "Trench coat belt?"

"No. Dirtier, nastier. I don't know what. And I saw it on him. All over him."

"Well, you're good then," said Cheap Suit. "'Cause Lanni's got some dark pals in prison."

When the detectives left, I rushed from the kitchen to find Mrs. O'Leary still seated at her favorite table near a pile of magazines she'd quickly gathered when she saw them enter.

"I only needed *her* dead," said Mrs. O'Leary. "Poor lad."

She shifted the papers before her, and that's when the image assaulted me. That's when I saw the article I'd read the month before only to satisfy her, the one in which casino chairman Terrance Lanni's wife denies having an affair with a handsome local, the one that speculates she will lose her fortune if the affair is confirmed, the one that's wrapped around a color photo of a woman with a thick bowl of black hair sprouting from a sharp widow's peak, blunt red talons, a smile like a blade in her teeth.

Did Mrs. O'Leary know that the following month Terrance Lanni would resign as MGM Grand's CEO after his wife was strangled to death in their Riverfront Towers apartment, that Bruce Donegan would bleed to death in a dark corner of the prison's laundry room after being stabbed twenty-six times? "It was bound to happen," was all she'd say, though I still wonder if things would have been different had I not turned that fateful card, if I'd refused to continue the reading, left my post at the table and ran home under a black sky that would bleed ice for the next two days. If, if, if. Despite her visions and machinations to save Detroit, the following year Mrs. O'Leary's tearoom closed as the casinos opened, and she packed her china sets and her wooden plaque for the long journey back to Cork.

Her obituary said she was a member of the Gaelic League and a secretary of the local Preservation Society, known for the cuisine she served at her long-term Irish tearoom in Corktown. *She will be missed*, the article stated, *for her kindness, her generosity, and her willingness to help everyone who crossed her doorstep.* Mrs. O'Leary died yesterday, and today I can tell a different story.

# PART IV

## EDGE OF THE PAST

# OVER THE BELLE ISLE BOUNDARY

BY LOLITA HERNANDEZ

*East Grand Boulevard*

*for Pops*

*All of the Antilles, every island, is an effort of memory; every mind, every racial biography culminating in amnesia and fog. Pieces of sunlight through the fog and sudden rainbows, arcs-en-ciel. That is the effort, the labour of the Antillean imagination, rebuilding its gods from bamboo frames, phrase by phrase.*
—Derek Walcott, *The Antilles: Fragments of Epic Memory*
(Nobel Lecture, December 7, 1992)

I t was a hot sun and breezeless day. Solar rays pressed relentlessly against the fourth-floor nursing home window facing East Grand Boulevard. The home really had no recourse from the sun in its treeless section of what was called *convalescent row* only a spit north of Belle Isle. The rays penetrated the panes, boldly thrusting themselves far down the hall, some almost to the utility room. Some reached just to the nursing station, located midway on the floor, weaving over and under papers and medications on the countertop. Others lingered on the edge of the bare ceiling-almost-to-floor window where all of them had entered. Some settled by the exit door just by the window. But one wide and gentle ray curled around the corner of the first resident room, where it crept up on the bed of a sleeping fawn-colored old man and flopped across waiting for him to rouse.

As it waited, strands of it began wrapping around the old

man's toes and his fingers and caressing his lightly whiskered face. He whispered, *Ooooh aahhh,* and rubbed eyes crusty where the sands of sleep lodged; he hadn't been bathed yet. He passed his hands up and down his cheeks and for no reason at all called out softly to his wife, the woman he called *Mummy* in life and in death, and she called him *shuga-plum.* She had been wife and mother to him and was good to their only child, a son who had become a world traveler; Lord in heaven knows where he is now. *Mummy, you see how I come? Dog betta dan me.*

But if Mummy were alive, not even she could have understood his stroke-slurred speech, further hampered by a tongue lightly purpled and slightly swollen from lack of use. The stroke took him quick and left him slumped and drooling in a pool of his own urine in the stairwell of the building he migrated to after his wife died. *Tang God* for the man who came by and found him.

Mummy would have said, *Tang God,* but that's not what he thought through stroke-laced brain waves as the ambulance personnel arrived to carry him off. *Oh Mummy, how could you leave me like this?*

Then, as they strapped him on the stretcher, *Oh Lorse, take me now,* he silently pleaded with the heavens.

*I comin, Mummy,* as the ambulance rolled toward Henry Ford Hospital. *I comin by you.*

But he didn't meet Mummy then. The medical staff kept him from her, tidied him up and released him to the nursing home, where he hasn't spoken one single intelligible word to one living soul since, except for silent prayers to his Mummy, beseeching her to come for him. He spoke not an intelligible word to the rotating crew that fed him the nursing home pap through his feeding tube and changed his dydee after feeding, not to the head nurse who often came in to pinch his big toe for a sign of life. In response he would grunt words she couldn't understand, *What de ass you want in here now?* To the Catholic priest who came weekly to pray with him, he moaned. But he communicated fluently to the motes that swirled around in his room on sunny days as he mumbled messages for them to carry to Mummy.

More awake now, he blinked; the sun was so bright. *Wait, nuh, where am I? Is as if, wait, nuh; where de hell am I?* he asked a cluster of dust that settled on the back of the wide sunray; then he slipped into a dream of *pelau* on a Sunday beach and the crab he would catch between platefuls of the rice dish. He was seeing himself in this dream, nice and slim and handsome, catching the eye of a young Mummy rushing out to meet the waves at Mácuri Beach, between his legs getting hot as he chased after her, and just then a crab came from nowhere and bit his toe.

—What are you smiling at old man? It was the nurse pinching his toe. He *cheups. Why de ass she can't leave me alone?*

She scanned the room as he eyed her through slits. *Ah, chut, what she want now?* Then he drifted off again to rejoin Mummy on the beach; she was dishing out the *pelau* and he was holding a bottle of *peppa* sauce waiting to dash it on the rice. It was he and Mummy for so long. She giving the *peppa*; he getting the sauce. And now he was on this bed in this shit-ass nursing home waiting to rejoin Mummy.

All of a sudden the dream shifted to the dusty yard of his boyhood home in Oronuevo Village. His brother Toli comes along with a flat stick whittled from the coconut tree in the front of their house, and running up to him is their friend Alfonso, bowling a ball he had fashioned from a rock and some twine. Toli hits the ball but Winston, another friend from down the road, picks it up, pivots magnificently, and breaks the wicket. *Well played, bhai!* Alfonso yells out to Winston. *Well played. Yuh finally break a wicket, bhai.* The three of them, all early teenagers, smile big at the sexual innuendo and wave at the old man. Then Toli says, *You're up, brother,* and the old man, who appears in his youth, is now batting. He is younger than Toli and taller; Toli is fairer; both are slim. Alfonso turns his back to the old man in the bed and begins running toward the young man, chest thrust forward, head high, ball in his right hand, left touching it, and almost leaps into the air to begin the hand-over-hand movements that add thrust to the bowl. *Perfect, perfect. Yes, buddy, I can well remember those days as if dey were yesterday.*

The Young Terrors of Oronuevo consisted of eleven regulars and a few alternates. Both he and Toli batted, they were usually in partnership. Toli was a better batsman. In truth, Toli was better than him all around in cricket. Winston Ramkeeson and Alfonso Luces from the other side of the junction practiced cricket with them in the front yard morning, noon, and night when school was out. They played at school during recess and after school. Alfonso was their star bowler, but they all switched up batting and bowling and playing the field. Winston was another all around player. At any one point, one of them might brag after a good play, *Worrell ent have nuteeng on us, yuh know.* Yes, cricket is a sunshine game and a hot sun day like today always reminded the old man of airborne bowlers, broken wickets, and dramatic overs.

*Yes buddy, is a nice game, nuh, a nice game. Oh, what I wouldn't give to see dose boys again, Toli, Alfonso, and Winston. It was eleven of dem in all. Dey made deir own pitch right dere to practice in de yard and made the wicket from dat same coconut tree. Well, in de first place, since cricket is played with two persons at de same time against all eleven of de other team, Toli and me were de lead batsmen. So whoever was de bowler would bowl to us first. You hit de ball and according to de distance you hit de ball you can make one run or two runs, or three runs or four if it roll on de ground and hit one of de boundary. When Toli hit dat ball and it go over de boundary, dat's a six. It's a game you really have to understand but it is a real nice game.*

He tried many times to explain the game to Detroit people, but they never understood.

*Yes, buddy, three men, six wickets; three wickets on dis end and three on de other end no, two wickets and six stumps. Yes, dat's it. And when de bowler hits de wicket dat man is out and he hits de ball and*

*it goes up in de air and it didn't go far enough and one of the fielders
pitching dat man is out, and if he hit de ball and don't, ah, if he hit de
ball . . . What de hell am I talking about?*

Just then his eyes flew open, fully connecting him with buzzing activity in the hallway just outside of his room. While the sun
played with the old man and he followed the shadows dancing
across his memory, the nursing staff bustled up and down the
hall, stepping over rays, walking right through them, completely
oblivious as they cleaned every corner and reorganized this and
that in anticipation of a surprise walk-through visit from the
State Certification Board. Mainly, they wanted the joint to smell
good, so bouquets of silk flowers sprayed with a potpourri scent
appeared everywhere to brighten things up and help camouflage
the urine odor that had sunk into the walls, under the paint,
and behind the baseboards. Every staff member practiced sporting a wide smile while changing the loaded dydees of old and
forgotten souls, vacant faces with drooling mouths. Staff cooed
lovingly to them as if they were newborn darlings, deftly cleaned
bottoms, switched stained or heavy dydees for fresh ones, and
then made airplane noises to the darlings as encouragement to
eat the colorless pap that would soon refill the dydees.

Not one hint of urine smell would escape from this home
on this Sunday morning, certainly not on the fourth floor where
staff prided itself on being the most efficient and most attentive
team in the entire building. Staff squirted extra deodorizer in
corners along the bed edges, in utility closets, and wherever used
dydees congregated.

A young woman staffer, starched and pleasant with hair
slicked into a neat little bun, entered the old man's room, brush-
ing past the section of the sunray that hugged the door frame.
She quickly arrived at his side at the point the ray began its as-
cent to the bed. Whistling an elevator tune through bright red
lips she stepped directly on it, startling the old man. He squinted
up at her. She smiled cheerily at him.

—Good morning, sweetie.

It was the last day of her first week of employment there, and her first solo dydee change. But with eight brothers and sisters under her, she had performed enough diaper changes to feel absolutely confident that she could handle this resident. In addition, she had received a day's worth of training on the art of changing adults.

Still, she wondered if the coming weeks would find her searching for another job. The nursing home, where her mother had worked for years, was hopefully a temporary stop for her on the way to community college and later maybe university. She wanted to be a doctor or a lawyer, someone successful, anyone but an aide in a nursing home where she was beginning to realize old people steal whatever years they can from young people. Look, in only one week, some of her had aged. She certainly felt it. How could she enjoy her youth looking at those old faces every day?

—Come on, sweetie, it's time to clean you up. She patted him on his arm, while surveying the room to see what she would need for his sponge bath.

By this time, the old man's reverie took him down East Grand Boulevard to Belle Isle. That's where he and his wife spent many summer Sundays observing cricket matches with others from the small West Indian community in Detroit. Mummy would carefully wrap a cast iron pot full of *pelau* in an old dish towel, lovingly securing the four corners of the towel with a large safety pin. She would nest a couple of avocados in the corner of the picnic basket, along with *peppa* sauce, sweet cakes, and utensils. Others would bring fruits, rum and sugary drinks, ice, cookies, chips, and so on. One time someone brought a manual ice cream maker and everyone took turns churning. But always his loving wife would bring the *pelau*, her specialty, long-recognized as the best in the Detroit island community.

Ah, those were the days, when the cricket teams would

come in from all over—Windsor, for sure, and as far as Chicago. Toledo and all had a team back then. All those brown bodies clad in white flannel and white shoes on the green field. They bowled and batted, broke wickets and often sent balls way over the boundary of the cricket field by the casino to shouts of, *Well played, bhai, well played!*

When the cricketers took a break for liquids and food, the fans gathered at the picnic tables clustered across a small path east of the field. The men dribbled *peppa* sauce on platefuls of *pelau*, drank the rum straight with lime, and rehashed the innings just played.

When fielders returned to the field, and batsmen and bowlers returned to the pitch, the fans retook their positions on the bleachers by the river side to cheer all of the players on without real team allegiance; after all, they were now all citizens of this island in this city. So, they shouted out appropriately to whichever team: *Good running, or, Cool down, bhai, cool down. It's a bowler's game.*

*Well, maybe luck's allowed, maybe, maybe. I'll be able to go to Belle Isle one of dese days to see another game. Yeah, buddy. Yeah. Yuh run with de bat when one guy hit de ball, he's going to run to try and score as many runs as he can. It depends on how hard yuh hit de ball; if yuh hit it real hard, it go over de boundary, dat's a six. If yuh don't reach to de end, dey run yuh out; dey call it runout. Some of dem bhais can't make it. Dey try to make one run and sometimes dey don't; dey don't make it. Den dey want to make two runs and so on. And when one guy hit de ball and he don't hit it hard enough and he hit it in front of one of de fielders and he have to run with de bat in he hand and he run, run, and what de hell, yes, buddy, run, run.*

And he began groaning. —Whan go, whan go, whan go.

—What, sweetie?

Louder and louder. —Whan go, whan go, whan go.

Was he speaking some foreign language, fragments of a tribal vocabulary that had been suppressed over the years? And then the stroke problem? She turned to find the head nurse. She wanted to know where this man was from. Maybe she could figure out a way to understand him if she knew the language he was speaking.

She found her by the central station. —Ms. Nurse, Ms. Nurse, she called out. Ms. Nurse was preparing meds for distribution.

—That man doesn't talk. I ain't got time now to fool with his grunting; gotta pass out meds. Let me see, does he get anything now? Nope.

And Ms. Nurse shuffled to the room at the other end of the hallway to begin distributing medications.

—Whan go, whan go, whan go.

—I can't understand you, sweetie. What do you want?

Back and forth they went, the old man and the young woman. A janitor on the way to take the exit stairs passed by the two. He listened to their exchange for a couple of minutes then interjected, —You'll never understand what he's saying. Then he opened the exit door and disappeared.

The young woman and the old man continued their frantic exchange. Realizing something was really bothering him and that he was trying to say something important, the young woman leaned over and addressed him face to face, almost exchanging breaths with him.

—I'm trying to understand. What do you want, sweetie? She put her hand on his shoulder.

He turned his face away from her and stared at the opposite wall. He was trying to call up a vision of him sick and then him doing much better. Him playing cricket in Oronuevo and him eating *pelau* at Belle Isle. For a moment he was perplexed. What was happening to him? He slipped into a deep stillness to ponder yet again the smell of freshly turned funeral soil, so far from where his navel string was buried.

Finally, she remembered that he was wheeled to the window every day after lunch. Who knows how that ritual began, but he sat in that same spot almost daily, beginning with the first winter he arrived and then spring and summer and fall and winter and again and again, once more, until he had marked a little over three years by the window. Through frost and snow and spring rains he watched out of it while he finished digesting his food. He followed the pedestrians heading to the liquor stores and other notable neighborhood destinations and absently glanced at cars crossing the Kercheval intersection on the way to perhaps Belle Isle? He contemplated navel strings and final resting places.

Maybe that's what he wanted now? she thought.

—Do you want to go to the window, sweetie?

Gratefully, the old man looked up at her and nodded. Finally, she understood and smiled back at him.

Now how to get him there, since she couldn't lift him by herself to put him in the wheelchair and everyone else was so busy. Conveniently, the one-ton white crane used to lift residents was already in a corner of the old man's room, likely in readiness for his afternoon window appointment. Luckily, she had been trained to use it yesterday. So confidently she marched over to get it. With its boom pointed toward the floor she maneuvered the lift near the old man's bed and removed the halter left dangling on the hook. He was almost smiling as she leaned over him to place his arms through the halter, pull a strap between his legs, fasten it in the back, and check the placement of the loops for the hook.

Then she stood back to look at him.

—You're a mess, sweetie. At least let me wash your face. He nodded, a crooked little smile developing.

After she washed his face and combed his few strands of hair, she wheeled the chair by the bed and locked it into what she thought would be the perfect spot to receive the old man when she was ready to lower him.

She was almost ready with everything and then . . .

—Oh my God, sweetie. I bet your diaper needs changing. She rolled the wheelchair aside and unfastened the halter. His crooked little smile turned into a look of alarm.

—Don't worry, sweetie, I know what I'm doing, and she began to change and wash him with the adroitness of an old pro.

He closed his eyes at the feel of the young hand covered by a warm washcloth wiping Mummy's territory. *There's nothing there anymore, Mummy. It's all gone.*

With the halter and wheelchair back in place, she moved the crane into position parallel to the bed. All of this activity occurred over and around the sunray, now angled slightly off the bed. The young woman darted in and out of its range as she prepared the crane without paying any attention to the motes traveling up and down the ray and the intermittent sunshine that caused her to squint. At last she felt the sun's warmth.

—Hey, sweetie, you're going to have a warm day at the window. You may not even be able to stand it.

She placed a pillow on the wheelchair seat for comfort and rolled him on his side. Now she was ready. She turned the directional knob on the lever to move the boom up and pumped the lever until it reached a good level for hooking the halter. Then she slid the base of the crane under the bed and pumped again, gently lifting his once-hefty body, guiding it all the way. He was now almost facedown and moving his heavily wrinkled arms and thin legs as if he was winding up in the yard to bowl to Toli.

—Hold on, sweetie. Don't move so much. I'm going to roll you over to the chair. We don't have far to go; hang in. Oh, you know what I mean.

He nodded, his smile having returned.

As she positioned the old man over the wheelchair, she pulled his legs down and around to make sure his bottom hit first. She reached to change the directional knob so that she could now lower the boom when she pumped the lever. It was jammed. It wouldn't move at all, not to pump up, not to pump down.

—Oh my God, what am I going to do? She looked up at the man, who was moving his arms left over right and right over left, his legs in running formation and said firmly, —Be still until I figure this thing out.

She was able to reach the emergency cord by his bed and pulled and pulled and pulled. But no one came to the room. The room had no phone because no one ever called the old man. She began yelling.

—Ms. Nurse, Ms. Nurse! Someone! Help!

No one came. All she heard were responses from other residents. —We're here, they yelled out. One lady down the hall began screaming. The young staffer yelled back.

—Everything is fine; don't worry.

So she patted the old man on his shoulder and said, —Okay, sweetie, don't let them upset you. You're going for a ride now. And she rolled the entire contraption, Sweetie and all, over to the doorway and looked up and down the hall. No one, not a soul was in sight. She yelled again, —Ms. Nurse, Ms. Nurse, someone!

No one.

The nursing station was midway in the hall. She thought to roll the crane to the station and use the phone to call for help, but the machine's pivot wheel suddenly locked tight. She pushed her foot on the wheel lock, then lifted up on it, then kicked it. She kneeled down to jiggle it, but it wouldn't loosen. So now the crane wouldn't move out of the room or back into it.

—We're stuck, sweetie. She smiled. He smiled too, and nodded, but thought to himself, *Man must live.*

She realized she had to chance it at this point. He wasn't so high up in the air; things looked relatively stable if she could get him to keep absolutely still.

—Sweetie, I have to call for help. You have to be real good

and be still. Don't move your hands or feet. What are you doing anyway? You look like you're pitching in a baseball game. Be still; I'm going to call for help.

He hung there, his brown body against the white crane, and watched the young staffer rush down the hall.

*Well, maybe luck's allowed today, maybe, maybe. I'll be able to go to Belle Isle to see another game. Yeah, buddy, yeah. Yuh run with de bat when one guy hit de ball, he's going to run to try and score as many runs as he can. It depends on how hard yuh hit de ball. If yuh hit it real hard, it go over de boundary, dat's a six. Yuh score big, den. If yuh don't reach to de end, dey run yuh out, dey call it runout; some of dem bhais can't make it; dey try to make one run and sometimes dey don't; dey don't make it den dey want to make two runs and so on, and when one guy hit de ball and he don't hit it hard enough and he hit it in front of one of de fielders and he have to run with de bat in he hand and he run, run, and what the hell. Yes buddy, run, run.*

She ran to the telephone, and in the instant she turned her head to grab the receiver, knocking over a silk floral arrangement in the process, and hit the button for security, she heard a loud snapping noise. —Oh my God, and she whipped her head around, expecting to see the old man on the floor.

But the crane was completely upright in the doorway and the boom in the same position she had left it. Only he was gone, halter and all. She froze, not able to respond when security finally answered the phone.

She dashed over to the crane and passed her hand under where the old man should have been hanging. He really wasn't there. —Sweetie, sweetie, where are you? She squeezed past it to enter his room and looked under the covers, under the bed, in the closet, in the restroom. She ran from room to room, like a mad woman; residents called out to her, each with his or her own need for food, water, diaper, conversation.

—Not now! she hollered back to them. Not now!

She pushed open the exit door. She ran down the stairs

yelling, —Old man, old man! She ran from floor to floor, past the staff, looking into each bedroom and each utility closet. When she returned to the fourth floor, Ms. Nurse, the head of security and most of the floor's staff were calmly standing by the lift, looking at her quizzically.

—The old man is gone, Ms. Nurse. He left.

—What are you talking about?

—He's just gone.

The huddle of fourth-floor staff and a few from the other floors, along with the head of security, began prowling the halls, peering behind the nursing counter and into the other rooms searching for the old man. The head of security, a rather large beefy man, tried to push the lift into the room, and when it wouldn't roll, he picked it up and moved it aside. Another staff went to the wheelchair and shook it. This unnerved Ms. Nurse who yelled out, —He ain't there, fool!

Bewildered, the young woman stood in the middle of the hallway in front of the old man's room. She began sobbing, long tears descending like a waterfall. Snot fell freely from her nose. She stared at the lift and at the wheelchair and at the bed and at the window in his room. It was then she remembered that the room had been sunny before; now it was gray. She looked up and down the hall and the whole place was gray. Didn't she tell the old man as she was preparing him for the crane that he would have a real sunny day at the window?

She walked slowly to the hall window, put her knee on the ledge and peered up and down the boulevard.

—What the hell you looking for, girl? He damn sure ain't out there.

To the astonishment of Ms. Nurse, the young woman, said, —Hush, and squeezed her eyes enough to be able to peer through the bright sun. She looked up and down trying to spot the old man. The sun was coming from the south, bright like a new beginning. Traffic was riding into it. But she saw nothing.

No old man. She pushed her wet face against the window and stared openly into the sun.

—Old man, how could you do this to me in my first week? I didn't want to stay here forever, but I need this job now. What have you done? They'll fire me for sure. How did I lose you? Why did you do this to me? I was trying to help you.

But if she had heard the commotion south of the nursing home, just inside the island on the north side of the casino. If she had known the jubilation all of them there were experiencing as the last batsman hit the last ball in the last innings, over, over, over the boundary so far it couldn't be recovered. All of the players stood with arms outstretched and knees slightly buckled, wonderment and joy on their faces; women and men fans clutched their hearts, clutched each other, and clutched their children as they watched the ball's trajectory over the road, past the sun, over the river heading west and out of view. And then this tremendous release of clapping and crying and rummy shouts coming from the entire casino area, pitch and oval, picnic benches, across the road over to the riverside. Had she heard the chorus, loud as one voice:

—Well played, old bhai, well played, well played!

If she had heard all of that, she would have well understood.

# THE DEAD MAN'S BOAT

BY PETER MARKUS

*Delray*

U s brothers, we took us our mud and our fish-fishing poles baited with worms and rust and mud and we hopped up into the dead man's boat, that boat that we found washed up on our dirty river's dirty shores, and we headed ourselves upriver, up past the shipwrecked mill where our father used to go inside to work, it sitting dark and silenced and fireless there on the river's muddy bank, up around the bend in the river, past the other string of mills farther north along the river, mills with fires still burning there inside them, up toward where the beaded lights of that big steel bridge stretching from our side of the river all the way over to the river's other side, it was all lit up in the night like a constellation of sunken-ship stars, each star shining out in the nighttime's dark like the shiny heads of nails hammered into some backyard telephone pole. We were chugging along, us brothers, with Brother sitting up in the bow, holding up a lantern's light for us to better see the river by, and the brother that I am was kneeling in the back of the boat, what's called the stern, with one hand on the outboard's tiller, the other hand hanging itself over the edge of the boat, the fingers of that hand dragging themselves across the muddy skin of the river. We were on our way upriver, up to where the dirty river that runs through our dirty river town begins, it runs all the way up through the city, us brothers heading up there to see if we might catch us some of the big city's big dirty river fish, when out of nowhere in the night and in the river's muddy dark we heard, then saw, a boat, much bigger than ours, it was cutting across and down the river, it was heading right for us brothers. There's a boat coming right for us, Brother turned his head and said, as he held up the lantern light with that fire glowing inside it so that his face flashed full like the moon. I looked up at Brother then. There was a look that us brothers sometimes liked to look at each other with. It was the kind of a look that actually hurt the eyes of the brother who was doing the looking. Imagine that look. Do I look like a brother born blind? was what I said to Brother then, and I cut the tiller hard and to the right. But that boat, that other boat much bigger than ours, that boat with us brothers not sitting down inside it, it kept on coming toward us brothers, as if it didn't see us brothers, as if us brothers weren't even there. But it saw us, this boat, the people sitting there inside it: this, us brothers, we knew. When we moved it, our boat, it moved closer toward where it was we moved. And before we knew what to do next, because we knew we couldn't outrun it, this boat, it was soon coming across our bow, it was doing what it could do to hit us, this boat, even though we didn't, we couldn't, know why. What did we, us brothers, do, to a boat like this boat? Us brothers, all we ever really did out on the river was fish. We didn't know what we should do, other than what we ended up doing. Us brothers, the both of us brothers, we both jumped, headfirst, out of our boat, the dead man's boat, the dead man who fell into the river pissing into the river for luck, we headed down into the river, and we swam ourselves down to get us away from this coming-after-us boat. When we stuck our boy heads up out of the river, to see if we were both of us still alive, to see where our boat was, to see where that other boat was, all us brothers could see was our boat drifting its way back and down the river, back to from where us brothers, ourselves, had just come from. That other boat, it seemed, had all but disappeared, and not even the sound of it could be heard by our ears. Our boat, the dead man's boat, away from us brothers, it had drifted too far away from us brothers for us to be able to swim back to it for us to get back in it. So, us brothers, we swam ourselves toward the river's muddy shore, we swam ourselves out of us brothers' breath, and plopped ourselves down in the mud at the edge of the river. Yes, like a couple of out-of-water fish, us brothers, there in the mud, we sucked in at the air until the sky above us, it helped us brothers to begin breathing again. We stood up, in the mud, out of the mud, but we did not wipe the mud off us. Us brothers, we liked mud and the fishy river smells that always smelled of river and mud and fish. With mud in our eyes, us brothers, we turned to look one last time back downriver, to where our boat, the dead man's boat, it had floated downriver and down around a bend in the river and almost out of sight, this boat with our fishing poles inside it, our buckets empty of fish. Us brothers, we didn't know what we were going to do, or how we were going to get back home, now that we didn't have us brothers a boat to take us back home in. So what us brothers did was, we figured it, in our boy heads, that it was too early in the night for us to head ourselves back home. We'd gone out, that night, out onto the river, out on the river in the dead man's boat, to spend the dark night fishing. It was what us brothers did, at night, and in the morning, and sometimes, too, in the day: we fished. Our mother and our father both believed that we were brothers sound asleep in our beds when we stepped outside through our bedroom's window and slipped, as we always did, down to the river. We had until the sun's rise for us brothers to get us back home before our father would call out to us to wake us with the word, Son. When our father called out to us brothers, Son, we both knew, we were crossing that dirty river together. But us brothers, we didn't want to go back home, to bed, in a room in a house with our mother and father asleep in it. Our house, with our mother and father in it, it was not the kind of a house that us brothers liked to go back to. The river, out fishing on the river, that was where us brothers liked to be. But now, us brothers, we didn't have a boat to be out on the river in, we didn't have us our fish-fishing poles for us to fish for our fish with, we didn't have us our buckets of mud and rust and worms for us brothers to bait our hooks with. It was just us brothers now standing on the upriver banks of a river and a city that was not ours. Our mother and our father had often told us brothers that the city was not a place for us boys to be. Don't ever go, was what our mother told us. But us brothers, we didn't much like to listen to what our mother liked to tell us. Our mother, she was the kind of a mother who told us brothers not to walk through mud, a mother who told us to wash our hands before we ate, our hands that always smelled of fish, our hands with mud dried hard in our palms. We liked mud and we liked it the way the fish's silver scales stuck to our hands. These were fish that we fished out of the dirty river that runs its way through this dirty river town, fish that we took back home with us and we gutted the guts out of those fish, we cut off the heads of those fish, and then we hammered them, those fish, those fish heads, into the backyard telephone pole out back in the back of our yard. In the end, there was exactly a hundred and fifty fish heads, hammered and nailed into that pole's creosoted wood. Each fish, each fish head, us brothers, we gave each one a name. Not one was called Jimmy or John. Jimmy and John was mine and my brother's name. We called each other Brother. Brother, Brother said to me then. What do you want to do? Brother was the brother of us brothers who always liked to ask these kinds of questions. To Brother, I did not know what then to say. Us brothers, we stood there like that on the dirty river's dirty banks, and we looked around this place that us brothers, we'd been told, this was not the kind of a place for us brothers to be. But this place, this city with this dirty river running through it, it didn't look much different than the town that was ours with its dirty river running through it and with its dirty river mill built up along its dirty river banks, its smokestacks that stained the sky the color of rust and mud. We liked a sky that was stained the color of rust and mud. Our mother once let it be known to us brothers that there was a sky, there was a sky, our mother told us, bigger than the sky above the river that was ours. Us brothers, we couldn't picture this, a sky bigger than the sky that was our backyard. We couldn't picture a town without a dirty river running through it where us brothers could run down to it to fish. This is our river, was what we said to our mother then, and this was what I said to Brother too. This is our river, I said, then. There's no place else for us to be. We stood there, like this, for a while, like this, just standing there along the edge of the river. The moon in the sky had not yet begun to rise. The sky, it was mostly dark. Behind us, away from the river, most of the houses sitting side by side in the dark, these houses did not have lights lighting them up from inside them. We stood there, on the edge of this river, but us brothers, we couldn't fish. We reached down into the mud and found us some stones and we threw them out and into the river. Sometimes the stones skipped. Sometimes, in the dark, the stones made a sound like a fish leaping up out of the water. Us brothers, we knew more about fish than most people know about fish. Us brothers know that when a fish jumps up out of the water, what that means is that that fish, it isn't a fish for us brothers to fish for and catch: not with our fishing hooks baited thick with mud and sunk down to the river's bottom. Us brothers, we didn't know how to fish for fish that were fish that jumped up as if to bite the sky. It's true, sometimes us brothers, we could walk out into the river and reach with our hands down into the river and fish us up some fish with our bare boy hands. It's true, too, that we could sometimes dunk our buckets into the river and like this we'd fill them up with a mix of fish and mud. But it was not one of those kinds of nights for us brothers. We didn't have us our buckets or our poles or a boat for us to fish from. And our hands hanging down by our legs, they were all four of them balled up into fists. Let's go for a walk, was what I said to Brother then, and we both of us turned and started walking in from the river, up past houses that did not look like anyone was living inside them. There were no lights lit up and burning on the insides of these houses, there were no streetlights lighting up the streets outside. But us brothers, we had us eyes like the marbly eyes of fish, eyes that, like moons, could see in the river at night. And so, us brothers, into this dark, we walked. We walked and we walked, it didn't matter where, until the mud on our boots had all of the way been walked off. That's how us brothers liked to wash the mud from off the bottoms of our boots. We didn't like it when our mother made us wash the mud off with a brush held in our hands. So we walked, and we walked, but we didn't see a face that looked like the faces that were ours. It was as if we had walked into a dead town, or maybe it was just a town that was early-to-bed asleep. Even the stars in the sky above this dead town seemed not to be shining. But still, us brothers, we walked. We did not talk. We just listened to the voice that was us brothers inside the each of our boy heads. In this town, even the cars that we saw, here on our walk, all of them seemed to be made out of rust. What us brothers needed was a couple of fishing poles for us to do some fishing with. Even though the fish were jumping, this night, maybe us brothers could get those fish to go back down to the river's muddy bottom. So we went looking around town for two poles for us to fish with. There was a store with a sign above the door that said on it, *Delray's Live Bait*, but the door, when we pulled on it to get it to open, it did not open up. There were other buildings with the same two words on it, *Delray, Delray*, some of them, these words, spray-painted on pieces of wood nailed into brick, *DELRAY, DELRAY*, but these doors, too, to these other buildings, they wouldn't open up for us either. So what us brothers did then was, we turned back around and we decided in our heads to head ourselves back downriver. If we started walking along the road that runs its way along the banks of the river, we'd get home before the night began its turning into day. We were walking back this way, back downriver, back toward where we lived in a house with a mother and father inside it, when Brother turned and said that he was tired of all this walking. Would you rather swim back home? was what I said to Brother. Brother said what we both knew, it was too cold for us to be all the way back home in the river swimming. What we need, Brother said, is another boat. I looked at Brother. I nodded with my head at what Brother said. Brother was right. Us brothers, we did need us a boat. It didn't have to be a fancy boat. The dead man's boat, it wasn't a fancy boat. It was a boat that floats is all that it was, a boat that we found washed up on the river's dirty river banks one day when the man that it once belonged to had fallen and drowned when he pissed into the river for luck. What other kind of a boat did brothers like us need? So we started looking with our eyes into the backyards of these unlit houses to see if we could find us a boat to get back on the river. But in the backyards of these houses, houses not far from the banks of the river that runs itself down and through our dirty river town, there were cars rusting in the backyards of these houses—cars with no wheels and cars with the windows in them busted out and cars with weeds as tall as us brothers growing up on all sides so that the cars were hard for us brothers to see. But boats: there were no boats to be seen in these backyards for us brothers to see, no boats for us brothers to get back out on the river, to take us brothers back home. Us brothers, we were standing out on the corner of Jefferson, that road that runs along the river, all the way from the big dirty city back to our dirty river town, when out of the dark, us brothers, we could see the shadow of a man coming on toward us. This man, this shadow, who here in the near river dark did not seem to have a face that us brothers could see, he walked right up to us brothers, as if he knew us, and asked us what were we looking for. Who says we're looking for something, was what Brother's mouth opened itself up to say. When Brother said this to this shadow of a man, this man without a face, I shot Brother this look. There was this look that us brothers sometimes liked to look at each other with. It was the kind of a look that actually hurt the eyes of the brother who was doing the looking. Imagine that look. When this man didn't say anything to this, I stepped in front of Brother and said that it's true, we were looking for something. A boat, was what I said into this man's shadowy face. This man, when I said this to his face, the look on his face seemed to lighten. It was like a light winked on when I said the word *boat*. Then he turned his face away from us brothers and he started walking down along the river. Come, this man said. Stay close. Us brothers, we did what we'd been told. It's true that, us brothers, we'd been told, by our mother and father, like most boys have been told: Don't talk to strangers, don't talk with your mouth full, don't walk into the house with mud on the bottoms of your boots. But us brothers, we weren't the kind of boys who liked to listen to this sort of talk. When we heard our mother say the word *don't*, us brothers, what we did was, we *did*. And so, us brothers, we walked in the shadows of this shadowy man, this man whose face was more shadow than it was flesh or even fish. We walked down along the river, past bars with steel bars rusted on the boarded-up windows, past more buildings with the words DELRAY written on their sides. After a while, we found ourselves standing outside the fenced-in yard of a hardware store, its backyard filled with boats. It was a boatyard of boats, this backyard was, and it was, to our eyes, like finding a river in the desert for us to make mud with. Us brothers, with our eyes, we looked and we looked at all of those boats. There were boats made out of steel and boats made of aluminum and boats that were made out of wood. Us brothers, we liked boats made out of wood best because it was hard for us to figure out how a thing made out of steel could float. What, we wondered, kept it from down to the river's bottom sinking? This was something that us brothers, we hadn't yet learned the reason why this was so. So, the man turned and turned his shadow face to ours, which boat would you boys like? There was a wood boat there that looked like it had been painted with mud. Us brothers, we both looked at each other and knew that this boat was made for us. We pointed with our hands toward this mud-colored boat. The man who was more shadow than flesh or fish, he pointed with his hand, he pushed at this fence, and the gate of it swung away from its rusted lock. You boys sure you want that boat? the man asked. You could have any boat here. He waved at them all with his hand as if to say that they were us brothers' boats for us to take. It doesn't have a motor on its back, the man pointed this out. We're sure, we said, and nodded our boy heads. We don't need us a motor for us to get back home, we said. The river will take us where we need to go, we said. Then it's yours, the man said. I'll even help you walk it down to the river. And this, we did. Us brothers, we lifted this boat made out of wood, this boat the color of mud, this boat that almost looked like it might be made out of mud, we held up its back, and the man who was a shadow to us brothers, he lifted this boat up by its front. And then we walked it, like this, this boat, down to the river, down to where the river's edge was a mix of mud and stones and broken slabs of concrete. We set the boat down, there at the river's muddy-watered edge, and got in it. The man with the dark face dug his heels into the mud and pushed us brothers off and out into the river's dark. We paddled with our hands out into the river's swirling current. It was a good current. It wouldn't be long before we drifted ourselves back and to our town. Us brothers, we raised our hands above our boy heads to say to this man goodbye. Thank you, we said with our mouths, but only the river heard this. This man, at us brothers floating away, he raised up his hand at us too. He was a good man, us brothers, we knew. This man, like us brothers did too, he knew a good boat when he saw it. The moon in the sky was now rising up out of the river. This moon, it threw down its rope of moony light but still that man's face was a face that us brothers could not see. We could not see any eyes on that man's shadowy face. We could not see a mouth. His mouth was just a hole in his face that sounds sometimes came out of. Somewhere in there

there must have been a tongue, us brothers figured. Unless this man was the father of Boy, that boy who was a brother to nobody, born with a full head of hair but with no tongue on the inside of his mouth. We're going home, was what I said to Brother then, and I turned to look at him in his face. Brother's face, it was a face like mine, a face with a nose and two eyes and a mouth and a chin that sometimes had mud dried on it. It won't be long now, Brother nodded and said. Tomorrow, I said, will be a new day for us, Brother, with a new boat for us brothers to fish from. For this, we had that man, whose face we could not see, whose name we did not ask for or know, to thank. Us brothers, we turned one last time back upriver to wave at this man our thanks. In the moon's rivery light, we could see him walking, this man, out into the river, out onto the river, and the river, it was holding him, this man, up. He did not see us, this man, as he walked and kept on walking on, he did not turn to look our way, until he had walked himself all the way across the river to the river's other side, walking and walking and walking on until there was nothing left on the river for us brothers to see, there was nothing left for us brothers to hear, only the sound that the river sometimes makes when a stone is skipped across it.

# HEY LOVE

BY ROGER K. JOHNSON
*New Center*

The guy in the wheelchair looked like he had long since stopped measuring his life in years. He looked like he was a candidate for counting his remaining time on earth in days—more than likely he was down to hours or minutes. His right leg rested its foot on the chair's foot-pad, its knee bent at a right angle. The other leg stretched indifferently out with the foot on the floor, as if letting the world know, *I've been through enough, and I'm not sitting up straight any longer.* His upper body diverged as well. While the right side of his body seemed at least to make an attempt at sitting up, the left was twisted and out of whack. His liver-spotted left hand twisted backward—palm up—as if waiting for some unseen jazz musician to slide past and give him five. An over-stretched elastic cord wrapped around his head and held a clear rubber oxygen mask that rested on his beak of a nose. His labored breathing had fogged it. A clear tube connected his mask to a canister of oxygen that hung from the handle of his wheelchair. Every now and again a cough would rattle around from somewhere in his chest, scrape its way up his throat, and explode out of his mouth, sending wet flecks of spittle spraying into the mask. As the cough subsided, he would bend over as if he were about to take his last breath on earth. He'd take a couple of deep swallows of air and lean back in his chair again, slumping to one side, waiting for the next cough to knock a few more moments off of his life.

He looked old, but he was probably younger. Illnesses have that annoying way of adding years to you. His hair looked to be the only thing that hadn't aged. His goatee, eyebrows, and full head of hair were blond, not dirty-blond or white Scandinavian blond, just regular old Hollywood blond.

A light-skinned black woman pushed his chair. She could have been—probably was—mixed. I wondered if she was his granddaughter or another relative. I thought this more because of her looks—she looked mixed—not so much that she looked like him. She didn't have his nose—I'm sure she was grateful for that.

I stood in the Motown Music Museum—Hitsville, U.S.A.—observing this. The house that was converted into a studio, which was eventually converted into a museum commemorating the Motown Sound and Experience. I was trying my best to keep my kids from staring at the guy, but wasn't doing a good job of it. I found myself getting lost in wondering if he was going to actually check out, right there in front of us. My "kids" is a misnomer; I should have said my students. I'm an English teacher.

The public school system—in its finite wisdom—having given up on the theory that students might actually be motivated to learn something outside the confines of asbestos-laden school buildings, had developed a pretty laissez-faire attitude toward field trips. It was driven not by academics, but by insurance. As long as we were able to secure parental permission (a.k.a., insurance liability waivers), we could take the students on the Bataan Death March if we were so inclined.

The situation can lead to some fairly interesting and creative field trips if the teacher really cares—which I do. This was a trip for some of my students who showed more than passing interest or ability in poetry. Having tired of hearing why Puff Daddy should fear Suge Night, in between our discussions about how well Tupac, Biggie, and whoever was the hip-hop flav du jour could rhyme and flow, I decided to introduce my students to some musical and poetic roots.

That's why I was standing in the Motown Music Museum looking at a dying man.

I say dying because you don't look like this guy did on your way up the mountain of life. But he looked happy; you could see it so clearly in his eyes. Everything else about this guy said— was shouting—*I've seen better days!* His eyes, however, were right there; they were clear and wide. Both he and the young woman pushing him looked around the museum with an air of utter fascination and enjoyment.

I found myself taking a much longer look at the surroundings in the building. What were they seeing that I wasn't? Was there some hidden magic that these faded album covers possessed? Was there a mystical power in the autographed black-and-white pictures of Smokey, Marvin, Michael, and Diana? These two people moved with an air of giddy reverence that intrigued me. The girl caught me staring at them as she wheeled him on the other side of a glass case that separated us. Caught and embarrassed, the only form of explanation I mustered was a smile.

She smiled back, not the least bit aggravated, a genuine *Don't you love this place?* smile.

"Hi," I said, trying to return a smile that I hoped was at least as bright.

"Oi yaself," she said in a light British accent, still smiling.

"You know, you have a great smile. Thank you for sharing it."

"Anytime," she said.

"Are both of you from across the pond?"

"Yeah, mate," the guy in the wheelchair croaked.

"Well then, welcome to *Day-trois*," I said, affecting what I hoped passed for a French accent and trying to sound as much like an ambassador of goodwill as a Detroiter can.

"Thank you," they both said, looking past me as some of my students eased up behind me. My students were happy that someone had broken the ice with them. This allowed them to ask the questions that had been on their minds since we walked into the museum, albeit through me.

*Who's this, Mr. Blake? You know them? What's they name? Why he in that wheelchair? What're they doin'?*

The pair continued to smile, and affected a posture that let me know they were well-acquainted with these questions.

"Being a teacher has somehow liberated me from the name my parents gave me. Now I'm just Mr. Blake, instead of Terrance Blake." After introducing myself, I introduced my students and explained why we were there.

"'Ello there, glad to meet you all. My name's Elliot Taylor and this 'ere's my daughter, Diana. My wife and I named 'er after Diana Ross," the man in the wheelchair rasped out through his face mask proudly. His accent was a lot heavier than hers, yet not the cockney or cartoonish accent that we sometimes hear actors and actresses affect. He straightened up some in his wheelchair and extended his right hand. I took it gently and gave it a shake.

"So where in England are you two from?" I asked, relaxing.

"Spent my 'ole life in London . . ." He was about to say more but then one of those coughs cut him off.

His daughter rubbed him on his shoulder.

"My father is dying," she said matter-of-factly, and I did my best not to let my mouth fall open. She said it the same way someone would have said: *My father's name is Elliot*, or, *I don't like bananas.* I wasn't surprised. Helen Keller could see that her father was dying. Saying it out loud, however, was like spilling a deep, dark secret that no one wanted to talk about. *Psst, hey, I know he's dying and you know he's dying, but let's not talk about it.* I wanted to say to her, *I know that! You didn't have to tell me!* It seemed that by her saying what we all knew anyway, she somehow betrayed a closeness that we had developed in the short time that we had known each other. I was taken aback, but how does one continue that conversation?

*Oh, I'm so sorry to hear that.*

*Really? Well my father's still alive and healthy as a bull.*

*OhmyGod! Whatever he's dying from isn't contagious, is it?*

I just sat there not saying anything. I looked into both of their faces trying to ascertain whether or not they wanted to continue talking, or was this her way of killing conversation. Her smile was certainly gone. If this was her way of killing a conversation, it sure worked, her pronouncement being right up there behind, *I'm sorry to inform you, Mr. Blake, but it's malignant,* on the list of Great Conversation Killers of the twentieth century.

Elliot broke the uncomfortable silence.

"'S okay, mate, I'm living out the rest of my days the way I want to," he said, producing a genuine half-smile on his face. I looked at him closely, trying to see any sign of a man who was patronizing and didn't.

"I'm . . . I'm sorry," I said, not really knowing what I was saying.

"My father grew up listening to Motown music," Diana began, thankfully moving the subject in another direction. "I guess I did as well," she said, lifting the pall out of the air with her smile. "The words, the beats, the singers, and the way they danced, they were all so . . . so magnificent. I remember 'aving always 'eard this music when I was young." Diana looked around lovingly. "'E and my mum were always singing and dancing to this music." At this she threw her left hand on her hip and stuck her right arm out with her hand up like a crossing guard. She began shaking her hips to an unheard beat. "*Stop! In the name of love, bee-fore you break mah heart,*" she sang. She didn't sound like Diana Ross. She sounded like a British teenager trying to sound like Diana Ross.

Behind me a couple of my students finished the song off for her, doing a pretty fair job of sounding like TLC trying to sound like the Supremes.

"*Think it oh-oh-ver.*"

Elliot tilted his head and began nodding to the beat, his eyes glazed in dreamy memories. Looking at his face, I saw in it his love for the music. Elliot looked a lot less sick than he had when

I first laid eyes on him. What was he seeing in his mind's eye—
Diana Ross singing on *The Ed Sullivan Show*? Or was he possibly
reminiscing about himself and his wife during a younger, happier
time? What was it like to experience the Motown Sound over
in merry old England? I wondered. Whatever he was thinking
about, it made a difference on his face immediately, and I was
thankful for that.

"This was a place my dad always wanted to visit. 'E always
talked about coming 'ere one day with my mum. When 'e took
ill, our family decided that 'e'd get to see some a the places 'e
always wanted to," Diana said proudly as she massaged her father's shoulders. "We got the money together and flew 'im over.
My mum couldn't make the trip. She's at 'ome with my sister and
brother. I took some time off from school 'cause 'e needs someone to be with 'im. We decided that this was one of the things
that dad would see . . ." Diana said, trailing off.

My students all sighed.

"That is sooo cool," I heard a couple of them say.

"This place 'as meant a lot to me. Being 'ere, in this city, in
this 'ouse . . . I feel like I'm standing in some sacred or 'oly place.
Ya know, when I was a young child, I used to look at pictures of
this building in old magazines that my parents used to keep back
'ome," Diana said with a voice that reverberated with real awe.

I was in awe as well, but for different reasons. I was trying
to work out in my mind why anyone would want to come to
Detroit. I was someone who couldn't wait to leave and generally
dreaded coming back. My mind kept flipping to the question:
*If I only had a couple of moments left on this earth, where would I
go?* Detroit was right up there, sandwiched between Bosnia and
Haiti on my list of gotta-see destinations! What about the Grand
Canyon, Africa, the Alps, or taking a swim in the Caribbean,
where the water is turquoise and the temperature of bath water?
My God, I could think of so many other things to do and certainly other places to see.

"Hitsville?" I said.

"Ummm-huh, 'itsville, Motown, Dee-troit, Michigan. I know Detroit, Michigan doesn't show up on a lot of travel brochures, but ya should see 'ow many people travel to Liverpool all the time!" Diana said plainly, as she was obviously picking up on my amazement. "I mean, I know a lot of people who travel from England to Memphis every year, just to visit Graceland!" Now it was her turn to be incredulous.

"Yeah, and that's just the place where Elvis died," Elliot said.

"Different stuff means different things to people, don't it, Mr. Blake?" one of my kids said.

"Some people used to say: *Diff'rent strokes for diff'rent folks,*" Elliot added, grinning knowingly at me.

"Ya know, for people who cared, for people who loved the artists and the music, there's bunches to see and do 'ere. My dad wants to see the places where they grew up—to walk where they walked, eat where they ate. 'E wants to see and feel what made the music," she said happily.

What made the music.

What made the music?

That statement clung to my thoughts suddenly. Yes, what about this city got the people to sing and harmonize the way they did? You know, like certain places out west in this country inspired beach music, yet nothing else sounded like Motown. Berry Gordy, a Young African American Male (this group of adjectives tends to send people scurrying to their statistic sheets on drugs, crime, and death) who worked in a factory and lived in the city where I was born, decided that the music that he would create would have a certain sound. He did whatever it took to get it done. In creating that Motown sound he affected a city, a generation, and countless lives. In the process of making music, he not only affected the lives of the people he knew but the lives of people he would never meet—people from half a world away.

I was stunned at the significance of that revelation.

I remembered looking at the 45s that my parents owned. The shiny black disc, larger, more pliable, and much less foreboding and antiseptic than the metallic-looking CDs that we listen to today. The funny-shaped little yellow thingy that you popped into its center to play it on the stereo, that was surrounded by the blue label with a little map of Detroit with the red star, showing the entire world where both I and the Motown Sound were born. People who otherwise may have never given Detroit a second thought discovered the city that way, through hearing the music. Young American soldiers found respite as they listened to it while they lived and some died in murky rice paddies and jungles far away from the streets and the house parties of their youth.

There are many times that I look around this city and see nothing other than burned-out and dilapidated old neighborhoods. Neighborhoods filled with homes and buildings whose usefulness has become nothing more than insidious schemes. Lately, whenever I drive around the city where both of my parents as well as all of their children were born and raised, I no longer see the city of my youth, the one that once vibrated— literally—with sounds. The coffee-and-cream voices of Marvin and Tammy crooning, *Ain't no mountain high enough*, that wafted up from the convertible Deuce-and-a-Quarters and finned Caddies that rolled up the streets. They are now replaced with hoopties that pump out Jay-Z as he tells me about *Big Pimpin'*, while his sampled soundtrack, that measures 8.5 on the Richter scale, rattles the windows of the homes that are left standing. I see a city that I once loved creeping along in its fifth renaissance, a town trying to find an identity without the virtue of direction. A town that reflects its citizens, or did its citizens reflect the town? Am I black, African American, or a person of color? Am I angry, upwardly mobile, or just a sellout? A playa, a hoe, or a man? A sinner or saint? Who or what was my town right now? Did my perspective allow me the blessing to care?

Elliot saw none of these things. For Elliot, this wasn't Detroit, 1999. It was Motown, circa 1960s. Elliot and Diana saw the specters of a lost time that brought joyful memories to their minds and warmed their hearts. Elliot saw the town that spoke to his teen and young-adult years, producing the perfect aphrodisiac to woo the love of his life and eventual mother of his children. He saw Detroit—pre-riot—when downtown radiated with life; when groups with names like The Temptations, The Marvelettes, and The Miracles danced—in the Motown style—in suits and shimmering dresses; when every Friday night the Fox Theatre presented the Motown Review, the proving ground where young men and women perfected the love songs that they performed on street corners and school talent shows. Motown, the city that nurtured the hope that they would be the next Smokey or Marvin, or that their words would join "The Tracks of My Tears" or "Love Child" on the airwaves that floated even across an ocean to waiting ears. A glow rested on Elliot's face, replacing the shroud of death that had earlier hung on him like a ten-dollar suit. I thought of something from the Bible: *Rejoice young man in thy youth.* That was what Elliot was right then, this scripture transformed into flesh.

I thought of the times that I had asked—that's too soft of a word, *implored!*—my students to "watch what happens when you change your perspective." At what point had I lost mine? Feeling a bit like the Pharisees, I looked around the house—the house that Berry, Diana, and Smokey built—once again trying to see it through Elliot or Diana's eyes.

"Ya never realized ya lived in such an interesting city, did ya?" Diana looked me straight in the eyes triumphantly. She seemed to be gloating just slightly, as if she were letting me know that she saw things that I didn't.

"Thanks for the reality check," I said sincerely.

"Anytime."

"You like this music, do you?" Elliot asked.

"Yeah, I grew up just like your daughter did, listening to the music of my parents. They neglected to name any of their children after any of the artists, however. Man, I wish my name was Tito." We all laughed.

Elliot coughed and cleared his throat. Doing this caused him some pain. He shut his eyes tightly. He sat there motionless for just a few seconds. A lone tear emerged slowly from beneath his eyelid, then slid down his leathery right cheek as if it was in fear of being discovered. The grim, pained expression on his face melted into the calm that he had shown only moments ago when his daughter and my kids sang their rendition of "Stop! In the Name of Love." His eyes were clear and his face showed no sign of death at that moment, then he spoke. It wasn't rough and scratchy like it had been previously, a voice that was being infected by the same sickness that had bent his body. He spoke in his voice, clearly yet softly. He sounded distinguished and learned as only the British can.

"Back in '68, I took my wife—well, she was just a girl I liked at the time—out to a pub one night. We 'ad been dancing to a lot of music, you know, the Jerk, the Twist—my favorite dance was the Camel Walk . . . Then they put on some Stevie Wonder. She and I socialed together to it."

Elliot took off his face mask, closed his eyes, and leaned his head back, taking in a deep breath, as if he smelled the fragrance of his girl—his love—right there, his memories having become incarnate.

"Aaah, I can still 'ear that song," he said, his eyes still closed in dreamy retrospection. His right hand began to snap his fingers to a melody that played inside his mind, a slowdance for him and his love.

Then Elliot did something that I was totally unprepared for, he began singing. Not a croaking, raspy-voiced whisper, but actually a pretty good imitation of Stevie Wonder.

"La-la-laa-la-laa-laaaa, La-la-laa-la-laa-laaaa. My cherie ahhmour, lovely as a summer's day . . ." He went on and sang more of Stevie's love song. As the last of the lyrics eased from his mouth—"Mah cherie amour, pretty little one that I ah-dore. You're the only one mah haarrt beats for, how I wish that you were mine"—I began to finish the song off for him, and in the middle of the La-la-laa's, Diana joined me and we finished together.

For a moment Elliot had left his sickness, his twisted body, and his leathery skin. He had become Elliot Taylor—Motown Sound Casanova—singing love songs softly into the ear of his girl as he slow danced with her. A brief respite from reality as he went back to a point in his life when face masks, bottled oxygen, and a wheelchair were as far away as the moon. Elliot's memory freed him from the confines of the wheelchair, something that doctors, their orders, modern medicine, and technology had failed to do.

"That was the night I fell in love with your mum," he said to Diana, taking her hand and rubbing it against his cheek tenderly. She smiled the smile of a well-loved child and replaced her father's face mask, just in time for another coughing fit that knocked a few more moments off his life.

Some people walked into the museum. Their eyes were instantly drawn to our group. They made a point to look at all of us, making sure not to stare too long at Elliot, clearly something difficult to do. Invariably their eyes lingered on the wheelchair, the oxygen bottle, the mask, and then on Elliot. The faces of the people spoke loudly: My God, look at that poor man. He looks like he's dying. Isn't that so sad?

I smiled as my eyes went from Elliot to them and back to Elliot again. I smiled because I knew better.

# THE LOST TIKI PALACES OF DETROIT

BY MICHAEL ZADOORIAN

*Woodward Avenue*

I was on the bus, heading down Woodward Avenue. We had just stopped at West Grand Boulevard and I craned my neck to check out the former site of the Mauna Loa. I probably do this once a week on the bus on my way to work. I try to imagine how the place must have looked there in the New Center: a massive Polynesian temple, its thatched A-frame entryway flanked by flaming torches and swaying winter-proof palm trees on a gently rippling man-made lagoon—nestled amongst the cathedrals of twentieth-century V-8 Hydromatic Commerce, just across the street from where they decided the pitiful fate of the Corvair.

I have an extensive collection of Tiki mugs. My rarest are from the Mauna Loa. I own the Polynesian Pigeon, a section of ceramic bamboo with an exotic bird for a handle. Also the Baha Lana, an ebony Tiki head sticking his tongue out at the drinker. Both say *Design by Mauna Loa Detroit* on the bottom.

There were high hopes for the place. It was to be the largest South Seas supper club of its kind in the Midwest. (Second only to the majestic Kahiki of Columbus, Ohio, now fallen to the wrecking ball since greedy owners sold to Walgreen's.) Over two million dollars were spent on this paradisiacal bastion of splendor, a lot of money in the late '60s.

There were five different dining rooms at the Mauna Loa (Tonga, Papeete, Bombay, Lanai, and one other that I forget), as well as the lavish Monkey Bar, which featured a Lucite bartop with 1,250 Chinese coins embedded in it and tables made from brass hatch covers from trading schooners. A waterfall scurried down a mountainette of volcanic lava into a grotto lush with palm trees and flaming Tikis. The waiters wore Mandarin jackets and turbans as they served you.

The Mauna Loa opened in August of 1967. Barely a month after the worst race riot in Detroit's history. It lasted not quite two years.

"I'm invisible!"

That's what the homeless man on the bus kept saying. He boarded at West Grand Boulevard and none of us dared look at him. But then you never look anyone in the eye on the bus. All gazes are cast peripherally, on the down-low. With the homeless man, we simply examined the air around him. Even the bus driver, a large man, blue-black and stoic, who never says more than a word or two to anyone as they board, looked away as the guy paid his fare. We all knew someone got on, but we weren't sure who it was. He could be smelled but not seen. The homeless man must have walked down the aisle defiantly, as if daring anyone to say something to him.

"That's right! I'm invisible!"

What could we say? We had all looked away. We had made him invisible.

I was pretty sure that he was sitting three aisles up from me on the other side. The bus wasn't nearly as full as it usually was on a Monday—President's Day or some such nonsense. I kept my eyes on my newspaper, but they kept straying out the window searching for landmarks, lost ones as well as those still standing. I gazed upon a beautiful old abandoned factory from the '20s, with a sign that read: *AMERICAN BEAUTY ELECTRIC IRONS.*

I kept my ears open. I felt the homeless man's eyes on me. I wanted to look, but didn't want him to catch me looking because I wasn't sure what he would say. When I felt his eyes leave me, I glanced forward into the bus, at the spaces around him.

A little boy, about two years old, sitting in the seat in front of him, was the only one who truly acknowledged the homeless man's existence. The little boy looked over the back of the seat at the homeless man, and started playing peek-a-boo with him. The man cracked a bitter half-smile at the child.

Then he said it again: "I'm invisible!"

I was frankly kind of impressed that the guy would say something like this. I don't expect a homeless guy on the bus to say such things, strange and existential—an awl to the heart. It made me think, *He understands his condition.* I thought about Ralph Ellison.

The homeless guy looked around and repeated it yet again, as he peered around at the rest of us on the bus.

The bus driver turned, scowled, but said nothing.

I glanced away just before the homeless man saw me looking. He knew I had looked. Luckily, the child distracted him again. When I turned back, I saw him smile again at the child, wider this time, a grisly green and yellow smile, the school colors of the university we were now passing.

Then the child's mother, reading her own paper, realized what was going on. She sat the little boy straight down in his seat, flashing a harsh glance behind her.

This set the man off. His gestures suddenly grew more animated. It was if he had decided he would show us what an invisible homeless man on a city bus could do. He pointed out the window at a young woman in a short skirt and yelled to everyone in the bus: "Look at the titties on her! Lookit those titties! Let me off!"

The bus didn't stop. Everybody stayed quiet. An older man across the aisle from me sighed and looked out the window. A cane was leaned against the empty seat next to him.

As we continued down Woodward, we approached the Fox Theatre. A block or two behind it, down Montcalm, I could catch a glimpse of the old Chin Tiki. By all rights, I should not have been able to see three blocks behind a major building to spot another, but behind the Fox, save for a fire station and an abandoned party store, there are mostly empty fields, now used for parking for the new stadiums, baseball and football, on the east side of Woodward. For that moment, I could see the Chin Tiki's Polynesian façade, its doorway arched and pointed, the shape of hands praying. To whom? Some great invisible Tiki God? Perhaps Chango: God of fire, lightning, force, war, and virility.

That would be a good guess. For Marvin Chin actually opened his Tiki bar when the riots were going on, around the same time as the Mauna Loa. Fires were everywhere in the city then, but not at the Chin Tiki. It would survive to become quite the popular place. Our parents ate there (when they dared venture downtown), as well as the stars: Streisand, DiMaggio, Muhammad Ali.

It held on until 1980, when it too closed up. But unlike the Mauna Loa, which suffered an ignoble end as a lowly seafood restaurant that eventually burned to the ground, the Chin Tiki was simply shuttered, all its Tiki treasures packed up and mothballed inside. To this day, it is still sealed up, a Tiki tomb of Tutankhamen, still owned by the Chin family, who are supposedly waiting it out, waiting for the inevitable gentrification. It will happen. Or it will become another parking lot. In the meantime, the place had a brief resurrection when Eminem used it to film a scene for 8 Mile.

Chango works in mysterious ways.

"Hey, white man!"

Without thinking, I turn and look at the homeless man. Apparently, I'm not so invisible to him.

"What you doing here?"

Everyone on the bus is obliquely looking at me now. I have to say something.

"I'm going to work," I reply coolly.

"What you on our bus for?"

"I'm just going to work," I repeat, then turn away and look out the window at the old Tele-Arts. It was a newsreel theater in my mother's time, but now it's been turned into some sort of swanky nightclub.

"Motherfucker on our bus."

"Shut your mouth," says the woman with the child in front of him. She's not sticking up for me, I know. She means that language in front of her child.

"Motherfucker."

Slowly she turns back to him, eyes like smoldering carbon. "You want to be invisible? I'll *make* you invisible."

She says it in that way that many black women have, that way that makes most anybody shut up if they know what's good for them. It certainly works on me, not that I invite that sort of thing. I mind my own business. It's the only way to be when you're the only white person on the bus, the *cue-ball effect*, as a friend of mine calls it.

The homeless man quiets down for the moment. We're further down Woodward now. I look out the window at the storefronts, façades ripped off, gaping wide open into the street. They are being gutted for new lofts, many of them right across from the old J.L. Hudson's site, where the behemoth department store was imploded. It is now replaced by a giant new skyscraper built by a software billionaire.

When things like this happen, the world starts to pay attention. Detroit is a city again! Back from the dead! Rising from the ashes! They can see us again. We were always there, but transparent, the way you can see right through the exoskeleton of the Michigan Central Train Station.

To the rest of the world, Detroit was just a place where Japanese film crews showed up every year to photograph the house fires on Halloween Eve, a.k.a., Devil's Night. Other than that, they hardly saw us. We don't even show up on the city temperature listings on the Weather Channel.

Further up, through one of the construction sites, I catch a glimpse of the old Statler Hilton Hotel, once proud home of Trader Vic's. The building has been ignored for so many years, the windows are no longer even boarded up. The Michigan weather is not kind to a man-made tropical oasis. Inside, columns of bamboo once seemed to shore up rattan-wrapped walls. Glowing blowfish and a native kayak hung from the ceiling, along with colored globes encased in fishnets. At the front door, where a stoic Moai once stood sentry, there is rubble. Long pieces of terra-cotta tile still surround the front door, ragged with metal mesh, depicting the faces of Tiki gods, mouths contorted, faces squinched into impossible, pained grimaces.

A Tyree Guyton lavender polka dot has now been painted on the door. He of the Heidelberg Project, a block-long art project composed completely of discarded objects: a gutted polka dot Rosa Parks bus, a backyard of vacuum cleaners, a tree of shoes. These dots appear on abandoned buildings all over the city. Cheery carbuncles that make sudden art of blight. What else can you do?

The story for Trader Vic's is much the same as the Chin Tiki and the Mauna Loa. When the white folks disappeared from downtown Detroit at the end of the workday in the '70s, the clubs and restaurants foundered. The building is now slated for demolition, but it's been a ghost for decades. "Demolished by neglect," as the preservationists like to say around here. They say it a lot.

I am chagrined to relate that I have been part of that demolition as well. One night, in a drunken Tiki frenzy, some friends and I brought crowbars to this very site and ripped terra-cotta tiles from the façade of the building. No one was using them anymore, right? That's what we told ourselves. It was wrong, and I knew it. I think of my offense to the Tiki gods when I look at my filched tile, which now resides in my backyard. Shame on me, I say. Shame. Yet these agonies of all our pasts will soon be ground into dust in the middle of the night, the preferred time to start the demolition of historic buildings here in Detroit.

Down one street, there is a sign on the side of a car wash: *HAND WASH TO THE GLORY OF GOD.*

"Motherfucker on our bus," I hear the homeless man mutter. I really wish he would stop saying that.

We pass by more construction sites. Things are changing here. New buildings push out the grand old ones, like bullies in a big rush. When you go downtown at night there are people there now, suburban people, city people, doing things, spending money.

"Hey, white man! Why don't you go back to Livonia?" says the homeless man.

I ignore him. Nothing bad is going to happen—for some reason I know this. Yet it alarms me when I hear a startled inhalation, a collective *Huh!* roll through the bus. I turn to look at the invisible man and I see that he has now dropped filthy trou and is displaying his penis to me and everyone else.

Frankly, I'm kind of relieved. An act of aggression, but a harmless one.

"I ain't too invisible now, am I, motherfuckers?" he yells, waving his spotted peter at everyone on board. To be on the safe side, I clutch my thermos, figuring it will work well as a cudgel if I need to use it that way. Taunt me, yes. Piss on me? I don't think so.

Still, it's a relief when the driver pulls the bus over right next to a construction site, stomps down the aisle, and tells the now-very-visible homeless man to walk his raggedy ass off his bus. *Right now.*

With great dignity, the homeless man pulls up his pants, turns, and exits. When the pneumatic doors close behind him, there is only the smell of him left. The woman with the child looks sternly at me. She is holding her child closely, protecting him, her lips squeezed tight.

For a moment, I try not to laugh about what just happened, but just can't help myself. She looks at me, puts a hand over her mouth, but soon her head is shaking and she can no longer hold it in. Everyone on the bus starts laughing. Up in the rearview mirror, I can even see the driver smiling.

# ABOUT THE CONTRIBUTORS

Joshua A. Gaylord

**MEGAN ABBOTT** is the author of *The Song Is You, Queenpin*, and the Edgar Award finalist *Die a Little*. Born in Warren, Michigan, she grew up in Grosse Pointe Woods, a suburb of Detroit. She lives in New York City.

Craig Bernier

**CRAIG BERNIER** became enthralled with Detroit—its culture and nuance, its dread and hope—after returning from a stint in the Navy to attend Wayne State University. Most of his published works have focused on the city's denizens. He teaches composition and writing on the adjunct faculty of Duquesne University in Pittsburgh.

Yukiko Krolicki

**JOE BOLAND** was born in Detroit, and has lived and worked in the area his entire life. He is currently writing a crime novel.

Patrice Chapman

**DESIREE COOPER** is a columnist for the *Detroit Free Press*, a frequent contributor to National Public Radio's *All Things Considered*, and cohost of American Public Media's *Weekend America*. She did anticrime and affordable housing advocacy work for New Detroit, an urban coalition that addresses the city's social problems. She lives in the city with her husband and two children.

Deborah Morgan

**LOREN D. ESTLEMAN**, a Michigan native, has received four Shamus Awards from the Private Eye Writers of America for his Amos Walker, Detroit P.I. series, which he's been writing for twenty-seven years. In addition, he is the author of a historical Detroit series that includes *Whiskey River, Motown, King of the Corner, Edsel, Stress, Jitterbug,* and *Thunder City*.

*Pedro Hernandez*

**LOLITA HERNANDEZ**, born and raised in Detroit, is the author of *Autopsy of an Engine and Other Stories from the Cadillac Plant*, winner of a 2005 PEN Beyond Margins Award. She is also the author of two chapbook collections of poems: *Quiet Battles* and *Snakecrossing*. Her family hails from Trinidad & Tobago and St. Vincent.

*Cinda Hocking*

**JOHN C. HOCKING** obsessively reads, writes, edits, and collects pulp and noir fiction. He lives outside of Detroit with his inspiring son and superhumanly tolerant wife. He thinks more people should read Dan J. Marlowe's *The Name of the Game Is Death*.

*John Foley*

**CRAIG HOLDEN** grew up in the shadow of Detroit and went to sleep most nights with a transistor radio under his pillow—listening to the Tigers and Red Wings or experiencing the late '60s via the old CKLW. His most recent novel is *Matala*.

*Life Touch Studios*

**ROGER K. JOHNSON** is a native Detroiter who still lives in the city with his beautiful wife and their three lovely daughters. A graduate of Wayne State University and a middle school science teacher, he is committed to making sure that all the children he encounters realize their full potential.

*Rebecca Markus*

**PETER MARKUS** is originally from the southwest side of Detroit. He now works with the InsideOut Literary Arts Project, which sends writers into Detroit public schools. He is the author of three books of short fiction, *Good, Brother, The Moon Is a Lighthouse*, and *The Singing Fish*. His novel, *Bob, or Man on Boat*, is forthcoming in 2008.

Jeff Sciortino

**JOYCE CAROL OATES** is a recipient of the National Book Award and the PEN/Malamud Award for Excellence in Short Fiction. Author of the national best sellers *We Were the Mulvaneys, Blond,* and *The Falls,* which won the 2005 Prix Femina, Oates is the Roger S. Berlind Distinguished Professor of the Humanities at Princeton University and has been a member of the American Academy of Arts and Letters since 1978. In Detroit, she lived on Sherbourne Road north of Seven Mile, 1962–1968.

Pat O'Brien

**DORENE O'BRIEN** was born and raised in Detroit and currently teaches writing at the College for Creative Studies and Wayne State University. She won the *Red Rock Review* Mark Twain Award for Short Fiction, the *New Millennium's* Fiction Award, the *Chicago Tribune* Nelson Algren Award, the Bridport Prize, and she is the recipient of a creative writing fellowship from the National Endowment for the Arts.

Angie Semler

**E.J. OLSEN** comes from a long line of sturdy Michigan folk, and has lived in the Detroit area for most of his life. He works as a freelance writer and editor and is currently writing his first novel.

Barbara Parker

**P.J. PARRISH,** the *New York Times* best-selling author of the Louis Kincaid series, is actually two sisters, Kris Montee and Kelly Nichols. Their books have been nominated for multiple Edgar, Shamus, and Anthony awards, and they have won an International Thriller Writers Award. They were born and raised in Detroit, and return home as often as possible—both in person and in their fiction.

Detroit News

**MELISSA PREDDY** traces her Detroit ancestry to the late 1800s and grew up absorbing family lore about mid–twentieth century life in the city's working-class neighborhoods. She is currently a business editor for the *Detroit News.*

Eileen Gunn

**NISI SHAWL** is a native of Kalamazoo, Michigan. Her short horror story "Cruel Sistah," which first appeared in Isaac Asimov's *SF Magazine,* was reprinted in the nineteenth volume of *The Year's Best Fantasy and Horror.*

John Roe/Roe Photo

**MICHAEL ZADOORIAN** is the author of the novel *Second Hand,* and his stories have appeared in *Literary Review, American Short Fiction, Beloit Fiction Journal, North American Review,* and *ARARAT.* A graduate of Wayne State University, he grew up on the northwest side of Detroit.

CPSIA information can be obtained at www.ICGtesting.com
Printed in the USA
LVOW07s0928300615

444408LV00001B/6/P